TRACK THE WOLF

ALEX STEWARD: BOOK 4

To Rich,
AH-WOO!

STEFANIE GILMOUR

Copyright © 2025 by Stefanie Gilmour

All rights reserved.

No part of this publication may be reproduced, distributed, or transmitted in any form or by any means, including photocopying, recording, or other electronic or mechanical methods, without the prior written permission of the publisher, except as permitted by U.S. copyright law. For permission requests, contact the author at writing@stefaniegilmour.com.

The story, all names, characters, and incidents portrayed in this production are fictitious. No identification with actual persons (living or deceased), places, buildings, and products is intended or should be inferred.

Printed in the United States of America
First edition 2025

Hardcover 979-8-9904623-5-9
Paperback 979-8-9904623-6-6
E-book 979-8-9904623-7-3

For Arthur.

1

I ASKED GRANDMA if I could take the forgotten shoebox once belonging to my grandfather, not for the old photos and article clippings collected inside, but for the key. It was attached to an aluminum ball chain with Grandpa's dog tags. My fingers found the smooth metal object, chain and all, in my jacket's pocket. The tarnished key seemed heavy for its size.

In the flurry of repacking my car, my grandmother waved me away with a nod, not even asking about the box's contents. I pushed aside a duffle bag full of clean clothes in the car's trunk to make room for the cardboard box. The well-loved army jacket I wore was the only thing of my grandfather's that I'd taken after his death.

"Your mom gave me this." The pleasant timbre of Ben's voice pulled me from my thoughts. Removing his tether restored the full use of his voice and, therefore, his ability to cast magic. But no charms or spells were needed to cause the fluttering in my chest while around him. Smiling, he held out a sandwich bag stuffed impossibly full of cookies. "She said it's for the ride home."

I chuckled. "Put it up front with us. I give it until the New York border before it's empty."

He gently nudged me aside and wedged another bag into the trunk. "You alright? You've been quiet this morning."

Since Ben was a wizard, I could share my *Surviving Life as a Werewolf* challenges with him. I wasn't sure yet how to communicate the odd mix of curiosity and discomfort the box and the key caused. I went for the more easily identifiable ache in my heart.

"I'm bummed we're leaving." I looked at the little two-story house I'd known since childhood. "After staying away for so long, it was nice to be back with my family." I closed the trunk. "But I'm also ready to go home to Hopewell. I miss Em like I'm missing a limb. I miss Trish and Nate a lot, too." I still missed Anne even though our fractured friendship was beyond repair.

Ben's arms closed around me, his touch causing another bout of that silly feeling, this time in my stomach.

I leaned back into his embrace and the comforting, spicy scent I associated with him. The warmth of his body against mine was all the more cozy with the autumn chill in the air. "What about you?"

"Honestly? I could keep traveling. I enjoy being with you and seeing anywhere that isn't Hopewell."

I turned in his arms to look up at him. It was important to me that he understood why I preferred to return rather than travel more with him. "After the Committee collapse, there's a lot of work to do in the supernatural community. I want to get back so I can help. "

The corners of his mouth twitched downward, and he looked away. "I know you do." A red smudge marred the lower part of his cheek.

"What the hell is on your face?" I blinked. "Is that . . . lipstick?"

Ben's brows gathered. He wiped his hand over his cheek and jaw, smearing the makeup, and then looked at his hand. "I don't know what—"

"Alex!" My grandmother strolled down the walkway from the house, carrying a folded knit blanket. "Don't forget this." Her white hair was curled, and her lips were a deep shade of red.

"Oh no. I'm so sorry." I wiped the remains of Grandma's lipstick from Ben's cheek with my thumb. "It won't happen again."

His skin warmed as color flooded his cheeks. "She asked for a hug and suddenly she—"

I turned on my grandmother. "You can't kiss every guy you meet! You're going to make people uncomfortable."

"It was a quick peck on the cheek." She passed me the blanket and winked at Ben. "A thank you for making my favorite granddaughter laugh and smile so much."

"I'm your only granddaughter." Now my cheeks were warm. I blurted a question to direct the focus away from Ben and me. "Are Mom and Dad on their way out?"

Grandma nodded. "Will the two of you visit us for the holidays?"

"I'm not sure yet." I tried to gauge Ben's reaction to the question. There wasn't one. He remained silent, allowing me to answer for us. "It'll depend on how everything is going at home." I gave Ben the blanket, and he packed it into the car's back seat.

The screen door on the front porch banged open, and my parents came toward us down the walkway. Grommet, our family dog, bounded ahead of them. Ben crouched, and Grommet nearly bowled him over. I laughed as Grommet tried to exchange wet kisses for ear scritchies. It warmed my heart to know my whole family had been won over by my guy during our visit.

Ben glanced around, a quick scan for any bystanders not clued into the supernatural, and then back at Grommet. He pressed his hands together. The energy he gathered for his magic tickled my skin. Ben whispered words in a language I didn't understand, grinned at Grommet, and slowly pulled his hands apart. A perfect blue sphere of light the size of a tennis ball formed between his palms. Grommet lunged, barking and wagging his tail. Ben stood, drew his arm back, and threw the ball toward the house. Grommet tore after it, uprooting turf.

My parents stepped aside, allowing Grommet to rush past them. "Here's leftover lasagna for lunch." My mom handed me a Tupperware dish. The aroma of garlic reached my sensitive nose through the plastic container. "Do you two have everything you need? Is there something else I can get you?"

"We're good, right?" I asked Ben.

"Yeah. Thanks for everything, Mr. and Mrs. Steward." He held his hand out to my parents. "I had a great time."

Dad accepted the handshake but pulled Ben into a hug. "Kim and Scott. No formalities needed with us, Ben." My mom and Grandma gave him a farewell hug as well.

My turn for family hugs caused a lump to form in my throat. I hugged each of them, inhaling their scents deeply to keep them with me a bit longer. Dad: Irish Spring soap and aftershave. Mom: scented hand lotion. And my grandmother: the beautiful, light touch of lavender. I managed to smile and walk to the driver's side door before my vision blurred with tears.

Grommet bounded back, dropped the glowing ball at Ben's feet, and barked. The sphere disappeared in a streak of light. A gentle current of energy, released from the spell, brushed over my skin.

"Great job!" Ben gave Grommet more scratches around his ears before my parents called Grommet back.

Ben and I finally got into the car. I honked the horn as we pulled away. My family gathered together at the end of the walk and waved to us until we were out of sight.

"They're nice," Ben said. "I'm glad we came out here to spend time with them."

"Yeah, they're pretty great." I wiped my fingers over my damp cheeks. "I'm going to miss them."

ON THE FIRST leg of our trip to New York from Hopewell, Ben and I stopped multiple times at different bars, concert venues, and warehouses for him to play EDM shows. Now on the return leg, we had a nine-hour trip west and one show left in Detroit before we could drive the two and half hours back home.

The cookies lasted beyond New York State but were gone by the Michigan border. Ben and I reached Detroit, our destination for the day, several hours before the evening's show. We took the opportunity to check in to the motel.

"Be sure to thank your parents for the cash to get a room. I should make enough tonight to repay them." Ben, a bundle of clothes in hand, looked up from his duffle bag. "Alex?"

"Mmm-hmm." I'd brought in my bag and the cardboard box. At one point it might have been a shoe box for men's boots. The corners were worn, dented, and retaped a few times after the glue failed. The scent of old newsprint clung to the box's interior. I meticulously unpacked its contents like ancient treasures or relics onto the generic bedspread. The metal key sat beside the odd collection.

"What are you doing?" His tone curious, he looked over my shoulder at the display I'd assembled on the bedspread.

"I found this box of Grandpa's in the basement." I gestured at the articles with one hand while I casually slipped the key back into my pocket with the other. "There are these weird newspaper clippings collected inside. Photos. A pine cone."

"Pine cone?"

I held up the pine cone, even now still smelling of sap. It was about 8 inches and slightly curved. "I don't remember Grandpa being a crafter."

"Huh." Ben's gaze moved from the pine cone to me. "If you don't know what it is, why didn't you leave it there?"

"Because it belonged to Grandpa, but I don't understand it. I thought if I brought it with me, I could puzzle it out," I said. "He grew up on a farm in Michigan, but his family moved to New York City when he was a teenager."

"And now you're back here calling Michigan home," Ben said.

"Yeah." I inspected one of the photos, taken with a Polaroid camera. A younger version of my grandfather stood in front of a log cabin with his arm around the waist of a woman. It was before

I was born, but Grandpa wore the jacket I currently wear, so the photo was taken after his tour in Vietnam. He would have been married with a son, my dad. I frowned and squinted at the blurry photo. "Who is this random woman?"

"You didn't show your grandma any of it?" Ben asked. "She might know the people."

"We were busy packing up the car when I asked if I could take the box. I'll call her later about it." My hand slipped in my pocket, and my thumb ran over the key. It was large enough for a door but didn't fit any locks in my parents' house. I'd checked. Did it even belong to Grandpa? I'd found it attached to a chain with his dog tags, so it seemed to, but maybe I was putting too much hope into it.

"Alex?"

I was jerked from my thoughts. "Huh?"

Ben stood in the bathroom doorway. "I asked if you're coming to the show tonight. That was a long drive. I don't mind if you stay in and rest."

"Of course I'm coming." I *was* tired and would rather hole up in the motel room and sift through the box's strange items. But I also wanted to support Ben at his last performance before we returned to Hopewell.

He smiled and jabbed a thumb over his shoulder. "I'm going to shower before we head over there."

I nodded. The bathroom door closed. I reached for my phone but then hesitated, not sure what to do. Should I ask Grandma about the box? Growing up, I viewed my grandparents as a team. Inseparable. The love and respect they had for each other was relationship goal material. I'd thought about it often as my relationship with Ben continued to grow and develop. Would my questions about the box tarnish those memories?

My grandfather was also my favorite playmate and coconspirator. My parents worked but couldn't afford childcare, so my grandparents were a large part of my childhood. I remembered Grandpa as a quiet man with a deep laugh. Kind and gentle. He was a loving grandparent and a doting husband. A high bar to meet for any man I allowed close to me.

The werewolf gene, activated in my body years after Grandpa's death, was passed to me through his bloodline. Any insight into his life could offer a glimpse into my future as a werewolf.

I snatched up the Polaroid again and narrowed my eyes at the unknown woman. A growl rumbled in my chest. "Who are you?"

I flipped through the remaining photos. There was another shot of the cabin. It was set somewhere in an evergreen forest. A photo showed my grandpa and two other men in flannel shirts and jeans seated at a campfire. Another had one of the same men in it, only he wore camo-patterned clothes and held a rifle. Who were these people?

Setting aside the photos, I carefully reviewed the yellowed newspaper articles. They were dated from the mid-seventies through the late eighties. I didn't recognize the city names. A quick search on my phone revealed the majority were smaller towns located north of Hopewell, somewhere I'd never traveled.

And then there were the headlines, as disturbing as the last time I'd read them. "Midnight Massacre: Entire Herd Lost" and "Horror of the Northern Woods: Is the Legend True?" Farmers of these towns were financially ruined by the slaughter of their livestock by an unknown creature during the night. Descriptions of the predator varied, but all accounts included a large monster with fur and glowing eyes.

The hair rose on the nape of my neck. The door to the bathroom clicked open. Startled, I dropped the article I'd been reading. Humid air and the scent of soap reached me.

"Ready to get something to eat?" Ben called from the bathroom.

"Yes." I packed everything back into the box and replaced the lid. The puzzle from my grandfather's past would have to wait.

I tried to keep Ben's show front of mind, wanting to be fully present for him since performing brought him so much joy. As we left, hand in hand, the mysterious key was a heavy weight in my pocket.

2

THE NIGHT WAS dark, rainy, and chilly. Ben and I ducked into the downtown building once used as a meat-packing plant. The venue reminded me a bit of Hopewell's older architecture but carried with it an emphasis on industrial manufacturing. An arts and music nonprofit converted the space for installments and shows. During his last Midwest tour with the band Derezzed, Ben had chatted with a founding member of the nonprofit. He was invited to perform in the space whenever he happened to be in the area next.

"Ben!" A silver-haired man dressed in stylish clothing strode across the room toward us. "Welcome to the Makers' Space." He gestured around him with a sweep of his hand. "We're so glad to have you here."

"Thanks." Ben's smile was easy. Only minutes after entering the place, he was already comfortable. "Alex, this is Nick."

Nick shook his head and grinned. "It's amazing how they restored your voice." He held his hand out to me. "Sorry, Alex. Hello. That must be old news for you by now."

"Hello." I briefly shook his hand. Strong scents of aftershave and hair product surrounded us. "I'm still getting used to it."

"I'm going to chat with Ben about the video tech he requested," Nick said. "Feel free to wander around and explore if you want."

Ben's smile faltered. "Or she can come along, right?" I found most new spaces unnerving, and he didn't want me to feel abandoned.

"No, that's okay." The thought of being a tagalong girlfriend made me more uncomfortable than the new surroundings. I lifted onto my toes and kissed Ben's cheek. "Do what you need to do. I was going to make a phone call anyway. I'll see you when the show starts."

Nick motioned Ben to follow. I blew out an exhale and scanned the nearly empty room. The rain outside had settled into a drizzle, so I opted for the fresh air despite the cold. There was something about the interior space that didn't sit well with me . . . something dark covered by the layers of fresh paint and investors' dollars.

Outside a side entrance to the building, I got my phone out of my pocket and called my parents. My mom answered. "Hello! You two make it okay? We were getting worried."

I'd waited too long to call. Mom's persistent anxiety about my safety came from a place of love, but it got pretty damn exhausting fast. "Yeah, we checked into the motel first. We're at the venue now, so I thought I'd call while he's getting ready."

"What's wrong?" she said.

"What?" In my peripheral vision, I caught someone jogging across the puddle-filled crosswalk.

"Something's wrong."

I bristled, already growing impatient. "No, nothing is wrong. Can I talk to Grandma?"

"Oh-kay." She elongated the word, giving me space to explain.

"Please?" I closed my eyes and clenched my jaw.

"Sure. Hold on." I imagined my mother tracking down my grandmother in the house. There was a muffled exchange.

"Hello, Alex," my grandmother said.

My chest warmed and tightened at the same time. "Hey, Grandma. I had a few minutes and wanted to ask you something."

"Go ahead, dear."

"I went through that box of Grandpa's," I said. My attention darted to another pedestrian walking my way. "It had old photos and articles in it."

"Oh, he was a pack rat," she said. "You wouldn't believe how many magazine back issues I threw out after he passed."

"The photos were of him and people I don't recognize. And there was a key." The man from the crosswalk passed by me. I turned to watch him continue down the sidewalk. There was silence on the line. I thought my call dropped. "Grandma?"

"I'm sorry," she said. "You should have left that old stuff here so I could get rid of it."

"Do you know anything about the articles? The people in the photos?" I asked. "The key?"

"No, I don't."

"Isn't that weird?" Since my grandparents were nearly insufferable with their adoration for each other, Grandpa keeping anything from Grandma didn't sit well with me.

There was another break in the conversation. "Alex, your grandfather faced his share of challenges in his lifetime."

"I know," I said. "He told me in his letter." The letter, worn from me unfolding and refolding it so often, lived in my go bag. He wrote it for me shortly before his death, certain the latent werewolf gene would still awaken in my body. "Sometimes he left Dad and you when he wasn't feeling well . . . when his wolf was uneasy. I thought this key might have something to do with that. You don't know where he went?"

"No."

I stood in silence, trying to process what she said.

"Alex—"

My chest burned and my throat was dry. The wolf in me turned to anger. "So, what was he doing all those times? He just left without telling you where he went? Why in the hell didn't he tell you?"

"Alex, dear—"

"No." I shook my head. "Did he lie to you? Make up stories?"

"I don't believe your grandfather ever lied to me." She paused. "There were things from his life he didn't tell me."

A growl slipped into my question. "What was he hiding?"

Her words sharpened. "Alexandria, you of all people should understand there were many things from his life he was forced to hide. I know you loved him deeply, we all did, but he was far from perfect."

The cold had crept in on me, chilling the end of my nose and causing it to run. I sniffled and wiped what could have been rain from my cheeks. "It's not like him."

My grandmother's tone softened. "He was a wonderful grandfather and loved us, especially you, with his whole heart."

I stepped back into the covered entryway to escape the rain. It started falling harder, adding to the ongoing street noise. My pulse pounded. The scent of winter lurked in the chilly air.

"Alex?"

I cleared my throat so my voice wouldn't crack. "Yeah, I'm here."

"Throw away that box and enjoy the rest of your trip with Ben," Grandma said.

"Yeah, okay." I sniffled again. "Thank you, Grandma."

"You're welcome, dear," she said. "I love you."

"Love you, too." I ended the call and turned to reenter the building. Being warm inside with Ben was preferable to standing out in the cold and rain, alone, with my thoughts. When I pulled on the door handle, the door clunked against its frame. Locked.

Another growl sprung into my throat. "Shit."

The sound of jangling metal reached my ears before a voice asked, "Here for the music tonight?" A stout woman stepped into the entryway before turning and shaking the water from her umbrella.

I stepped back from the door. "Yeah. I came out for a phone call."

She wore a canvas coat with the words Jessie's Auto Repair embroidered on the breast pocket. With her came not only the expected scent of damp fabric, but also something like burned metal and grease. She looked past me at the wall. "I have a key."

"Thank you." I pressed back against the wall to give her more room. "I'm Alex. It's my first time here."

"It's a great space. Lots of room and equipment to make shit." She selected a dongle from a bundle of keys. She lifted it to a keypad, the keypad beeped, and the door unlocked. She pulled it open.

"You work here?" I asked.

"I used to, but not anymore. When I visit my parents, I like to help out here." She nodded at the doorway. "Are you going in or not?"

"Oh, sorry." I slipped past her into the warmth and light of the building's interior. "Thank you."

She studied me in silence for a moment. "You're welcome." Her glasses, the lenses perfectly round with the tiniest of wire frames, started to fog. She snatched them from the end of her nose to wipe them with a rag tucked into the back pocket of her overalls. In the light, I noticed all the zippers, clasps, and pockets on her person.

"My . . ." I paused. "I'm here with Ben Sharpe. He's the one performing—"

"You're the girlfriend." She put her glasses back on. Her study of me grew uncomfortable. "The arm candy."

My hackles raised. "Excuse me?"

"No?" Her gaze twitched toward my left hand. "Wife?"

My face warmed. "You're being rude."

She paused, cocked her head, and then shook it. "I do that. Working on it." She smiled, but it seemed painfully put on, like a performance. "My name is Jessica."

"Of Jessie's Auto Repair?" I asked.

She tilted her head again.

I motioned at her jacket.

"Oh. Yes. It's where I build and fix cars in Traverse City." She held out her hand. Grease lined the creases of her skin and lay under her fingernails.

"Nice to meet you." I shook her hand. Her skin was surprisingly rough.

Jessica checked a complex wristwatch. "Are you a maker, too?"

"A what?"

"Do you make stuff? Do you build? Create?" she said. "This space is for makers."

The question hit a bit hard. While Ben and I traveled, I thought about that question a lot. Ben thrived on stage, playing the music he wove together like a tapestry. Audiences loved him. I knew because I stood in the audience each time.

But what exactly did I do? Or want to do? So much of my adult life had been spent running and hiding. That was no longer necessary. "I—"

"You know what?" Jessica checked her watch again. "That's all the time I have to talk. I need to check the video setup before the show starts."

"Oh. Sure, I didn't mean—"

"Do you want a business card?" She handed one to me.

"Um, thanks."

Jessica gave a nod as if checking off another thing on a task list. Turning on the heel of her paint-splattered Doc Martens, she strode off. I pocketed the card and found my way back to the venue's entrance to leave my jacket at coat check. I looked forward to dancing, one of my favorite forms of escape from anything weighing on my mind or heart.

WHEN THE LIGHTS went down for Ben's show, the performance space was filled with people. Many pop-up spaces in older warehouses or dark clubs hosted him into the early morning hours. This show had a more planned and refined look to both the space and the attendees. The metal ceiling beams were exposed like Trish and Nate's place, Hell's Bells, but the floor was blonde wood . . . and clean. Scents of sweet cocktails, smoky liquors, and expensive perfumes clung to the people in the room.

I stood aside at first, holding up a wall and a drink while I familiarized myself with the sounds, scents, and bodies in the space. The venue worked with Ben to include video loops with his requested lighting. He scanned the room, seeking me out in the crowd, before smiling at me and starting his first set. The steady, ribcage-trembling beat, layered with a Sisters of Mercy track, filled the air. Ben became a moving silhouette, different planes of his face and body highlighted briefly with pulses of light. I wished my best friend Emma were here. We'd already be in the thick of the crowd, dancing together.

There was a flash of reflected light up near the stage. The woman I'd met, Jessica, wore a large pair of goggles and headphones as she adjusted wires at a box attached to the wall.

I thought of our brief conversation and realized I wanted more than ever to get back to Hopewell. I'd rested, but now it was time to work. I wasn't a person who did well sitting still, and I'd finally found something I was good at. I was going to help the werewolf community of Hopewell weather one of the most major overhauls in governance they'd seen in decades.

I threw back the rest of my drink, set the cup aside, and gently elbowed my way closer to the stage. The closer I got, the more the crowd turned from individuals watching a concert to a moving and breathing being, its heart beating in time to the rhythm. I was about to give myself over to the music, and then a new scent crept up my nose. It was a primal earthy scent I was intimately familiar with.

Turning in place, I scanned the crowd. My nostrils quivered. I'd caught the scent of other lupine while Ben and I traveled. Some had noticed me. We'd even hung out with wolves during his first run of shows on the way to visit my family. This lupine aroma raised the hair on the nape of my neck. My whole body tensed, alert. It was somehow . . . different. Off.

The stuttering lights obscured the other dancers' features. Everyone was an intricate pulse of dark and light. Flashes of glowing eyes and teeth flickered around me. I slunk toward what I thought could be the direction of the scent. Large ceiling fans mixed up the air in the room and made it difficult to identify the exact origin.

Suddenly the odd scent was potent and surrounded me. It was an unpleasant odor of something stagnant or decomposing. A large hand closed over my upper arm, and sharp nails bit into my skin. I spun, but the shifting figures took away whoever had been there. The fans diffused the scent. A growl sprung up into my throat.

I quickly elbowed my way toward the edge of the crowd. The wolf in me was agitated being in close quarters and unable to identify what I was smelling. I waded from the pool of dancing people and turned to face it. Another pulse of light and the following darkness revealed a set of glowing eyes across the room.

They stared back at me. Whoever it was, they were tall, standing a head above the crowd. Then the light pulsed again, and the stranger was gone.

I remained on high alert for the rest of the show, pacing along the room's edges. The scent vanished along with any further glimpses of the stranger. I kept an eye on the stage to make sure no one advanced on Ben. The lights came back up, and the concertgoers began to disperse. I reclaimed my jacket and wandered among the people in the lobby, trying to find any trace of whoever had grabbed me.

One of my favorite aromas, a spicy warm one, reached my nose.

"Alex?" Ben caught me lurking in the corner of the lobby, sniffing the sleeve of my shirt. He stood watching me, an eyebrow raised and forehead wrinkled. "What're you doing?"

I realized how odd I probably looked. Embarrassed, I blurted, "Someone smelled funny in there."

"Smelled 'funny?' That's a bit judgy."

"No, not like that. Well, kind of. They grabbed me." I pulled my shirt sleeve up to show him my forearm. Four raised welts were scratched onto my skin.

Ben frowned. "What the hell?"

"Yeah." I pushed my sleeve back down. "I could tell it was someone like me, but . . . not."

Ben glowered and scanned the lobby. "Did you get a good look at them?"

"No. The lighting was too erratic." I gave him a nudge in the arm. "Don't worry about it. I can't detect them anymore, so I think they're gone."

"Are you sure?"

"Yeah. It could have been a weird accident." I remembered the pair of glowing eyes focused on me from across the room. That'd felt very intentional, but we'd be gone tomorrow.

"Okay," Ben said. "What'd you think of the show?" He always asked since we were both music junkies, and he constantly tweaked his arrangements.

"It sounded great. I liked what you changed with the Sisters of Mercy transition."

"Yeah, I think it worked better. When I play tomorrow night—"

"Tomorrow night?" Disappointment soured my stomach. "Ben, you've already played so many places on this trip, and we agreed to leave tomorrow morning."

He reached for my hand. "Yeah, but Nick asked if I could play again since they had to turn people away tonight. Kind of like a pop-up show. And since we aren't in a rush—"

"No." I moved back, my desire to support him warring with my need to return to Hopewell.

He dropped his hand to his side, his previous frown returning.

"I've had a great time traveling with you," I said, "but I'm ready to go home."

"Yeah." He backstepped. "No, you're right. I got excited and didn't think it through. Sorry. I'll go tell Nick and then I'll be ready."

I watched him leave, irritated he'd made me feel like the bad guy. Was it selfish of me to pull him away when there was another opportunity to promote his talent? But we'd made the decision together to leave the day following this performance. Instead of silently fuming while I waited, I took out my phone and texted Trish.

Ben and I are on the east side of the state. We'll be leaving for Hopewell tomorrow morning. See you soon.

My phone rang not even a minute after sending the message. Trish's name displayed on the screen. She never called unless it was important.

"Hey, Trish," I said. "Everything okay?"

"Alex, you're not able to come back yet," she said.

My stomach dropped. "Why not? What's wrong?"

"A lot of our time has been invested in debating and outlining new guidelines. Since the Committee collapsed, many supernatural citizens who previously hid their identities have appeared at our community meetings. More than we expected."

"But that's great!" Only the werewolves and wizards had participated in the Committee, the previous governing body for Hopewell's supernatural population. Supernatural citizens were allowed to live among Commoners, but many kept low profiles to remain safe. "What does that have to do with Ben and me, though?"

"We haven't been able to address the situation with Fillip," Trish said.

This time my stomach gave a sickening twist. "Is he still pissed about losing half his arm? I thought vampires grew bits and pieces back, like a starfish or something."

Trish wasn't amused by my attempt to lighten the mood. "He's ancient and dangerous, Alex, and you humiliated him. He will be waiting for you."

"If he's so angry, wouldn't he have sent someone to find me by now?"

"No," she said. "Vampires are extremely territorial. He wouldn't enter another's domain to follow you. And Fillip cares too much about his flock to endanger members by sending them to another vampire's hunting grounds. Instead, he more than likely posted flock members at the corners of his territory. They will be waiting to alert him when you return."

"I'm getting a bit stir-crazy, Trish. I miss Em. I miss you, Nate, and the other wolves." Ben's scent tickled my nose again. He stood several feet off, his arms wrapped about himself as he waited. "When can we come home?"

"I don't know at the moment," she said. "I hope to secure a meeting with Fillip and broker a deal for your safety."

Guilt soured my stomach. Nate and Trish had already given a lot to help me get settled in Hopewell, and deals with Fillip were expensive. I couldn't imagine how much that one would cost. "I'm sorry you have to do that."

"It's something we're willing to do. You're family,' she said. "Give us a few days. Nate or I will contact you when we have an update on our standing with Fillip."

"Okay, good luck. And thank you." I ended the call.

Ben walked to me, the edges of his mouth turned down. "We're not able to go back. Fillip?"

I shrugged on my jacket. "Apparently he holds grudges?"

The corner of Ben's mouth twitched. "Vampires have a lot of time to do so."

I chuckled and held out my hand for his. The earlier tension between us diffused.

Ben laced his fingers with mine and drew me into a hug. "Do you think the person who grabbed your arm was one of Fillip's people?"

"Trish said he wouldn't risk hurting any of his flock by sending them outside his territory." As a type of matriarch for the wolves in Hopewell, Trish had her fingers in a lot of political pots. She knew the ins and outs of how supernatural citizens operated in the city.

"I'm sorry you can't go back yet." He pressed a kiss to my hair.

"Good news is you can perform that second show after all."

"Nah, it's alright. I already told Nick it wouldn't work."

"Are you sure?"

Ben broke our embrace. "You were right. I've already had a lot of opportunities on this trip. Let's do something tomorrow that doesn't involve performing at shows or fixing Hopewell. Any preference?"

The box and its mysterious contents. Answers about what my grandfather was up to away from his family.

The key.

"How do you feel about a pseudo treasure hunt?" I asked.

Ben lifted his chin and narrowed his eyes ever-so-slightly. "Is this a trick question?"

I laughed. "No. Not at all. Since we're not able to go home, maybe we puzzle out Grandpa's mystery box together. It could be fun."

"Ah, the box." His opinion of the idea was difficult to discern.

It left me feeling defensive and self-conscious. Maybe it wasn't something I could share with Ben. He wouldn't understand. "Do you have a better idea?"

"This treasure hunt... Will there be research? Possibly books?"

I blinked. "Um, probably?"

He grinned and pushed his glasses up his nose. "I'm in."

We walked a few blocks through the spritz of chilly rain to the public parking garage. The end of my nose was cold by the time we reached our level. I slowed as we drew near to my car. The odd scent from Ben's show lingered in the air.

Ben stopped and scanned the poorly lit and murky space, his voice lowered. "What is it?"

I released Ben's hand. "That funny smell I caught a whiff of inside? Whoever it was, they were here, too." My ears and nose straining, I crouched to look under my car and those parked next to it. Scattered trash and the scent of oil and gasoline were all I found. I stood and crept between the cars to the driver's side door.

The hood came into view and I froze. My pulse thudded in my ears. Scratched into the paint in large scrawling letters were the words "YOUR FAULT."

3

I SPUN IN place, eyes narrowed, teeth bared, and a growl rumbling in my chest. Was the vandal still here? Were they watching us?

Ben's eyes widened at my reaction. His gaze darted over the other parked cars.

Not spotting anyone or smelling a stronger scent, the wolf in me receded. I ran my fingers over the ruined paint. "Someone graffitied the car."

Ben scowled at the sight of the wrecked hood. He looked up at me for an explanation.

I shook my head. "I don't know anyone around here."

"It seems pretty personal."

"This whole night is creeping me out." I swallowed. "Let's get to the motel."

We quickly got into the car. I looked in the rearview mirror and backed out of the parking space. A humanoid figure slipped through the shadows of the cars behind us. They had glowing eyes. My heart lurched and instinct kicked in.

Run.

I put the car in drive and rapidly accelerated.

The figure ran along the line of parked cars, their identity obscured by the poor lighting. I took the garage switchback tight and too fast. The car's wheels squealed.

Ben grabbed the passenger door handle, his eyes wide again. "What are you doing?"

"There's someone following us." White-knuckled, I took the next switchback just as fast.

Ben twisted in his seat to look behind the car. "Where? I can't see—Holy shit!" He flinched away from the passenger window, raising his arm to shield his face.

A large figure had leaped forward through the dim light. It landed on the hood of a parked car as we zoomed past. Glowing eyes. A flash of elongated teeth. Claws.

The unmanned parking garage booth and lowered arm blocked the exit ahead. My mind ran through different scenarios. The hood was already wrecked. I pressed down further on the accelerator. "Hold on."

"What!"

The hood of the car went under the gate arm. The arm struck the windshield and snapped. Wood ricocheted off the car in pieces. I wrenched the steering wheel. The car bounced over the curb and onto the street. We sped along the street in the sparse early morning traffic.

Ben turned to look at the garage entrance. "Was that the person from the show?"

"I think so." My heart pounded. "Are they still there?"

"No. I can't see anyone." He sat back, his eyes still rounded. "Alex, someone that big would draw attention. Are you sure?"

"Their weird scent was lingering around the car." My mind spun. Who would know me here? I had no ties to Detroit. "They smelled a lot like a wolf, which would explain the size."

"Are werewolves territorial?"

"Not really?" I couldn't be one hundred percent positive. Whenever I thought I'd made strides in learning my lore, more info would surface, making me feel like an outsider again. It was so damn frustrating. "I don't want to stay at the motel tonight."

"It's two in the morning. Let's get a few hours of rest first."

"But they know our scents now. If they're a wolf, what if they track us? Or are you able to hide that with your magic? Your sister veils sight, scent, and sound." Since Ben's magic use was suppressed when we met, I was still learning what he was capable of.

He shook his head. "My area of magic is different from Joan's. You think this person would make a scene by breaking into a motel?"

"It doesn't feel right. I'm not staying," I said. "Do you know anyone on this side of the state? Maybe within an hour of here?"

"My parents are over here." Ben's features darkened. He rarely spoke about his parents or any past events of his life. My curiosity caused me to pry here and there, but I usually backed off at the first sign of discomfort.

"Would they have wards on their house?"

"Yes."

"Can we crash there?" Maybe he could briefly sideline the tension between them.

He frowned, shifted his weight, and pulled at the seatbelt across his chest like it was suddenly too tight.

"We put distance behind us now," I said. "The wards let us rest without worry. We'll be out of your parents' hair later this morning and driving farther away from whoever the hell was in the parking garage."

"Yeah. Alright." Ben sent a text to his parents. A few minutes later, he received a reply and entered an address into my phone for navigation. The location was about a thirty-minute drive away. Ben's long body seemed to contract. He fell silent, and his focus rested far beyond the road we were traveling.

I'd never met Ben's parents or older brother, only his sister Joan and his grandfather Reginald. The gene for using magic was passed down through his mother. Ben and Joan were both wizards, but the gene didn't become active in his older brother. Since Ben never really talked about his family or growing up in Hopewell, I didn't know how our impromptu visit would be received. He once made the offhand comment that he wasn't as close to his parents as I was to mine.

"When did you last see your parents?" I asked.

His narrow shoulders lifted. "Not since they moved over here, so about thirteen years."

"Did you write?"

"No," he said. "Joan visits them."

Not communicating with my family that long would break my heart. When I was in hiding, my family and I limited our calls. Speaking to them was the highlight of my month. I hesitated, but my curiosity got the best of me. "The tether restricted you to Hopewell, but Joan drove up to visit you from Chicago. Why didn't your parents—"

"How the hell should I know? They're busy people." Ben slipped down in his seat. His arms settled around himself.

Read: Conversation over.

Like my best friend Emma, Ben came from a wealthy family. Unlike Emma, he didn't deftly wield his family's wealth to his advantage. He seemed to avoid doing so at the cost of a drafty studio apartment, threadbare clothes, and a fridge that was nearly empty on a regular basis. Even after nine months together, I still wasn't sure if it was pride or distaste that caused the behavior.

We swung by the motel to grab our belongings and were on our way. The signs of industry faded as we left the city and entered Grosse Pointe. The streetlamps illuminated well-manicured lawns and hedges with long drives leading back to redbrick colonial-style mansions. The car windows were up, but I could smell the money. The navigation directed me to turn into a drive outside an iron gate. The property was surrounded by a redbrick wall.

I checked the house number on the gate to our destination. "This is the place."

"I have the code." Ben checked his phone and read the numbers aloud. I punched them into a console. The gate shuddered and started to retract. We drove up the circular drive. The gate rattled and closed behind us.

At the top of the drive, we parked near the front door. We extracted our duffle bags from the crowded trunk. I also grabbed my grandfather's box, not wanting to spend a night without it near me. Ben reached out to ring the doorbell but quickly withdrew his hand when the door opened.

An older woman wearing a housecoat stood in the doorway. The scents of baby powder and something floral clung to her. I glanced at Ben, but no recognition lit his face.

"Hello, Mr. Sharpe. I'm your mother's assistant, Ms. Williams." She stepped aside and held the door for us. "Please, come in."

"Thanks." Ben followed me inside. "I'm sorry you had to get out of bed for us."

Ms. Williams's smile was tight. "It's no bother." She closed the door. "If you'll follow me, I'll show you to your rooms."

"We only need one room," Ben said.

"Mrs. Sharpe requested two rooms be prepared, one for you and one for your guest," Ms. Williams said.

I raised an eyebrow at Ben.

His grip tightened on the duffle bag. Ben didn't stay in contact with his parents, but he'd said Joan was in touch with them. Surely she would have told them about Ben and me by now.

We climbed a wide staircase to the second floor. Ms. Williams opened a door along the hallway and gestured into the room. "Miss, this is where you'll be staying."

I gave Ben another look. Were we going to play along with the sleeping arrangements? He answered with a helpless shrug.

"Thank you." I entered the spacious guest room and shut the door. The bed frame was exquisitely carved wood, and the decorative rugs were the size of Ben's apartment. I sat on the bed, sinking into the plentiful textiles to wait. My sensitive hearing picked up murmuring down the hall as Ms. Williams took Ben to his room. A door clicked closed. Soft footsteps passed by my room.

I grabbed my bag and box again. Cracking open the door, I peeked into the hallway. No Ms. Williams. I snuck out and quietly closed the door. My vision sharpened in the low light. I walked further down the hall, my nostrils quivering. Ben's warm and spicy scent was one of my favorites, next to lavender, vanilla, and freshly brewed coffee. I followed it to the hallway's end and knocked lightly on the last door.

Ben opened the door. "Sorry about that."

I winked. "Whatever I need to do to get into bed with you."

He chuckled, pulled me into the room, and kissed me.

The guest room assigned to Ben was twice the size of mine. The four-post bed had a canopy, and heavy embroidered curtains covered the windows. "Is that a fireplace?" I walked over to the hearth and turned toward him. "You have a fireplace in here."

He didn't respond and was undressing beside the bed.

I ditched my clothes and pulled on another band t-shirt Ben had surrendered to me. "Hey, have you told your parents we're dating?"

"No, I haven't. Like I said, I don't really talk to them." He got into bed. His head hit the pillow and a relieved sigh left him.

I climbed into bed as well and shimmied closer to Ben. It took a while since the bed was wider than any I'd slept in before. "Not because I'm a werewolf."

He slipped his arm around me. "Alex."

"Okay, okay." My thoughts returned to the stranger at Ben's show and the fact they found my car in the garage. Did someone follow us from Hopewell? It didn't make sense. We'd been at my family's place in New York before Detroit. "Ben?"

His voice was already groggy. "Hmm?"

"Whoever was in the garage, they won't be able to find us here, right? You double-checked that your parents have—"

"We're good. Mom said the privacy wards are set at the wall surrounding the place." He briefly tightened his arms around me. "No more night thoughts. Time to rest."

I snuggled against him in the comfy bed, my body gradually relaxing from the evening's frightening encounters. My sleep was fitful. I didn't have the recurring nightmare, the one of the wolf inside me awakening, but images of glowing eyes and ominous shadows haunted my dreams.

4

LIGHT CREPT AROUND the edges of the curtains when I finally gave up any hope of restful sleep. I slipped out of bed, sat on a chaise lounge, and rustled through my Grandpa's box.

One of the items was an old state map of Michigan. The towns circled on the map aligned with the article clippings. A vague trail formed between towns, first west and then north, through the state. Taking out my phone, I pinned the towns on the navigation app to get a better idea of driving times. I chewed at my thumbnail, wondering where we should go first.

"Find anything interesting?"

My attention switched to the bed I'd vacated.

Ben lay on his side, wrapped in the covers and wearing a groggy smile. "You're glaring at your phone like it offended you."

"These old articles . . ." I collected them up and tucked them back into the box. "I don't know why he kept them." I replaced the box's lid. "And there are similar articles over multiple years." Shivering, I left the chaise in favor of the bed and Ben.

He held up the covers so I could join him, then wrapped the warm sheets and blankets around me. I curled up beside him and inhaled deeply. Usually, his scent and touch helped to calm my mind, but the box agitated my thoughts.

"I called Grandma yesterday before your show to ask her about the box. She was a bit evasive, but she said she doesn't know anything about the articles, photos, or the key."

"A key?"

Dammit. I'd unintentionally let that detail slip. But why was I hiding the key from him in the first place? Since he was a wizard, I could share the more uncertain parts of my life as a werewolf.

He's safe.

"There was a key on a necklace with his dog tags," I said.

"What's it for?" Ben's tone wasn't angry, only curious.

"I don't know." I shifted to press my body closer to him. "And I don't understand why Grandma wouldn't know, either. It was almost ridiculous how crazy they were for each other. Why would he keep secrets from his partner?"

Ben chuckled.

I frowned and pushed myself up on an elbow to look down at him. "What?"

The covers shifted as he shrugged. "People can do pretty stupid shit to protect each other." He nudged me. "Right?"

So maybe I had a bad habit of keeping info from loved ones with the hope it would keep them safe. "But it's like..." My chest tightened. "It's like I had this idea of who Grandpa was, and now that's all messed up. Was he even the person I thought he was? It doesn't feel good."

Ben brushed the back of his fingers along my cheek.

I leaned into his touch. "I have a map of the towns mentioned in the articles. Maybe you can look ahead and find a few more venues to play."

His eyebrow arched. "It sounded like you were done with that. I think the word 'stir-crazy' was used."

"I meant that about traveling in general. I'd prefer to go back to Hopewell, but that isn't an option right now."

"Sure, I can do that." With a few groans, he sat up. "Can we get breakfast first?"

"We're eating here?" My stomach gave an anxious twist at the thought of meeting his parents. There was a tiny part of me that'd hoped we could sneak out before they woke up.

"We'll be expected to since we stayed here," he said. "And it's a free meal."

"Free is good." I slipped out of bed and padded to the adjoining bathroom. There wasn't time for my hair to dry, so I bundled it up in a towel and quickly showered. I could at least ensure I wouldn't smell bad. After emptying my entire bag on the bed, a growl rumbled in my chest. "I have nothing to wear. Is your mom as judgy as Em's?"

"Alex, it's going to be okay," Ben reassured me from his perch at the edge of the chaise lounge. He'd simply changed, pulled his hands through his hair, and was ready. "We've been traveling. They won't expect anything more than comfortable clothes."

"It's the first time I'm meeting them. I want to make a good impression." I didn't want to be a point of contention between Ben and his parents. I settled for a pair of jeans and a black t-shirt. Basic. Unassuming. Hopefully acceptable. A ponytail was all I could do for my frizzy curls. Taking one last look in the mirror, another growl rumbled inside me.

"No frustrated growling." Ben stood and offered me his hand. "You look great."

I held tight to Ben as we went into the hall together. Sounds of the household already in the swing of the morning routine reached my ears. At the top of the stairs, the aroma of breakfast caused more rumbling inside me. I placed my hand over my stomach.

Ben chuckled. "Same." At the bottom of the stairs, he hesitated. "I haven't been here before, so I don't know where—"

"The food is that way." I pointed to a side hall.

He gave me a suspicious glance. "Were you already—"

I tapped my nose with my fingertip.

Ms. Williams bustled into the entryway, her smile warm at the more reasonable hour. "Good morning, Mr. Sharpe. Miss. I hope you slept well."

"Good morning," I said. "It's Alex."

"Steward," Ben said.

"You can just call me Alex."

Ms. Williams nodded. "Mr. Sharpe, Miss Steward, please follow me."

Ben's fingers tightened around mine.

I gave his hand a gentle tug to get him moving. I lowered my voice. "Together, we got this."

He swallowed and nodded, but the faintest odor of fear drifted around him.

We followed Ms. Williams to a long dining room with tall windows, chandeliers, and another fireplace. High-backed chairs surrounded a table set with pretty serveware.

A woman with salt-and-pepper hair stood when we entered. She wore a simple blouse, shawl, and pair of slacks. Smiling, she opened her arms to Ben. "There you are. I wanted to let you sleep as long as you needed. You arrived so late."

Ben released my hand when she enfolded him into a hug. He tentatively raised his arms and placed them lightly around her. "Hey, Mom."

I clasped my hands and remained quiet, not wanting to intrude on their reunion.

"We've missed you." She held him at arm's length and beamed up at him. "You look healthy! Your eyes are so clear." Her gaze moved over his throat, but she didn't comment on the recently removed tether. I thought it was strange since Ben's tethering severely impacted his mental health.

Footsteps approached from behind us. A tall man with brown hair and glasses entered the room. "Benjamin! Good to see you." He grinned. "When your mother told me you'd be at breakfast, I wasn't sure whether or not to believe her."

Ben exchanged a handshake with the man. "Dad."

Ben's mom gestured at her son. "Can you believe it, Noah? Our youngest is a grown man."

"Yes, so I see," Noah said.

"Where did the time go?" His mom reached up to push hair away from Ben's eyes. "If you'd like, Benjamin, we could schedule you an appointment with your father's barber before you leave."

Ben tipped his head back out of her reach. "No, thank you. I'm good."

"Hope you're hungry." Noah clapped him on the shoulder. His gaze fell on me. "Can you introduce us to your friend?"

"This is Alex," Ben said.

I waited a beat before conjuring my *I'm a Polite Young Woman* smile for his parents. "Hello. Thank you for letting us stay here."

"Welcome, Alex." His dad shook my hand. "I'm Noah. This is my wife, Linda."

"Alex." His mom startled me by hugging me as well. "Welcome to our humble home. It's nice to meet you." She gestured to the table. "Let's eat."

The kitchen staff brought in steaming dishes of breakfast foods. We passed the platters of bacon, eggs, fruit, toast, waffles, and pastries around the table. I tried not to overfill my little plate. In my experience, wealthy people tended to have either ridiculously small plates or huge plates and comically tiny food portions.

Linda, stealing glances at Ben as he ate, cleared her throat. The behavior immediately brought Ben's grandfather, Reginald, to mind. "Your father and I were chatting earlier, and we tried to remember what career you'd wanted to study in college."

Ben didn't look up from his meal. "Architect."

Noah snapped his fingers. "I'd thought it was something with design or building."

"Are you still interested in that field?" Linda asked.

"No," Ben said.

"I think you'd make a great architect," Noah said.

"Your father and I would help with school expenses," Linda said. "We don't want money keeping you from what you love."

"No thanks," Ben said.

"Could I send along something so you can buy new clothes?" Linda asked.

I tried to catch Ben's eye. The money would be nice for our trip. Linda didn't need to know we spent it on something other than clothes.

"My clothes are fine, Mom," Ben said.

"They're a tad . . ." She cleared her throat again. "They're looking well worn."

"No, thank you," Ben said.

I was refilling my plate when the question I'd dreaded was asked. Linda, finished with her meal and drinking tea, smiled at me. "Alex, what do you do with your time? Tell us about yourself."

I paused, a forkful of eggs halfway to my mouth. Why weren't they more interested in what their son had been up to? "Um . . ." I glanced at Ben and realized at the moment he might not have the stamina. He stared down at his plate, pushing a piece of sausage around. I lowered my fork. "Well, right now we're coming back from visiting my parents and Grandma in New York State. We were talking about traveling north next."

"How far up north? We have a dear friend living in Bellaire." Linda looked at Ben. "Maybe you can stop and visit him."

"Why up north?" Noah asked. "Going for the fall colors? I'm not sure if they're at their peak yet."

"If we see any, that'll be a bonus." I didn't want to share the puzzle of Grandpa's box with people I'd just met. "We thought Ben could pick up a few more shows."

His dad raised an eyebrow. "Shows?"

Linda's smile slipped. "Joan told us you were done with that silly band, Benjamin. She promised you'd found a real job to support yourself."

"I am, and I have." Ben set his fork beside his plate. "This is something different."

Noah didn't bother to mask his concern. "Do you still have your job? Weren't you working in retail?"

"Yes." Ben wiped his hands and set his napkin aside. He looked across the table at me, his features dark. "Ready to go?"

My mouth full of toast, I looked down at my half-full plate, at his parents, and back at Ben. I wondered if it would be a faux pas to bring the plate back to the bedroom as we packed.

"Leaving already?" Noah asked.

"We haven't seen you in years," Linda said.

"You could've visited any time." Ben stood. The edges of his mouth turned down. "I sure as hell wasn't going anywhere."

"Let's not ruin today with rude behavior," Linda said. "Please sit down so we can talk."

Shaking his head, Ben backed away from the table. He gave me one last glance, turned, and left the room.

"Thank you for breakfast." I stood and grabbed half a bagel from my plate. "It was nice to meet you." With a final smile for his parents, I jogged after Ben. I caught up with him on the stairs. "We don't have to rush out if—"

"No, I'm ready to leave." We walked back to our guest room.

"Hey, talk to me." I caught his arm. "What's going on? Was it all their picking at you?"

"I don't want to be around them. Not once did they visit me while I was trapped in Hopewell. I was alone for years, and now they're acting like nothing . . ." He shook his head and gestured to his throat. "I don't know why I thought it'd be different with the tether gone. It's not like we were ever close in the first place."

I set the bagel aside and hugged him.

"Sometimes I wish they could be . . ." His hold tightened on me. "Your family is so close. Mine is so fucking . . . absent."

I kissed his cheek. His skin was wet and salty. My heart ached for him. "Your sister adores you. I know because she was a bitch to me at first. She didn't want anyone messing with her little brother."

He grimaced. "Sorry."

"I know Em, Trish, and Nate aren't your siblings or parents, but they'd all be bummed if you weren't around." Slipping my hands down and into his back pockets, I grinned up at him. "And hopefully you know how much I enjoy having you as close as possible to me."

A small smile brightened his features. He kissed my forehead. "Thanks."

I caught his chin and gave him a proper kiss. I loved the taste of him. I continued to give him lingering kisses as I backed him toward the bed. We weren't in *that* much of a rush to leave.

Ben chuckled, the sound causing a different type of warmth inside me. It wasn't the hunger for him my wolf reveled in, which was definitely firing deep in my navel, but a more delicate and nuanced one in my chest.

The back of his legs bumped against the edge of the bed. He broke our impromptu makeout session to scoop me up, turn, and toss me atop the mattress.

"Hey!" I laughed. "How am I supposed to seduce you if you're stealing all my moves?"

Grinning, he crawled onto the bed after me. When we first met, his behavior would have triggered the protective wolf in me in an extremely bad-for-Ben way. But through frustratingly slow steps and a hell of a lot of patience on both our parts, my body's comfort level with him improved. I understood his flirtatious and goofy hijinks for what they were.

He's safe.

He crawled over the top of me and searched my eyes. His voice was low. "This okay?"

"Yes." I squirmed, wanting contact again. "It'd be better if we were closer."

He leaned down and teased me with a soft and lingering kiss. A low hungry growl sounded in my chest. His focus remained on my mouth, and a small smile turned up his lips. "That's my favorite one."

I was moments from pulling him down on top of me. "Then less talking and more touching."

The sound of footsteps in the hall reached my ears. My body tensed beneath Ben. He immediately sat back. "Are you okay? Did I do something wrong?"

A light rapping on the door startled him. Linda's voice came from the other side. "Benjamin."

His attention switched to the door. "Great timing," he muttered.

"Please," Linda continued. "I want to talk before you leave. And I have something to give you."

Ben's jaw clenched. He left to open the door. I sat up and scooched to the edge of the bed, quickly straightening both my ponytail and my shirt. As an afterthought, I tried to smooth out the bedspread.

Ben opened the door. Linda's eyes widened briefly when she noticed me sitting on the bed. "Alex. I thought you were staying down the hall."

"She stayed with me," Ben said. "We're together."

I gave Linda a little wave, which I immediately felt like an idiot about. *Hi there! Remember me? Yup, I'm having sex with your baby boy.*

She frowned and entered the room, carrying a small book. "Can I have a moment to speak to my son in private, please?"

"Alex knows about us," Ben said. "She's lupine."

Linda flinched and glanced back at me. "How long—"

"Nine months," Ben said.

Linda recovered and then addressed me. "I'm sorry. Our son doesn't feel the need to keep us informed of the important events in his life."

I bit back my reply, not wanting to cause any more friction between Ben and his parents. Remaining silent was difficult since everything in me wanted to speak up in Ben's defense.

Ben not sharing information about himself wasn't limited to our interactions. Even his sister, whom he was close with, expressed annoyance over the character quirk. But his parents never even asked. Was Linda attempting to change that?

She looked at his throat and asked the question I expected earlier. "How are you feeling since your tether was removed?"

Ben shifted his weight. "Like I can breathe. Like I'm complete."

"Have you considered resuming studies with your grandfather?"

"I kept up my studies," Ben said. "I don't need him."

Linda watched her son. "What's your plan moving forward? Will you be joining Joan and her work in Chicago?"

My pulse skipped. He'd never mentioned wanting to move closer to Joan.

Ben shrugged. "I don't know yet. Alex and I—"

"This is your second chance, Benjamin," Linda said. "Don't squander your gift."

His grandfather, Reginald, had told him the same thing.

Ben's face flushed and his jawline tightened.

I clenched my hands, and a growl rose in my throat.

Linda's gaze returned to me. "Are you the reason he's calling at all hours of the morning asking for a safe place to stay?"

"Mom, stop." Ben scowled. "Alex and I are traveling together. We're making decisions together. Like I said, we're together."

Linda's voice rose and she pointed at him with the book she held. "You've always been an awful judge of character. Too trusting. You must be more guarded around people." She spared me a glance. "No offense, Alex. You seem nice. I'm only concerned for the welfare of my son."

"I wouldn't have guessed that." I internally winced. In my defense, I'd lasted a hell of a lot longer than I thought before voicing my opinion on how they'd abandoned their son.

"I'm sorry?" Her eyes narrowed at me. "You don't know—"

"That's enough, Mom. We're going." Ben started to stuff his things into his duffel bag. I did the same with my bag, all while struggling to withhold some snarling.

"Wait," Linda said. "Before you leave and we don't see you for another ten years, I wanted to give you this." She offered him the small book she'd brought with her.

Ben cautiously accepted it and turned it over. "What's this?"

"When Joan, then you, were awoken to magic, I wanted to guide your apprenticeships. But your grandfather took it upon himself to assume that role. There wasn't room for debate. So instead, I transcribed my spellwork for you." She motioned to the book. "I've never achieved the level of spellcasting my father expected of me, but I'm far from awful."

A part of me felt bad she was shut out of her kids' apprenticeships. I waited, anxious, watching Ben for any sign I should commence with the snarling so we could get out of there.

"You want *me* to have this?" Ben asked. "Not Joan?"

"Joan has her copy," Linda said. "This was supposed to be a present for your sixteenth birthday, but we were out of the country on business. Then you were tethered."

Ben opened the leather cover and flipped through the pages. "Why did you keep it from me? I could've been studying this." He looked up, his eyes stormy.

"You weren't well, Benjamin. I thought having this, without access to your magic, would cause you more grief than good. I didn't realize you'd kept up your studies." She reached out for his arm, but Ben pulled it away. She sighed and clasped her hands together. "I'm glad I can finally give it to you."

Ben snapped the book closed and tossed it in his bag.

We stood in awkward silence before Linda continued. "Can I ask why you had to hide here overnight?"

I spoke up. "Someone was harassing me at Ben's show in Detroit. We think the same person vandalized my car and chased us from the garage. They smelled like lupine, but somehow different."

"Were you followed from New York?" she asked.

I shook my head. "We didn't notice anyone."

"The lupine population is smaller on this side of the state," she said. "Perhaps they didn't approve of someone from out of town visiting without notifying them. The complete mess on the west side due to the dismantling of the Hopewell Committee is a common conversation here. We wouldn't want anything or anyone upsetting our peaceful cohabitation."

My gut was telling me, wizard or not, Linda wouldn't be any help identifying who'd tried to jump us in the garage. But maybe she was right. It was someone who didn't want a strange wolf bringing trouble to their home range. The message scratched into the hood of my car felt personal, though.

"Hopefully we'll leave whoever it is behind us," I said.

Linda's brows were pinched. "Please be careful, Benjamin. You've just had the tether removed."

Ben shifted the bag on his shoulder.

I zipped my bag and grabbed my grandfather's box. "I'm ready."

Ben tolerated another hug from his mother.

"Thank you again for letting us stay, Linda." I hesitated before adding. "It was nice to meet you."

She nodded, her smile unsure, reminding me of her son. "You're welcome back anytime."

Linda walked us to the front door. We didn't see Noah anywhere. By the time we were in the car, the door of the large home was already closed.

"I didn't know she wanted to be a part of our apprenticeships." Ben looked as exhausted as when we arrived. "I thought she was too busy. That we weren't important to her."

I reached over to squeeze his hand. "How can I help you?"

He swallowed, shook his head, and looked away from me. "Get us as far from here as possible."

"I can do that."

5

WE FOUND A gas station and I refilled the car. Ben went to the trunk to dig out a notepad and Linda's book. When I rejoined him, he was already pages deep into the book and scribbling on the notepad.

The money Ben made from the night before would cover tonight's motel stay, wherever that might be. A lot of hassle could've been avoided if he'd accepted the money Linda offered, but I wanted to respect how he chose to deal with his family.

He looked up from the notepad as I passed him the small bag from the gas station store. "Snacks?"

"Yes." I started the car. "They didn't have the flavor of Combos you like, but I got the Cheez-Its. White cheddar, right?"

"Yeah, thanks." He pulled the bag out and opened it despite the breakfast we just had at his parents' house.

Traveling was a fairly new activity for Ben. Since I'd been intermittently on the run for five years after becoming a werewolf, I took it upon myself to mentor him in the finer points of the road trip experience, such as appropriate music and snacks.

"So, wait." At first, he'd looked mildly confused. "I want snacks I wouldn't usually eat?"

"Yes," I'd explained. "I would never eat gas station beef jerky otherwise. Mini donuts? Awful unless devoured on the road."

"Huh." He'd still appeared baffled, but caught on fast during our trip.

"Can you pass me the Funyuns?" I asked.

Ben wrinkled his nose but handed over the requested snack. "Did you remember the—"

"Garlic rye chips? Of course." I winked. "I know what you like."

He leaned toward me, and I met him halfway for a kiss. His voice was a whisper. "Wanted to get one last taste of you before you eat that shit." Laughing, he shied away from the playful punch I gave his arm.

"Says the guy who's going to stink like garlic!" Grinning, I pulled out of the gas station lot and onto the road. "How far until our first stop?"

Ben consulted the map on my phone. "About two and a half hours northwest on the expressway." He looked over at me. "It'll add time to the trip, but there might be more interesting things to see if we go the back way."

"Agreed, and we have the time. The back way it is."

The gas and snack stop teased out Ben's usual smile, and his mood improved. We passed the expressway and drove northwest, through more suburbs, into the rural stretches between towns. Fields of concrete gave way to fields of corn, interspersed with pastures and lone farmhouses.

"It's like there's a weird battle going on." Ben's attention had wandered from his studying. Munching on the cheese-flavored crackers, he watched the scenery pass. He pointed at a farmhouse with a crumbling barn and silo. "Like that one. It's surrounded by crops and then suddenly there's a cluster of identical homes crammed into a field with no trees and a fake water feature."

"Last man standing and the enemy's army waiting at the gates." I crunched on a Funyun.

"When you moved around before settling in Hopewell, did you ever travel up this way?"

"No, but this feels similar to other areas of the Midwest. Farmlands slowly being eaten by pods of cookie-cutter homes with cities few and far between."

"Yeah, that's what I noticed during the spring tour." Ben settled back in his seat. He raised his hand to point out the window again. "Cows."

We zoomed past a herd of dairy cattle. I started laughing.

He smiled and looked over at me. Dark shocks of hair stuck out from beneath his knit beanie, encroaching on his thick eyelashes and gray-blue eyes. "What?"

There was a fluttering in my chest, and the wolf in me stirred. It happened often when Ben looked at me. It was embarrassing how effortlessly he drew that primal part of me forward without even meaning to. I shook my head and focused on the road. "There are going to be plenty of those on this trip."

Multiple small towns we passed through displayed banners strung across the main street announcing a harvest festival. The same was true of our first stop on the state's map. Bales of straw, cornstalks, scarecrows, and every shape of gourd imaginable decorated Alma's downtown district. People bundled in hats, scarves, and heavy coats strolled the sidewalks.

"I'm not sure where to even start asking questions." I found street parking a block north of the downtown area.

Ben zipped up his coat. "What about the newspaper? Is their office here? Do newspapers have offices anymore?"

I pulled out a few articles from the box. "It's a county paper with offices located elsewhere, but the stories took place here."

"Let's take a look around."

We got out of the car. The fall afternoon filled my nose with the odors of crisp air and fallen leaves. Leaves and mud. The articles I held crumpled in my fist.

"Alex?" Ben's voice was distant.

The wolf in me drew forward, bristling. A low and threatening rumble sounded in my chest. I looked up through the sparse tree canopy. These were autumnal leaves, turned gold, red, and orange, not freshly emerged spring leaves. This was different from the day the man's attack woke the wolf in me.

"Alex." Ben's scent mixed with the fallen leaves. He touched my arm.

I flinched and my lip pulled back from my teeth in a snarl.

He yanked his hand away and glanced around us. "Shh, it's okay. Do you need a minute in the car?"

His words brought me back from the awful memory the odor of decaying leaves triggered. I rubbed my hands over my face. "No. I'm sorry." I gestured around me. "It's the smells."

Ben's features were a mix of confusion and concern.

"It was strong and all at once. I'm okay now."

"You're pale as a ghost." He scanned the area again. "Let's get coffee or tea. Maybe a bite to eat of something that isn't junk food." Ben offered me his hand. I took hold of it, and we walked back to the main street filled with historic brick storefronts and milling pedestrians. The odor of the leaves was overtaken by the aromas of woodsmoke, candy, spices, and warm hearty food.

The bright scents of cooking tomatoes and meat caused me to pull Ben toward an area roped off for pedestrians. In the street, rows of long tables were divided up into sections, each with its banner and a cook behind the table. Large bubbling pots sent columns of steam swirling up into the autumn air.

"It's a chili cook-off." My stomach took a turn at the growling. "I think we found lunch."

We purchased enough tickets for both of us to get a few bowls of chili. The price was substantially less than anything we'd get in Hopewell.

"Where're you two from?" asked one of the competing cooks, adding ingredients to his pot. Something spicy, if my nose was correct. He was tall like Ben, but wider with gray hair and a generous gut beneath his apron.

I frowned, instantly suspicious of the guy. I'd spent many years trying to blend in to the point of being overlooked. It was difficult not to default to old precautionary behaviors. When I didn't say anything, Ben answered. "Hopewell."

"West side of the state." The man adjusted his American Legion hat. He spoke to Ben even as he grinned at me. "Your lady can wolf down some food, can't she?"

My jaw tightened, and I forced an exhale through my nose. If I opened my mouth, I'd tell him where to put his hat.

Ben placed his free hand lightly on the small of my back. His touch soothed the anger the guy's rude comment sparked. "It must be this great chili." He gestured down the line of tables with the bowl he held. "Are all these entries . . ."

Their conversation faded. My gaze had fallen on a folded newspaper beside shopping bags of ingredients. I set my bowl down and picked up the newspaper. I unfolded it to find a gruesome full-page photo of a pasture filled with mangled cattle. "Senseless Slaughter" read the headline.

"That's Bill's herd." The cook's voice broke into my thoughts. "Damn shame."

Ben looked over my shoulder at the paper. "What happened?"

I couldn't help scanning the article even while the guy answered, "Not sure. The police think it's a large predator, but bear don't go after cattle and cougar don't come this far south."

The article mentioned an animal attack. A DNR officer suspected a pack of wild dogs. "The fatal wounds appeared canine in nature." I set the newspaper back down and searched my pockets for the two articles I'd pulled from the box. I laid them beside the article's headline and date.

"What you got there?" the guy asked.

I tapped on the article with my fingertip. "This one was from almost forty years ago. A farmer lost a large number of his cattle in a violent attack."

Ben looked between the three articles. "And the other one is from thirty-four years ago. A whole herd gone." He looked up at the cook. "Is this something that happens regularly around here?"

"Well, I haven't seen something like that since . . ." His eyes rolled upward. "Twenty years? Yeah, twenty years ago. Darcie lost her prize chickens. Now, don't tell me a pack of dogs can bust apart a whole chicken coop." He pointed to the older article I'd brought. "I remember that one happening. It was just after I moved here as a kid. Scared the hell outta me. Thought a monster was living in the woods."

I looked up from the articles. "Can I have this newspaper?"

"Help yourself!" He grinned. "Just leave the sports section."

"Thanks." I separated the sports reporting from the paper, folded the remainder, and tucked it under my arm. "Ready to go, Ben?"

His eyes widened, a spoon in his mouth. Ben swallowed the bite of chili and gestured to the bowl. "We can't leave yet. I still have a ticket. It's chili that's paid for and isn't in my stomach."

"Point taken." I eyed the steaming pots. They smelled delicious, but I was full. "Spend your tickets and then we'll take off."

He nodded, finishing the bowl he carried even as he sought out his next. Ben refilled his bowl, and we grabbed a few hot coffees. I steeled myself against the scent of the wet leaves on our stroll back to the car. It didn't catch me unaware this time, but still caused my muscles to twitch.

Ben's phone buzzed. He set the bowl of chili on the dash, leaned to get his phone, and scanned the screen. "One of the towns we're stopping at today, Big Rapids, has a show tonight. They can add me to the bill." When he looked over at me, his eyes were bright and he was smiling. "Maybe tomorrow morning we'll have the cash to get some diner food."

"Oh." I tried not to sound disappointed and started the car. "That was fast. Did you know someone there?"

Ben motioned to his phone. "It's a network that connects performers." He paused before adding, "I thought you said you were okay with me doing this. You were the one to suggest—"

"I know what I said." Having my words thrown back at me didn't feel good. I'd *thought* I was okay with the idea, but something petty and quite close to jealousy soured my mood. I pulled away from the curb in a lurch. "Can you bring up the map so I know where we're going?"

He grabbed the bowl of chili to keep it from sliding across the dash. "Hold on, can you pull over? I can't . . ." Ben tried to access the map with one hand while keeping the food from spilling with his other. He dropped the phone instead. "Shit." He scowled. "Alex!"

"What!"

"Pull over the car."

I jerked the steering wheel to the side. We abruptly stopped beside the curb. My face hot, I avoided looking at Ben, feeling foolish over my childish behavior.

"What the hell is going on with you right now?" he asked. "You're all over the place. Talk to me, please."

I wasn't sure myself. Why was I so irritated he'd found a show to play? I should be happy for him and grateful we'd have money for food. Flustered, I blurted, "We need to get to the next stop. With you taking this gig, we won't have much time to hunt down info on these articles, which is why we're going in the first place."

"I thought you were okay with this or I wouldn't have looked for anything." Ben swallowed. "The show isn't until later at night. We should have plenty of time beforehand. Okay?"

I felt all the more ridiculous that everything was upsetting me. Not being able to return to Hopewell. My grandfather's box. Ben's success and rising popularity. The scary parking garage stranger. Not knowing what the goddamn key would unlock. "Yeah, okay. I'm sorry."

The crease in his brow smoothed. "Okay." He retrieved the phone, brought up the map, and tossed the phone in the console. Then it was back to his chili. "Onward, Holmes," he said around a spoonful.

6

THE NEXT TOWN we stopped in was farther north and similar to the first. The same sort of festive autumnal decor lined the street into a downtown that lasted all of two blocks. Unlike the last stop, many of the storefronts were vacant.

Ben looked out the windows as I searched for a place to park. "Where is everyone?"

"Maybe the cold is keeping them at home?" I pulled the car over in front of an antique mall called *Another Man's Treasure*. "Where's the venue you're supposed to play?"

"It's outside town into the countryside a bit." Ben unbuckled his seatbelt and raised his eyebrows. "Ready to explore?"

"Sure." We got out of the car, and I walked to the trunk to dig through the old box. A blast of wind sent fallen leaves skittering across the street and around our ankles.

Ben shivered. "What news clippings do you have from here?"

"Only one." I passed it to him and closed the trunk.

He looked at the article and grimaced. "Sheep this time."

"Yup. Forty-three years ago."

Ben handed back the article. "It's a pretty gruesome theme for your grandpa to collect articles about. Why do you think he took such a personal interest?"

The darker part of my wolf had an inkling. I hoped I was wrong. "I'm not sure yet. Since he kept the articles together, he must have thought they were related."

"The same pack of animals traveling the state for years killing livestock?"

I avoided his gaze. "Or the same person."

We crossed the sidewalk and entered the antique mall. The temperature inside the building was toasty, almost too much. The seemingly endless space was packed full of so many items that it felt as if the walls were falling in on me. The aisles were vague suggestions rather than official paths. The scents of things forgotten—dust, mildew, and rust—lurked everywhere in the dimly lit store.

"Hello?" I walked further into the store, unsure where the register was located. "Anyone here?" I turned around to talk to Ben, but he was gone. "Ben?"

His voice, wound tight with excitement, came from the general direction to my left. "Over here. There's a huge stash of vinyl. How much money do you think we need for a motel? Probably not as much as in Detroit, right?"

I grinned and shook my head. "We only have so much room in the car, so choose wisely." Ben's record collection was massive, but that didn't keep him from picking up more vinyl whenever given the chance. Imagining the giddiness in his eyes as he sorted through the records gave me a jolt of happiness. "Though we have blankets for sleeping in the car if needed."

He chuckled, and I pushed farther into the store by myself. A large window, one of the few in the store, was filled with a colorful spectrum of vases and dishes, making it appear like stained glass. Tarnished broaches, necklaces, and racks of earrings were enclosed in a long showcase. The scent of musty fabric grew stronger. Racks of clothing, yellowed lace, crushed velvet, and brilliant patterns from the sixties and seventies hung on display.

I rounded the corner and nearly yelped. An entire shelving unit displayed dusty taxidermied animals. Some were wearing clothing. A pair of frogs were mid-leap on a tiny basketball court, complete with a small basketball and a hoop. "What the hell?"

The wood flooring creaked under someone's footsteps, and my attention jerked to the aisle leading to the front... or was it the back... of the store. Nostrils quivering, I tried to pick up who or what it could be. It wasn't Ben. My mind flashed back to the huge figure with glowing eyes at the Detroit show. I caught a whiff of sulfur and smoke. The scent was different. The floor protested with another groan as if under a great weight.

"Can I help you?" The raspy voice belonged to a petite round woman who somehow appeared beside me. Her gray hair was secured in a bun. She held a cane in one hand and a wooden pipe in the other. Her long nails were lacquered in a metallic gold polish.

"Hello," I stepped back. "I was just browsing. It's my first time visiting."

"It's a bit of a hunt, but we have many treasures here," she said. "Some you don't even realize you need until you find them."

I glanced around. "Yeah, there's a lot. Are you the owner?"

She nodded and took a puff on her pipe.

"How long have you had it?" If she'd lived in the area for a while, maybe she knew about the strange livestock killings.

The woman's shoulders lifted. "It depends on what you believe to be long. My shop has been here for over a hundred years."

She didn't look a day over sixty.

"Your family owned it for that long, right? Because you'd look great for over a hundred." I heard Emma in my head requesting the woman's skincare routine.

The woman smiled. A few of her teeth were gold. "Thank you." She waddled toward me to close the small space I'd placed between us. The smoke odor grew potent. "What a beautifully kept piece." She touched my jacket's sleeve. Her nails made a light scratching sound on the fabric. "A hand-me-down from someone important to you?"

"Yes." I looked from the patched sleeve to her. "My grandfather's."

Her gaze moved up and down me once. "Vietnam."

I nodded. She knew her history.

"Memories can make an otherwise invaluable item precious." She puffed on her pipe. "Would you consider trading the jacket?"

I opened my mouth to answer, but my Shield suddenly flared to life. The magical tattoo, protecting me against malicious magic, burned on my breastbone. My hand flew instinctively to my chest. A growl leaped into my throat, but I kept it contained. The act of a wizard gathering energy for a spell usually sent a tingling sensation over my skin.

Ben's scent drifted to my nose, and his footsteps sounded on the wood floor behind me. "I think I've narrowed it down to the necessary few." He wore a wide grin and held a box full of records. His attention moved from me to the shop owner. "Hello."

The woman made a reptilian-like hiss. Her shoulders drew up near her ears where long gold earrings hung. She studied Ben with narrowed eyes. "Don't think you'll charm me and escape without paying for those, young man."

Ben blinked, his smile tentative. "Yeah, I'll pay for them."

"Why don't we settle that right now." She pointed with her pipe. "The register is this way."

Ben gave me a glance before he squeezed past me and followed the older woman.

"I'm with him." There was no way I wanted him wandering off with a possibly dangerous magic user. I walked behind the two, getting the strongest noseful of sulfur yet. I lifted the back of my hand to my nose and mouth, my eyes watering.

The floor creaked and moaned as the petite woman shuffled along. I thought we were lost again, but the narrow path discharged us into an open space with an ornate rug. Two upholstered chairs faced each other across a small table. A wooden chess set, part of the board singed, was on the table. I lowered my hand and smelled faint traces of burnt wood.

Beside the small gathering of furniture was a counter with an ancient-looking scale and register. The woman walked behind the counter and pulled a step stool toward her.

Ben set the box on the counter and gave me a sideward glance, mouthing *What the hell?*

I mouthed back *I know!*

The woman climbed atop the stool, enabling her to see over the counter. Eyeing the tattoos along Ben's throat and neck, she said, "There are no returns. All sales are final."

He nodded. "I understand."

She flipped through the albums, noting the price of each fluorescent green dot sticker as she muttered to herself.

It was my chance to clue Ben in on what had happened. He had a far better understanding of the supernatural world than I did. I tugged on his sleeve. "Hey, did you see . . . um . . . the cute frogs over there?"

His brows gathered.

"We'll be right back. No one should miss seeing these frogs." I pulled Ben away by the sleeve. When we were out of sight of the counter, I lowered my voice. "She tried to use magic on me. My Shield stopped it."

Alarm flashed in his eyes.

"But it was different from your or any other wizard's magic that I've felt," I said. "Well, except Sebastian. I couldn't feel all of his spells. Is that a necromancy thing?"

Ben frowned at the mention of his ex. "They use material components like blood so they don't fully rely on gathering energy." He looked back over his shoulder. "I'm glad Sandra repaired your Shield before we left Hopewell. Do you want to leave?"

"No."

Ben's frown deepened. "You said she tried—"

"I didn't want you to be surprised if things escalated." I held up my newspaper clipping. "She said the shop is over a hundred years old. If she has been here that long, I want to ask her about this."

Ben licked his lips. "I don't know. Maybe we ask somewhere else. We don't know who or what we're dealing with here."

The shop's dim lighting flickered and faded. Shadows seeped out from shelving, nooks, and crannies like fog. The sulfur smell from before became overwhelming. I gagged and covered my nose. Even Ben made a face because of the unpleasant odor.

"Conspiring against me, are you?" The deep voice rattled items on the shelves. A pair of large, glowing, reptilian eyes shown from the dark. "Planning to steal my treasure? Wretched wizard."

I reached for the wolf in me, and heat charged my muscles. I stepped in front of Ben and released a low growl of warning directed at the stranger in the dark.

"Ah, a lupine lackey. How typical," the voice rumbled. "You wizards are never willing to get your hands dirty. Was she going to steal my treasures while you paid for the records? Do you think I wouldn't have noticed?" The eyes flashed. Smoke snaked along the floor from the shadows.

I glanced at Ben, hoping to gain a clue of what we were up against. He was practically cowering, his eyes wide and his thin body trembling. So . . . pretty bad, then.

"We're not here to steal from you," I said. "We're passing through, gathering information."

"Information?" There were clicking sounds, like talons against wood. "What kind of information do you seek?"

I thrust my arm forward, holding out the article like a paper shield. "A weird event took place outside this town fifty years ago, and we want to know more about it."

"Before your time," the voice said. "What event do you speak of?"

"Sheep," Ben sputtered.

"A killing of a herd of sheep," I clarified.

Another low rumble filled the shop, and I realized it was a chuckle. The floorboards creaked, and the old woman emerged from the shadows. Her pupils remained as slits.

Energy surged through the room past me, making my skin prickle. Ben stepped beside me, the readied spell causing a blue light to crackle around his clenched fist.

He was still trembling like a leaf.

I reached out and put a hand on his arm. "Wait."

"Yes, I remember." The woman took a large puff of the pipe, and smoke rolled out of her nostrils. "He tried to accuse me of that as if I'd be so uncultured as to slaughter livestock."

"Who?" I said. "Who accused you of it?"

The woman flashed her now sharp teeth. "A lupine like yourself who thought he could outsmart someone as old and clever as me."

We said Grandpa's name at the same time. "Alexander Steward."

There was a twisting sensation in my chest. Years ago, my grandfather spoke to the same shop owner I spoke to now. "What was he doing? Was he tracking something or someone?"

The woman studied me, puffing on her pipe again. "Give me the jacket and I'll tell you."

My answer was immediate. "No."

Her gaze slid past me and stopped on Ben. "Then give me the wizard."

I looked at Ben, biting at my bottom lip.

His voice quavered as he shot back. "You're not getting anything from us. We're leaving."

"Please, tell me," I said. "Alexander was my grandfather."

"Alex, we need to go." Ben took a step back. "We'll find this information somewhere else."

Smoke rose out of the woman's nostrils. She watched me, smug. "Do as he bids you. Follow along at his heels."

Anger flared in my chest. "What else?" I snarled. "What can I give you? You can't have my jacket or him."

She studied me with narrowed eyes.

The woman had told me that memories make items valuable. I grabbed my wallet from my pocket. "What about this?" I pulled out a picture. It was a cheesy photo, staged at one of the neighborhood department stores, but the only family photo small enough to carry in my wallet. My heart ached with loss even as I offered it up. "Would this work?"

The woman shuffled forward.

Ben tensed. His fingers twitched and the blue light crackled.

She received the slightly bent photo with her gold fingernails. Wrinkles deepened around her mouth as its edges turned up. "This will do." She tucked the photo away in her cardigan. The pockets were brimming with other small odds and ends, many sparkling. "Your grandfather was searching for who killed that flock. He arrived at my shop with a folder of those clippings. In the string of several stories he imagined he saw a pattern."

"You don't think there's a pattern?" I said.

"I didn't say that," she said. "But those acts against Commoners don't concern me. I work in the trade of treasures, magic, and memories, not livestock. Once he realized I wasn't responsible for the farmers' loss, he left."

"When he stopped in here, was he alone?" I asked.

"That will cost you," she said.

"I don't have anything else to trade." And even as I said it, I couldn't remember what I'd already given the woman.

She looked between the jacket and Ben. "But you do, don't you?"

Ben's lowered voice was a plea behind me. "Alex."

"I can't give you those." I swallowed. "They mean too much to me."

"Then I'll ask you to leave. Be sure to take the wizard with you."

I backstepped. "We'll try. It's a bit confusing in here."

The woman already walked away. The shadows retreated like a dark robe she pulled behind her. The lighting brightened, at least to the dim light previously reaching into the shop from outdoors.

Ben released the energy for the spell. It spread out like a wave, rippling over me. I shivered. "I guess you won't be getting the records, then?"

"Don't remind me." We wound toward the front door, and he threw a scowl back to the store's interior. "I found rare vinyl I've been searching for, and they're in the clutches of probably the single dragon squatting in the Midwest."

I stopped, staring at his retreating back. A dragon? Those weren't real. "Are you screwing with me right now?"

"No." He held the front door open for me. "There aren't many other reasons I'd leave those records behind."

I blinked and hurried out the door. "Aren't dragons supposed to be, well, bigger?"

"I'm thankful she didn't decide to go that route. I almost pissed myself as it is. If she'd decided to attack us, I don't think I could've held her off."

"Huh." I glanced at him. "Do *all* the other supernatural beings hate wizards? Because it seems like a lot of them do."

Ben stopped beside the car. "We don't have the best reputation. A lot of wizards believe they're . . ." He paused to find the word. "*More* than other supernatural beings."

"That's not obnoxious at all." No wonder Nate got so snarly about wizards. "Has it always been like that?"

"From how the books during my apprenticeship relayed our history, yes," he said. "I didn't notice until I was tethered and excluded from those social circles. Then it was so obvious I felt foolish for never noticing it."

"Because you were suddenly treated as an outsider and less than the rest of the wizards," I said.

He nodded.

I walked my fingers up his chest and kissed his nose. "I'm not sure it offers comfort, but I think you're pretty alright for a wizard."

Ben smiled. "Well, thank goodness for that."

WE CHECKED INTO the town's only motel, a relic from the seventies with decor that hadn't been updated since. I asked Ben if it was okay spending money on the hotel seeing as there was a box of records down the street we could buy instead. The sour expression he gave in return made me think the joke was premature.

We hauled our bags into the room. There was a barely-there odor of old cigarette smoke clinging to the walls. I sat cross-legged on the bed with my grandfather's box. Ben lay beside me on his stomach with his laptop, wearing a large pair of headphones. He wanted to make final edits on the music for that night's show.

I'd grouped the clippings by town and then chronologically within the group, adding the article I'd found at the chili cook-off. I chewed at my thumbnail, looking between them and willing it all to make sense. "There isn't an exact pattern, but they all occur in similar areas. Do you think it's a curse?" When I didn't get a response, I looked over at Ben. Music leaked from the headphones as he worked. I tapped him on the leg.

His attention jumped from the laptop to me. He pulled the headphones off. "Yeah?"

"Curses are real, right? Are they a type of magic?"

"There are many types of magic that could create what you would think of as a curse or hex."

I scanned the articles, neatly grouped on the bedspread. "Do you think that's what's going on here? It happened pretty regularly."

"But it moves," he said. "It doesn't happen regularly in the same towns."

"It's the same general areas, though." I picked up my phone and pulled up the map. "We have to be dealing with a person. But going that far back? They'd be pretty old by now."

"You're sure it's a person, then?"

I motioned to the articles. "The slaughtering of these animals appears mindless. They were killed for fun, not prey. The only creature I know that does that is a human."

"Well, that's grim," Ben said.

"It's true." I gave him side-eye. "Probably a 'wretched wizard.'"

He laughed. "Yeah? You think so?"

I lifted my chin and smirked. "Yeah."

Ben sat up, tossed his headphones aside, and tackled me. Delighted by his playfulness, I started laughing. Ben's scent, strong in our tumble, drew the wolf in me forward. I hooked a leg around him to keep his body pressed against mine. My glowing golden eyes shone in the lenses of his glasses.

"How much longer do you need to finish your work?" I asked.

He pressed a kiss to the edge of my jaw. To my neck. "I could be done. Why? What were you thinking?"

I pushed my hips up against him. "That we have a few hours before your show."

"We do." He grinned. "And?"

Heat already spread through my body as I imagined how to fill the time. "And I want you."

7

WHEN BEN SAID the show was in the countryside, he wasn't exaggerating. We drove ten minutes northwest of town, past multiple cornfields. The moon provided the only light in an otherwise inky-dark night sky.

"So, where is this place?" I said. "Is it even on a map?"

"Yeah. I downloaded directions before we left the motel." Ben's face was lit from beneath by his phone. "It should be coming up here soon." He looked up and pointed. "I think it's that dirt pathway going into the cornfield."

"*Into* the cornfield?" I frowned. "This is the part in the horror movie where the audience is shouting 'Don't go in there' to us."

Ben scanned the field. "There's a building back there."

"Yup. That's where we'll be murdered with a pitchfork by Bill in his pig shed." I pulled off the road onto a dirt path made wide enough for a larger vehicle, probably a tractor. Even moving slowly, the car pitched around from the uneven bumpy terrain. The bouncing headlights caught the edges of pale cornstalks rising on either side.

Headlights swung up behind us as another car turned onto the path. Ben looked back into the headlights, squinting. "Must be more people coming to the show."

I didn't like having the unknown car at my back, especially since we couldn't drive fast if needed. My nerves elevated the tone of my voice. "Definitely not Bill, here to murder us."

Ben turned to face forward again. "I wonder how often they use random locations like for concerts."

"Probably not much else to do around here."

"I didn't see any music venues, anyway. I like that they're creating spaces for events."

We finally reached the metal building. Unlike my prediction, it seemed to be an old storage building, not a home for livestock. Several cars and pickups were parked in a patch of empty field beside the building. The car following us pulled up beside us and parked as well. A group of people chatting with each other got out and headed toward the building.

Ben looked at me. "I think we have the right place."

We got out of the car, and the pungent scent of manure nearly knocked me on my ass. I gagged and pulled my shirt collar up over my nose. "Holy hell, that's foul."

Ben gave me a sympathetic smile. "It must be awful having your nose right now. Maybe it won't be as bad inside."

We followed the people through an entrance with a tall sliding door hanging from a metal track. Ben was right. The manure odors were muted inside the building, covered up by a grass-like aroma and dust. The building's walls were made of metal, streaked with rust, and rose high above us. It seemed like a modern version of one of those wooden barns. Two-thirds of the way through, there was an open loft with stacked bales of hay or straw.

Ben checked his phone. "I'm supposed to meet someone at the loft when we get here."

A young woman waited at the ladder to the loft. She grinned when she spotted Ben and stepped forward with her hand outstretched. "Hey, I'm Cathy, the organizer of this chaos. Thanks for filling in at the last minute."

I immediately recognized Cathy's scent. Each lupine had an individual scent, but the primal and earthy base was universal. The wolf in me was pleased because Cathy would detect my scent around Ben, letting her know where he and I stood.

Ben shifted his laptop bag on his shoulder and accepted the handshake. "Ben Sharpe. Thanks for adding me. This is my girlfriend, Alex."

Or, that worked, too.

Her attention focused on me, and her nostrils twitched. She grinned. "Welcome, Alex."

"Hello." I shook Cathy's hand. Hopefully, she was grinning because she was pleased to have another wolf at the show, not because of Ben's introduction. I wasn't sure why, but I found the label of "girlfriend" embarrassing and a bit juvenile. Ben and I hadn't formally settled on how to introduce each other. We'd figure it out later.

"Sorry about the fertilizer," Cathy said. "It's often rough on new noses."

"It doesn't bother you?" I asked.

"You don't even notice it after a while." She gestured up at the loft. "I'm sorry, but with all the sound equipment up there, we can only fit a couple of people."

"That's alright. I prefer to watch from the crowd." I exchanged a kiss with Ben and murmured near his ear. "Cathy is lupine." Unless it was out of urgency, I let Ben decide if he wanted to tell other supernatural beings he was a wizard. I parted from him. "Good luck with the show."

His eyes were warm with affection. He caught my hand and pulled me close for one more quick kiss. "Thanks."

My stomach cartwheeled. One endearing look and he made me feel like the most important person in the room. Ben climbed the ladder after Cathy to get ready for the show. More people filled the main floor below the loft.

Prowling about, I found a stack of solo cups and a keg. People were helping themselves. I poured myself a cup of what looked and smelled adjacent to beer. I took a sip and immediately leaned over my cup to let the beer run back out of my mouth. Hopewell had spoiled me with its large selection of delicious beer.

The lighting was pared down from Ben's usual shows, and there was no video, but the crowd went crazy anyway. As Emma would insist, the joy of music and dancing is universal. I squeezed into the crowd, losing myself in the music and the aroma of the warm bodies.

That's when the scent hit me, the one I'd noticed during Ben's Detroit show. The one from the frightening encounter in the parking garage. It powered its way past the odors of cheap beer and the dancing crowd. The wolf in me lurched to the surface, and I clenched my hands to keep them from shifting. I harnessed my heightened vision and the dark space brightened. Turning in place, I frantically searched for the scent's owner. Waving arms and moving bodies obscured my field of sight. A pair of glowing eyes watched me from not even ten feet away, but when I pushed my way toward them, they disappeared.

Was I losing my mind? I hadn't imagined the encounter at the show. The scratches on my arm were almost healed, but they were still there. And there was no way Ben and I made up the shadow chasing us in the parking garage. But why would the same scent be this far northwest in a random cornfield? Had the person followed us? I wished Nate or Trish were here to assure me I wasn't crazy. That the scent I'd caught, musky and putrid, was actually present.

The figure with glowing eyes appeared near the door. I shoved my way through the crowd toward them. When I reached the doorway leading outside, the stranger was gone. I stepped out of the heat generated by all the bodies into the crisp evening air . . . and was smacked in the face with the manure odor. I pressed the back of my hand under my nose, a frustrated growl brewing in my chest. There's no way I'd find anyone out here by scent.

The encounter set my nerves on edge. Instead of rejoining the dancing, I lurked near the wall, watching the door. I grew impatient as Ben chatted with Cathy after the show. Only a handful of concertgoers remained when he descended from the loft. I was waiting for him at the bottom of the ladder.

My expression or body language must have communicated my nerves because Ben immediately asked. "What's wrong?"

"The stranger from your Detroit show and the parking garage is here."

"What?" His gaze darted around the room. "How in the hell did they find us here?"

"I don't know."

He looked back at me with a frown. "They didn't grab you again, did they?"

"No. I caught their scent before they could. It was halfway through your second set. I got a glimpse of them, too, but couldn't track them after they slipped outside."

"If this person followed us up here, they must have an issue with us. Please don't go after them alone."

I had a reputation for pursuing questionably dangerous situations without him. It drove him nutty, but I did so to protect him. "They smell so strange. They're like a werewolf . . . only different. I'd never scented someone like that before. If it's the same person from Detroit, I want to know who it is and why they're following us."

Ben's gaze swept over the emptying space again. "We can watch for them while we're leaving."

Cathy called down, descending from the loft. "Everything okay?"

I waited until she stood beside us. "When you were getting ready tonight, was there anyone who didn't smell quite right?"

She lifted an eyebrow. "Like someone I didn't recognize? There are always new people coming and going at these events."

"But the scent would have stood out to you, trust me," I said. "Nothing odd?"

Cathy shook her head, but her gaze swept the space and her nostrils flared. "Is this something I should be worried about?"

I wasn't sure how to answer. The stranger seemed to be following Ben and me. We were leaving town tomorrow. "I don't think so."

She didn't seem pleased by my flimsy answer. "I'll call if I notice anything while cleaning up. I have Ben's number."

We thanked Cathy and left for the car. It was odd to rely on only sight and hearing once outside, my sense of smell shot from the manure funk. The last groups of concert attendees were getting into their cars. Conversations, the slamming of car doors, and the starting of engines punctured the otherwise silent and brisk night.

Not a trace of the stranger.

We got into the car and followed the drive back onto the road. A car passed us, cruising at a decent speed on the unmarked roads. I accelerated, wanting to get back to town as soon as possible. "Do you think we should still stay tonight?" I glanced in the rearview at the empty road.

"Look out!" Ben pointed ahead to the shoulder.

My gaze jerked forward. A large furry mass struck the front of the car. It bounced off the bumper and smashed into the windshield. Glass shattered. I released the steering wheel, raising my arms and hands to shield my face.

The car careened off the edge of the road, dipped down into the ditch, and lurched up onto the embankment of a field before stopping. Shaking, I lowered my arms. The front of my shoulder ached from where the seat belt had bit into it. The car's headlights illuminated a wall of corn.

I looked over at Ben, my chest quickly rising and falling. The scents of his blood and fear swirled around us. "Are you okay?"

Trembling, he stared at the corn. "What the *fuck* was that?"

"Ben." I brushed glass from his jacket sleeve. "Are you hurt?"

He turned his attention to me, his expression dazed before his mind caught up. He gingerly touched his cheek and forehead. "Only a few scratches. You?"

"Same with what feels like a bruised shoulder." I turned off the sputtering car but left the lights on. "I think we hit an animal. Maybe a deer?" My stomach twisted, not loving the idea we'd probably killed it.

He shook his head. "That wasn't a deer."

I wrestled with my seatbelt, but the buckle wouldn't release. The wolf in me warmed the muscles in my upper body. Tightening my hold, I snapped the clasp free from the buckle. I pocketed the keys and opened the door.

"Wait!" The passenger door creaked as Ben got out. "Where are you going?"

I held up a hand, signaling him to be quiet. Whispering cornstalks and crispy air lurked outside. My nose found rich dirt, rotting plants, exhaust from the car, and the damn manure odor that seemed to be everywhere. There were traces of blood and acidic accents of fear that weren't human... and the rotten scent I'd noticed at the show. The hair on my arms and the back of my neck rose. I crept up the short embankment.

Back down the road, a large animal lay in the opposite lane. My heart sank. "Dammit."

Ben stood beside me, shivering from the cold or the adrenaline crash. "Do we call someone about it?"

"I don't know."

We walked toward the fallen animal. I didn't want to leave it in the middle of the road to be dismantled by traffic. Soon we were close enough to recognize it as a deer. Ben shook his head. "That isn't what I saw."

"What?"

"No." His gaze darted back toward the rustling stalks of corn. "That wasn't what I saw at the side of the road. It was tall and broad."

I crouched beside the deer to get a better look. Long gouges of flesh were missing from its flanks. A nasty gash had opened its throat. My nostrils filled with the odor of stale blood. "It was already dead when it hit our car."

Ben stepped away, averting his gaze from the gruesome scene. "So we were hit by a zombie deer? I knew there was something off about this place as soon as we rolled into town."

"That isn't a thing, is it? Zombies?" I pulled the deer from the middle of the lane and down into the opposite ditch.

"In necromancy, there are a few spells—"

I growled. "Great. A necromancer with zombie deer." Never thought I'd add that to my *Shit-To-Deal-With* list. "I don't smell any tissue decay on the body, but the wounds aren't fresh." I swallowed. "And I've seen wounds like that before."

"Where?" Ben extended his hand to help me out of the ditch.

"I created them when Mitch strapped me to a chair and my shifting slipped." My mauling of Emma's evil ex wasn't a proud moment for me. "And when I fought with Fillip."

"So it's confirmed? We have a werewolf on our trail?"

"That's the best guess I have on the deer's wounds and the person's scent." My stomach soured. The person intimidating us along our impromptu road trip was someone like me. Someone who could be deadly to us, especially Ben. Wizards didn't have the physical stamina and accelerated healing inherent in lupine.

The cold gnawed at my fingers and the end of my nose. "If we brush the glass off the seats and drive slowly, maybe we can get back into town."

Ben grasped my hand tight as we returned to the car. I passed him the keys. He got behind the wheel while I waded through the tall grass and wildflowers to the front of the car. My shadow loomed large and menacing against the backdrop of cornstalks. I thought of the trail of livestock killings, and the fact someone like me could have done that.

"Are you okay?" Ben called out the window.

"Yeah, sorry." I turned and braced my hands on the front of the car. The words "YOUR FAULT" screamed at me from the hood.

"Ready?"

"Go ahead." I leveraged the wolf's strength in my body, and my muscles warmed. Ben put the car in reverse and attempted to back out of the ditch. I leaned into the car and pushed. The tires spun, but the car gradually backed away from the cornfield.

We seemed to be making progress until a loud clunk sounded beneath the car. Ben let off the accelerator. "Did you hear that?"

I nodded and passed through the headlights. Crouching beside the car, I looked beneath it. One of the front wheels was pointed straight ahead while the other was angled to the inside. "Dammit," I growled.

Ben stepped out and looked over the roof. "We're not making it out of here, are we?"

I shook my head. "Not with the car."

"I'll check for a signal so we can call a towing company." Ben moved to the road's shoulder and hunted for a cell signal. I shut off the engine, grabbed his laptop, and locked the car. When I joined him, he didn't look pleased. "Nothing."

"We should start walking. It's late, cold, and I'm tired." I surveyed the sea of cornfields. "Not sure we need to worry about the car being stolen since there isn't another human being in sight."

Ben's forehead creased "You want to walk back to town, in the middle of the night, with an angry lupine on our trail?"

"Do we have another choice?" Irritation was winning out over any anxiety I had about the situation. "It's freezing out here. And I should be able to pick up their scent before they can get too close."

Ben took his laptop case from me, and we zipped up our coats. The moonlight painted the pavement silver. Raspy whispers of dry corn stalks filled the air. I wiggled my fingers against Ben's tight hold on my hand. He was cutting off the circulation.

"Sorry." He frowned as his attention leaped from one shadow to the next in the field. "I keep thinking I'm hearing something."

I slipped my arm through his. "Don't worry, I'll protect you."

My attempt to lighten the mood fell flat. He gave me a fleeting glance, his tone serious. "Alex, this thing, or person, was big."

"Right. Sorry." I walked close beside him and focused on watching the roadside. My ears and nose strained to retrieve any other information. All I got was the continuous chorus of the wind through the fields and the stench of manure.

We were 30 minutes down the road when a pair of headlights blasted our backs. Ben and I moved to the road's shoulder, waving our arms. The car slowed and stopped beside us. Cathy, the show's organizer, looked across the passenger seat to us. "Everything okay? Breakdown?"

"Deer," I said.

"Oh, shit, sorry. Was that your car back there in the ditch?"

"Yeah."

"You guys alright?" Cathy looked between us. "Do you need a lift to the ER?"

"Just banged up a bit. No need for a hospital visit," Ben said. "We were walking back to the motel in town."

"That's a long walk but a short drive," Cathy said. "Hop in."

Ben looked at me and raised his eyebrows.

"Thank you." I took the front seat with Cathy, and Ben got into the back. I held my hands up to the heating vents on the dash. "Do you live here?"

Cathy tilted her head. "I sort of drift around the area organizing these shows." She looked in the rearview mirror at Ben. "My cousin does the same thing west of here on the lakeshore. I hope it's okay I sent him your info."

"Thanks," Ben said.

"Family business?" I asked.

Cathy shrugged. "Something like that. Between him and I, anyway. His Dad isn't quite on board."

She dropped us off in front of the motel. I scented the air outside and inside our room, searching for any trace of the stranger. Nothing. My muscles relaxed, relieved no hulking shadow was waiting to harm Ben or me. Only several hours were left until dawn.

Ben came up behind me while I was brushing my teeth for bed. He slipped his arms around my waist and nuzzled his cold nose against the warm curve of my neck. I chuckled and shied away.

"I found a place in town for the car. They open at nine."

"Thanks. How much did you make at the show?" I asked around my toothbrush.

"Two fifty."

I spat out the toothpaste and rinsed my toothbrush. "I think the repair is going to cost more than that. I'll call my parents and give them a heads-up." They'd given me a credit card for emergency expenses.

I left the bathroom for the bed while he brushed his teeth. Sitting on the extra bed was my grandfather's box. I returned the article clipping from the back pocket of my jeans to the box before changing and getting into bed. The only progress we'd made was discovering the bizarre killings had happened in similar areas of the state. There was a distinct trail leading to the northwest.

Ben jumped onto the bed beside me, causing my body to bounce. I laughed and fell back against him. He pulled me down onto the bed and the covers up over us. "No more thinking about the box or lupine creepers." His breath tickled my skin. "We'll deal with everything after sleep."

"Yeah, alright." I enjoyed the comforting warmth of his body against mine and listened to his breath. It eventually slowed and fell into an even rhythm. His hold on me relaxed.

Ever since Ben was tethered by his grandfather, Reginald, their relationship was nearly nonexistent. The punishment caused a chain of events that nearly resulted in Ben's death. Even after Reginald removed the tether, Ben preferred not to interact with him.

Could Ben understand how puzzling out Grandpa's box was meaningful to me? I needed to find out what my grandfather was up to all those years ago. What could be so important that he left my grandmother, someone he supposedly treasured, alone at home and unaware of what he was doing? What had he been hiding?

Across from us on the other bed, the box sat with its secrets.

8

THE FOLLOWING MORNING I called the local repair shop. I gave them the car's location, and after I described how the wheels looked, the mechanic predicted a broken tie rod. If that were the case, the repair would take the majority of the day.

I made the most of the situation by crawling back into bed with Ben to sleep in. When we finally roused ourselves, we decided to treat ourselves to a hot brunch.

A bell jangled over the door of the diner we entered. The delicious aromas of coffee, eggs, toast, and bacon hit me hard. There was a brief pause in the commotion of the place as everyone looked toward the door and us. A waitress with short blonde hair and heavy eye makeup straight out of an eighties film passed by with two pots of coffee. "Grab a seat. I'll be with you in a minute."

Conversations resumed.

We waded through the tightly packed space to a small two-top. Ben glanced above the table at the deer head mounted to the wood-paneled wall. He looked at me, the corner of his mouth twitching up ever-so-slightly. "Too soon."

I snorted and looked around at the rest of the decor. It was a mishmash of taxidermied animals, sponsored sports team photos, domestic beer signs, and pine tree curtains. I picked up the menu as the waitress approached our table. We ordered two coffees and food. The waitress wrote our order on her notepad, tucked it back in her apron, and bustled away.

Ben watched her leave.

"What's on your mind?" I asked.

"Just thankful I don't have to carry around a pen and notepad anymore to have a conversation." He reached across the table to take my hand. "And being able to travel wherever I want without needing anyone's permission? It's so freeing."

I rubbed my thumb over his fingers. "Ben, you don't want to go back to Hopewell, do you?"

He hesitated, which reinforced my suspicions. "I want to be where you are."

My chest warmed but ached as well. I didn't want to be the reason he was being held back. "But you'd prefer to keep traveling."

He lowered his gaze. "Yes."

The waitress set two steaming cups of coffee down on our table. Ben pulled his hand from mine to add cream to his coffee.

"We could still get a place together in Hopewell, you know. Even if you want to travel." I took the first sip of coffee. It was wonderful, black and strong enough to give me a jolt.

"You'd be okay with that?" His tone was a bit too incredulous for my taste.

My quick response was defensive. "Yes. Why wouldn't I be?"

"Well . . ." he hesitated again. "You seem . . . What I mean is, it seems—"

"I seem what?" It irritated the hell out of me when someone pussy-footed around an answer. I wanted Ben to be honest and straightforward with me. "Just say it."

"Lately you seem to be struggling with me wanting to book gigs. On one hand, you seem excited for me, but then on the other, it's like you aren't thrilled with me performing. That's what I'd be doing while I was away."

"I'm sorry. It's not you performing." Though part of it kind of was. The wolf in me wanted Ben for myself, and when he performed, he shared himself with so many other people. But it was more complicated than basic jealousy. "I'm anxious to get home where I can be useful. I like being at your shows, but there's nothing I can do to help you. I'm not accomplishing much by being the token partner waiting in the wings."

"Partner?" He arched an eyebrow and smiled. It broke the uneasy tension of our conversation.

"We do need to settle on something to call—"

"I like 'partner.' Is that the reason you're focused on your grandfather's box? You need something to keep you busy?"

"No." I turned my cup on the table. I wasn't ready to share that whole snarly mess of emotions with him. "That's something else."

Fortunately, the scents of bacon and pancakes wafted ahead of the waitress, and as soon as she set the two plates of steaming food down, we dug in.

The bell rang above the door and the room quieted again. A police officer, dressed in a brown and khaki uniform, stood by the front door. She spoke with our waitress, who nodded and pointed to our table. The officer started toward us.

My pulse skipped. Ben looked up from his meal at me and then in the direction of the officer. His features immediately darkened. Many of my interactions with the police were unpleasant, but Ben's were terrible.

The officer stopped at our table. Her uniform was crisp and her hair was pulled back into a tidy ponytail, but she looked tired. "Good morning. Alexandria Steward?"

"Yes."

"I'm Officer Miller. Do you own a blue Camry?"

I set my fork down. "Why?"

"We were called by White Pine Repair this morning," she said. "They told us they received a tow request from you?"

"Yes. We hit a deer last night."

Her eyebrows rose. "A deer?"

"Yes. A deer." The wolf in me was becoming agitated, sensing people in the restaurant watching us. "Why did they call the police? Was the car stolen?"

"No, ma'am. The car is at the station. If you and your friend could come with me, we have a few questions for you."

AFTER PAYING FOR a meal we had to take away in to-go boxes, Ben and I stood in a parking lot surrounded by a tall chain-link fence. My crippled car looked a lot like it did the night before. The front bumper was dented, and the windshield was shattered. But now swaths of blood were smeared up the hood and along the doors.

My skin crawled. "Who did this?"

"We were hoping you could tell us," Officer Miller said. "The car was abandoned in the middle of Doug Johnson's pasture. Part of his flock of sheep were also found dead."

Nausea soured my stomach.

"In a pasture?" Ben said. "We left the car in a ditch where it ran off the road."

"So you two were together last night?" She looked between us.

I nodded. My vision started to spot. I reached for Ben's arm.

"You're looking pretty pale, Miss Steward," Miller said. "Let's go inside, sit down, and talk."

We followed her into the station. It was sterile-looking and small with a single office labeled *Sheriff*. Officer Miller's desk, along with several others, was crammed into a space behind the receptionist. The receptionist's potent cologne mixed terribly with the lingering odors of cleaning products, not helping my unsettled stomach one bit.

The only items on Miller's tidy desk were a notepad, a closed laptop, and a framed photo of her with an older couple, the man also dressed as a policeman. I wouldn't have given the photo a second glance, but the woman looked vaguely familiar. Miller noticed me studying it. "My parents," she said. "Grab a seat and we'll get started."

Ben and I pulled up two chairs from a nearby table and sat down. Steam rose out of the Styrofoam cups set in front of us. The coffee smelled burnt.

Miller sat behind her desk and opened a notepad. "So tell me what you two were doing last night that led to us finding your car where it was this morning."

Ben stared at his coffee cup and didn't respond. His discomfort was palpable. I cleared my throat and took the lead. "We checked into the motel, visited an antique shop, and then drove to a show."

"A show?"

"A concert."

Miller's pen scribbled across the page. "Concert? There aren't any places out that way to hold a concert."

"The building wasn't even a five-minute drive from where we hit the deer," I said.

Ben rubbed his hand over his face. "It was an impromptu show being held at this metal barn structure. I was invited to play there."

"By who?"

Ben shook his head. "I don't remember their name."

The lie was so casually delivered, that I wondered briefly if he'd forgotten Cathy's name.

Miller fixed a flat stare on Ben and tapped the end of her pen on the notepad. "Okay. Then where did you go?"

"We started to drive back to the motel," I said. "That's when the deer hit the car."

"What time?"

"Um... I think it was between two and three in the morning."

"Okay. The deer hit the car, and then the car ran off the road into Doug's pasture."

I shook my head. "It ran off the road in front of a cornfield."

"Through the stand of corn to the pasture?"

"No." I struggled to contain a growl. There was something about Miller that rubbed me the wrong way. "The car went off the road, into the ditch, and stopped in front of the cornfield."

She jotted down more notes. "Had either of you consumed any illegal substances at this concert? A few too many drinks?"

"No," we both said.

"Would either of you agree to a drug test?"

"No." Ben scowled. "We don't know anything about that guy's pasture or his sheep. We're not even from around here."

Miller calmly continued. "Where's home?"

"Hopewell," I said.

"What did you do after the car went into the ditch?"

"The car wasn't drivable, so we started walking back toward town," I said. "Someone stopped and offered us a ride. We took them up on it because it was cold and we were tired."

"Can anyone vouch for your whereabouts at that time? The driver maybe?" She looked between the two of us, her pen poised.

We weren't Commoners, and I didn't know how local supernatural law enforcement operated. All Cathy would have to do was confirm she gave us a ride to the hotel. Despite Ben dodging the question, I wanted us out from beneath Officer Miller's microscope. "Her name was Cathy. I don't know her last name."

A slight frown passed over Officer Miller's lips. "Your height, stocky, early twenties, brown hair and eyes?"

"Yes." I glanced at Ben. Still scowling, he leaned back in his chair and looked away.

"I know her. I'll give her a call," Miller said. "Anything to add?"

"No," I said. "Can I get the car back so we can get it repaired? We were hoping to leave today."

Miller continued writing. "No. It's being held as evidence."

Ben cursed beneath his breath and shook his head.

"So we're stuck here?" I asked.

"You can leave whenever you'd like." Miller looked up from her notes. "You haven't been arrested."

"This is bullshit," Ben said. "We came in and answered your questions, but we're stuck here because our car was dragged into something we know nothing about."

I placed my hand on Ben's. "Where can we can rent a car?"

"Several towns over. About forty minutes away," Miller said. "I never asked, what brought the two of you up here to visit us?"

"Ben had a—"

"Yes, the concert at the venue that doesn't legally exist." She waved along my answer. "Is that the only reason?"

The wolf in me sensed something was off as if we were slowly being cornered. Officer Miller's study of us, even while she casually ran through her list of questions, was unnerving. I fell silent and shifted in my seat.

"What about the car's hood?" she asked.

Shit.

"It was vandalized in Detroit," I said.

Miller waited. "And . . ."

I swallowed and remained silent.

"Nothing?" She blew out an exhale. "Miss Steward, when I looked up your car's registration, your name threw up a flag. It sounded familiar. I couldn't quite remember why, so I did a bit of searching. It seems Alexander Steward was marked as a person of interest in a cold case in 1975."

The mention of Grandpa's name by Officer Miller caused the blood to leave my face. The police case was also three years earlier than the article from the box.

"So you know him?" She nodded. "I thought it was too much of a coincidence. The funny thing is, when Alexander passed through our humble little town, he was asking about a farmer who lost part of his herd. Several cattle were slaughtered in the middle of the night. Alexander made a real pest of himself for my dad, the investigating officer."

I licked my lips and looked at my untouched cup of coffee. So my grandfather was investigating the strange killings to the point of irritating the local police. And he'd possibly visited the town more than once. Was he trying to find someone? A twinge pinged in my chest. Or was he trying to cover up something?

"Nothing?" Miller sighed and closed her notebook. "If something gets jogged loose or you feel like talking, please give me a call." She handed me a business card.

"Thanks."

"Enjoy your stay. If you do get that rental car, have a safe trip."

Ben and I walked out of the station together. He glowered at the business card I held as if it were Officer Miller herself. "I'll text Cathy and let her know the police might be calling."

"Why did you lie about not knowing Cathy's name?" I asked.

"I didn't want her to have to deal with a cop. Cathy is doing something great for music fans in the area. She doesn't need to be hassled for it."

If Cathy confirmed our story, Miller would back off, and I could shake the anxiety Miller stirred up in me. "All Cathy would have to say is she gave us a ride back to the motel. That helps us."

Ben smirked. "It's never that simple with the police."

I let it drop, not wanting to argue the point. Ben's dislike for law enforcement was a consequence of his tethering. What I found more worrying was how easily he'd lied. Had he ever lied to me?

I bit at my lip, looking at the card. "I'm not sure what to do, especially with this unknown person following us. Should we stay and try to find out who it is?" I looked at him. "You said you saw something last night on the side of the road?"

He shivered, nodded, and zipped up his jacket. "It was much larger than that deer."

"If it's the person following us as we suspect, they were out there last night, too. They must have taken out that guy's sheep and tried to pin it on us," I said.

"Someone strong if they moved the car," Ben said.

"And why pull in the Commoner's law enforcement?" I tried to recall everyone I may have pissed off over the last year. Only Fillip would go so far as launching a deer at us. But Trish said that wasn't a possibility, and the attack did seem a bit clumsy for him.

"So . . . you feel we should stay?" he asked.

"We can leave tomorrow," I said. "I know we didn't plan on the expense of the room, but renting a car is going to cost a lot more. And maybe since we answered Miller's questions, she'll let us out of here with the car sooner."

I'd prefer to continue driving, but we didn't need more trouble by upsetting the local police. And if we were lucky, we'd find out who wanted to bring a terrible end to our road trip.

9

WE WALKED FROM the police station to the downtown area. Unlike when we arrived, people were out on the sidewalks. Similar to the small towns we'd passed through, a harvest festival was taking place. Shops had pulled out sandwich boards and sales racks. The aroma of warm foods and spiced drinks filled the air.

Ben spotted a display cart outside a bookstore. "Mind if I look?"

"No, go ahead." It would've been cruel to keep him from the books. He loved them almost as much as music.

He kissed my forehead and left to browse the cart. I wandered to the next business, a quaint bakery serving cups of steaming cider and freshly baked donuts in front of the shop.

While I waited in line, I watched a couple of young kids chase each other around tables set out for customers. The pursued was shrieking and laughing, while the chaser roared and howled. He wore a paper mask. The kids rounded a table and ran straight toward me. The boy's mask resembled a type of canine. The children crashed into the legs of a woman standing in front of me. The toddler she held shrieked and laughed, waving his hands.

"Settle down, you two." The woman turned with an apologetic smile. "Sorry! Their energy is off the charts this morning."

I shrugged. "It's okay. I get excited about donuts, too."

The child with the mask looked up at me and roared. He raised his hands, fingers curled. His bright eyes showed through the clumsily cut holes in the mask.

I feigned fright. "Ah! Don't eat me, Mr. Wolf!"

The boy's arms fell to his sides. "Dogman." He turned to the woman. "Mom, when do we get our donuts?"

"Sorry?" I asked. "Dogman?"

The woman rolled her eyes. "He's obsessed with the Dogman right now."

"You don't know about the Dogman?" The little boy pulled off his mask. He regarded me with a look somewhere between disbelief and disappointment.

"It's a local legend," the woman said. "His older brother told him about the Dogman, and now he won't stop talking about it."

"He's seven feet tall, taller than my dad!" the boy shouted.

The girl who'd been chased peered at me from behind her mother's legs. "But he doesn't eat people. He eats animals."

"He scares people to death!" The boy roared in glee. "He's like a dog on top, but a man on the bottom. The Dogman can walk on two legs like us." He stomped around in a circle, his arms lifted menacingly. "He has blue eyes and big teeth and long claws on his fingers."

"No!" The description was uncomfortably close to my reality, but I widened my eyes and held my hand over my mouth in mock horror. "That's so scary."

The boy giggled and nodded, clasping the flimsy paper mask to his chest.

The woman doled out donuts to the kids. "Go over and sit down. I'll bring your cider."

The two children tore off to sit at one of the outdoor tables.

"Thanks for humoring them." She tried to hold onto the wiggling toddler while getting their cider.

"No problem." I didn't mind. She was the sole wrangler of three young kids. She could use the help. "I can carry some of those."

"Oh, thank you."

"What'll you have, miss?" the guy behind the cart asked.

"Two donuts and a large cider," I said.

While my order was being put together, I helped the woman carry the ciders to the table and the waiting children. "So this Dogman is like a cryptid?"

"Yes. It's been around since I was little. It used to scare me when we'd have slumber parties. The story itself is old." She set the ciders down in front of her kids.

"Grownups have seen him in Paris and Big Rapids." The boy squirmed in his seat, his attention divided between his donut and me.

"Oh my! So the Dogman lives around here?" I recognized the names of the towns from studying Grandpa's state map.

"Supposedly the northern half of the lower peninsula within the pine forests," the woman answered.

The woman took the last cider "Thank you for your help."

"You're welcome. Have a nice day."

"You too."

I walked back to pay for my order. There were similarities between the story the family had shared and what I'd found about my grandfather and his articles. A werewolf-like creature. Recurring instances of dead livestock. I nearly jumped out of my skin when a light touch landed on my upper arm.

"Whoa, you okay?" Ben held a bag from the bookstore. "Donuts and cider? Nice."

I handed over his donut. "Couldn't say no to the books?"

He arched an eyebrow. "Couldn't say no to the food?"

"Not fair," I said. "We didn't get to finish breakfast while it was hot."

Ben glanced at the family at the table. "What's with the shouting and bouncing kids?"

We walked past the table. The boy had his mask on again, and cinnamon sugar stuck to the canine face. He roared at Ben.

Ben feigned away, giving the boy a theatrical expression of fear. I laughed. The little boy dissolved into giggles and started munching on his donut again.

"Beware the Dogman," I said.

"The what?"

As Ben and I strolled through the little downtown, I told him about my conversation with the kids and their mom. We sat down on a bench to share the cider.

"And you think this Dogman is real?"

"Maybe?" I handed him the cider. "What if there's a lupine who's been spotted by Commoners throughout the years? People use folktales all the time to explain things they don't understand."

"Or to scare people," Ben said. "Wouldn't a rogue lupine taking out livestock attract Hunters?"

"I don't know." The cold weather and the mention of Hunters made me shiver and scoot closer to Ben. Hunters believed it to be their holy mission to rid the world of poorly behaved supernatural beings. In my experience with Hunters, simply existing as a supernatural being made you a target.

Ben put his arm around me and gave my temple a cider-scented kiss. I leaned my head against his shoulder. "I wish I knew more about what my grandfather was doing that pissed off the police."

"He probably wasn't doing anything," Ben said. "Can you imagine how bored the cops must be around here?"

"He seemed to be tracking someone, and that person was connected to the case Miller's dad was working on." I sat up and looked at Ben. "Maybe it was this Dogman. If they're a cryptid that's been around for years, we should be able to find more info about them."

Ben's eyes lit up and he grinned. "Are you requesting a full-on research montage?"

I laughed. "I thought that'd make you happy."

Ben's phone buzzed. He read the incoming message, and his grin faded.

"Is everything okay?" I asked.

"I messaged Cathy and let her know the police might call," Ben said.

"Thank you for reaching out to her," I said.

He motioned to his phone. "This is her cousin contacting me. If we can leave here soon enough, he has a show in Silver Lake he'd like me to play tomorrow night."

"Tomorrow, already?" I fought the twinge of irritation, reassuring myself we could support each other in our goals. "Sure, if we can get the car in time. Ready for some research?"

"If I do this show tomorrow, I want to change up a few things with the music," Ben said. "Rain check on the research date?"

"Okay." I hid my disappointment as we walked hand-in-hand back to the motel. I'd get started looking up info on the Dogman while he worked. Maybe Trish would call with an update on the Fillip situation.

Ben set up his laptop at a desk and disappeared into his large headphones and sound software. I didn't get far into my research before I fell asleep.

I WOKE FROM a fitful nap of odd dreams. In one I was being tracked through a large crowd of faceless people by a large dark silhouette with glowing eyes. Everything smelled rotten, and I couldn't pinpoint where the person was in the crowd. I checked my phone at the bedside for the time. My stomach growled as if providing the answer: Dinnertime.

Our motel room was dark. Ben's computer was closed on the desk, and he'd fallen asleep on the bed beside me.

I rolled over, shimmied close to Ben, and nudged him in the side. "Hey. I'm going to get food."

"Hmm?" He didn't open his eyes.

"I need food."

"A half-hour?"

"I need food right now."

Ben cracked an eyelid. "What time is it?"

"Time for dinner. I can bring you something back, but the food would taste better with you there."

"Right. Okay." He stretched. "I'll come with you."

We found a bar that served dinner. The few other restaurants in town were closed because of the late hour. The bar had a narrow entryway and no windows. Usually, I wouldn't enter a bar that didn't have windows. In any enclosed space, the wolf in me was uncomfortable unless there were exits. Windows were considered exits.

Ben paused with his hand on the door handle. "Everything okay? Change your mind?"

"I don't know about this place."

He jerked his head toward the door. "Let's give it a try."

We entered the bar and my nose was assailed by years-old cigarette smoke, fried food, sour beer, and bleach. My chest tightened. I halted inside the door, and Ben ran into me.

"Sorry." He guided me forward so we weren't standing in the immediate entryway.

The stink of bleach brought back memories of my deadly encounter with a Hunter in Hopewell. He'd used the chemical to scramble the noses of any werewolves that attempted to track him. He'd also kept a trophy box filled with the canine teeth of the werewolves he murdered.

Ben lowered his voice and spoke near my ear, "If it feels off, we can put in a to-go order. Or maybe there's a vending machine outside the motel. I'm sure nothing in there is over three years old."

"No, I can manage." Especially since Ben would be by my side. His presence soothed the wolf in me.

A sign posted in the entryway read "Please seat yourself." We sat at a booth, Ben sliding onto the seat next to me. With the cold weather and only having pancakes and a donut for the day, I was tempted to get one of everything from the fried food choices.

"So, if I ordered these mozzarella sticks, will you expect me to share? Because I'm not sure we're at that point in our relationship."

That's more of a one-year anniversary thing." I stole a look at him to see how the joke landed. We were close to reaching that milestone, which was by far the longest I'd been with anyone.

"You see us together three months from now?" Ben's smile was affectionate, a good sign.

My stomach fluttered as always when he looked at me like that. He knew the real me I was required to hide from Commoners, and my presence brought him happiness despite it. I stared hard at the menu because, even with him, I struggled to be vulnerable. "Yeah, why not?"

He put his arm around my shoulders, pulled me close, and kissed my temple.

I never turned down the opportunity to get close to him, but the tender gesture could also be him avoiding the topic. "No, you don't get to charm your way out of answering the question. Three months isn't far away. I thought we were on the same page. Why did you ask that?"

"Purely selfish reasons," Ben said. "I wanted to hear you say it."

"Do you see us together?"

"Yeah, I do." He removed his arm from around my shoulders to hold my hand. "You and I were both dealing with other shit when we met. I feel like a lot of that has passed, and we can be more present for each other, you know?"

"What can I get you?" The waiter stood at the end of our booth.

I started, having not noticed his approach. I should've heard the waiter walk up to our booth. Why was I so stupid around Ben? He completely scrambled my senses.

We ordered burgers, fries, and sodas. I wasn't going to chance the beer again.

"How should we handle the car tomorrow?" Ben asked.

"I'll call Officer Miller in the morning. Hopefully, they're done with it, we can get it repaired, and then we can leave."

A tall middle-aged man walked by us, trailing the scent of alcohol and another aroma that made me tense. It was that strange odor, so close to a werewolf's, but not. He stopped at the booth ahead of us, and I studied his profile. He was about the right height. Was it our guy? But why would he walk right by us where we'd notice him? If the stranger following us was lupine, they'd know I was too.

At the booth, a girl of maybe fifteen worked at clearing dirty dishes. I recognized the tightening around her shoulders and the way she stepped to the side when the man leaned into her space. Her body was shifting into defense mode.

The man whispered, but the words rang clear in my ears. "How old are you, darling?"

The wolf in me rose violently toward the surface. I curled my fingers beneath the heels of my hands to conceal my emerging claws. Even when I believed my mind and body were in sync, the wolf could take me by surprise. My tightened jaw ached as I willed the spike of anger inside me to recede.

"Alex," Ben's hand closed over mine, hiding it from view. "What's wrong?" He followed my gaze to the booth ahead of ours.

The girl ignored the man, doing her best to pretend he wasn't looming over her as she tried to work. The acidic scent of her fear reached my nostrils.

"What time do you get off work?" asked the man.

I nudged Ben's shoulder. "Move, please."

He squeezed my hand and lowered his voice. His words were rushed. "Alex, no. She's safe here with all these people."

"Then why isn't anyone doing anything?" A low growl edged my voice.

"He'll leave. You don't need—"

"Let me out of the goddamn booth. Now."

Ben frowned and released my hand. He slid out of the booth.

I quickly followed. The wolf in me wanted to drop the guy where he stood. How else would these men ever learn? The girl deserved a job, even if it was a shitty one paying minimum wage, free of harassment.

The man carrying the strange scent left through the front door on unsteady legs.

I walked up beside the girl. "Hey, are you alright?"

She jumped and gave me a nervous chuckle. "What?"

"Are you okay?" I nodded toward the door. "I heard that asshole talking to you."

She blushed and went back to wiping down the cleared table. Her shoulder lifted. "Yeah, I'm fine."

"Tell your boss," I said. "You shouldn't have to put up with that shit."

She tossed the cleaning rag back in the bin with the dirty dishes. "It's part of the job. We should be thankful to have one. That's what the waitresses were told when they complained."

Telling the boss you were harassed at work was 'complaining?' No. This was not okay.

Anger roiled inside me. I left the girl's side and strode toward the door. If her boss wouldn't do anything about it, I would.

Ben's voice called out, "Alex!"

10

THE DOOR SWUNG shut behind me. In the parking lot beside the restaurant, the man wove toward a red Ford truck. I briefly surveyed the area, pleased only the two of us were outside. I was almost on top of him before he heard me. He glanced back. There was a brief moment of delayed surprise on his features.

My muscles warmed, and I shoved him into the side of his truck. He thudded into the door panel with his shoulder, grasping at the handle to keep himself on his feet.

I pushed my shifting further, my gums burning as my teeth grew sharp. My eyes would already be glowing the radiant gold of my wolf. I smiled for him as he turned to face me. His bleary eyes widened, and he pressed back against the truck. "What the hell?"

The fool didn't know how close to death he danced. If I fully embraced my wolf, I could use my claws to open him up. There'd be steam as his insides met the chilly outside. No other young woman would have to suffer his unwanted advances.

Instead, I struck the door panel near his head. It dented with a crunch beneath my fist.

He cried out. His arms rose to hide his face. The alcohol odor hung in a cloud around him, but the other scent I noticed inside the bar was gone. He wasn't the person following us.

I leaned forward, looked down at him, and allowed a snarl into my voice. "Don't ever go near her again."

The sound of footsteps and a familiar scent battled for my

attention. Ben had followed but waited at the bar's door, giving me space. "Let's go back inside."

His interference caused a growl to rumble through my chest. "Tell me you understand," I said to the cowering man.

The man briskly nodded.

"Say it!"

"I . . . I understand." His voice quavered like his body.

Leaning closer, I made a show of taking a long inhale through my nose. "I've got your scent now. If I ever smell you around here again, I'll track you down and gut you."

The man turned his face away and squeezed his eyes shut.

I straightened and walked back toward the restaurant. Deep calming breaths allowed my eyes, hands, and teeth to return to their usual state. I half expected an irritating comment from Ben about my behavior, but he remained silent as he held the door open. The teenage girl had moved on to another table.

Hot greasy food waited for us at our booth. It smelled delicious. I asked Ben to sit on the inside this time, something I should have done in the first place. He didn't object.

"I should get extra mozzarella sticks for not breaking his nose," I muttered.

Ben dipped one in marinara sauce and handed it to me. "You shouldn't get any for revealing yourself to a Commoner. It's rule number one." He'd waited to feed me before criticizing my actions. Clever.

"He's drunk. And he's an asshole." I took the deep-fried stick of cheese out in two bites. "He's a drunk asshole."

"That's beside the point. And with that cop questioning us, maybe we don't start shit with the locals?"

"He carried traces of that scent I noticed at your shows."

An anxious crease appeared between Ben's eyebrows. "Was it him?"

I shook my head. "Once we were outside, it was gone. Did you notice where he was sitting before he decided to harass the wait staff?" Several people were around a pool table, and a few more couples were seated throughout the room. Customers were perched along the bar, occasionally stealing glances over their shoulders at us.

My gaze landed on a bearded man sitting beside an empty barstool. A camo ball cap cast shadows that obscured his features, but he was looking directly at me. Not smiling, not frowning, but watching me with an unblinking stare. The hair on the nape of my neck rose. I fought to keep another growl contained. "The guy at the bar, fifth chair from the end. I think that's him."

"Should we try to talk to him here or go somewhere else?"

The man broke his stare to lay bills on the bar and stand. He was tall and broad, dressed in jeans, a Carhartt jacket, and work boots. He turned away and walked down a narrow hall toward the bathrooms.

"I think he prefers somewhere else." I tried to keep my eye on him. "I don't want to dance around this guy. I'll follow him and see if I can get him to talk. You don't have to come if you want to wait here."

Ben grimaced. "You know I can't wait here."

"Well, he isn't waiting for either of us." We started after the stranger and, sure enough, the odd like-a-werewolf-but-not scent filled my nose and grew stronger. At the end of the hall, past the bathrooms, was a solid gray door with a glowing exit sign. The door clicked shut.

I slunk down the hall, paused briefly at the back door, and then pushed it open into the chilly night. The sparsely lit parking lot extended behind the bar. A rusting, once-green dumpster sat beside the back door. I covered my nose to dampen the scent of rotting food.

Ben exited after me. "Find him?"

Movement caught my eye at the end of the little lot. A figure crossed the railroad tracks and started down into the woodline. A growl sprung up into my throat as the wolf in me urged my body forward in pursuit. I turned to Ben. "Are you sure you can't wait here?"

He scoffed. "No. You'd be alone. We don't know what the person wants from us. I assume it's nothing good since he's pitching forest animals at our car."

"I can move faster if I go alone. I'll have my phone with me."

His forehead wrinkled and eyes stormy, Ben cursed. "Go."

Scenting the air as I went, I jogged through the lot. The stink of the garbage faded. Across the road and along the railroad tracks, traces of the musky smell lingered on the crisp night air. I scanned the dark woodline for movement. When the scent disappeared, I doubled back and eased down the embankment toward the woods. Small stones clattered, creating painfully loud noises. So much for sneaking up on the guy.

I crept into the woodline, my vision adjusting further for the dark. The last bit of leaves the trees held onto rustled in the wind. Drifts of fallen leaves rustled with each of my steps. The damp scent of decaying leaves wafted up to me. The wolf in me bristled, and I paused to refocus. I concentrated on this moment and where I was in the woods instead of the slew of horrible images and sensations my body wanted to react to from my past.

Then the breeze shifted and the deteriorating leaves were overpowered by a waft of the strange scent I'd been tracking. I spun toward a stand of trees to my left. The outer edge of the tree's silhouette shifted. Glowing red eyes watched me.

I froze, my nostrils flaring, trying to pick up as much info as possible. "Who are you? Why are you following us?"

A guttural growl sounded from the shadows. Not much of a talker then.

I gave more of myself to the wolf in me. With popping cartilage, my fingers elongated and my nails formed into claws. My senses heightened further. The area lightened and the outlines of the tree and the person behind it sharpened. The odor of the damp ground reached into my consciousness, threatening to distract me.

I puzzled through the mysterious figure's scent, the strangeness of it. It was so close to the base primal scent all werewolves have, but it was odd. Spoiled, almost, like the food in the dumpster. What happened to alter his scent so drastically?

The next step I took was too far. The huge guy leaped at me from behind the tree. He'd shifted his form closer to wolf. His jacket and boots were gone. The seams of his shirt were split by muscular, fur-covered arms.

I jerked back. He barely missed me with a swipe of his claws. The dodge saved me from getting smacked, but I stumbled over a fallen sapling and crashed to the ground on my ass.

With a roar, the werewolf spun and launched himself toward me again. I rolled out of the way. The guy landed with another swipe of his claws, sending up a spray of leaves and dirt.

I scrambled up onto my knees. My body ignited with heat, warming and charging my muscles. The wolf in me wanted to fight back, to defend myself from the threat. "Stop! Tell me who—"

The werewolf turned. I got my first good look at our stranger. And I recognized him.

"Leo?" The last time Leonard Whelan and I had crossed paths, he wasn't sporting the beard or the camo. He'd single-handedly fended off multiple other werewolves at one time. If I hadn't tricked him during our last scuffle, he very likely would have killed me.

He was a tethered werewolf and partner-in-crime to wizard George Marino. Emma's evil ex hired them to haul in supernatural citizens to his brainwashing center. But I'd thought that mess was behind me when George was hospitalized and Leo disappeared.

Leo's lips pulled back from his large serrated teeth. One of the canines was broken.

I snarled. "Why the hell are you following us?"

Leo shook his head. His chest rose and fell in irregular bursts.

That sense that something was off, not quite right, caused me to hesitate.

My mistake.

A fist the size of a bowling ball knocked me back into the underbrush. Saplings and twigs snapped as I struck them. The side of my body lit up with pain. Leo crashed through the foliage after me. I found my feet a second time. His jaws opened and he lunged as if he planned to take a bite out of me even though he wasn't fully shifted.

I backed up against a tree and channeled my strength into a punch. It struck his nose. Cartilage crunched. He yelped and turned his face away. Another strike made him pull back.

I chanced turning my back to him and bolted for the woodline and the railroad tracks. Leo was stronger than me in his current form. The woods were too crowded. Where I was forced to avoid obstacles in my path, Leo crashed through them.

He gave chase, snarling and barreling after me with all the grace of a freight train. Breath burned in my chest as I pushed my body harder. Leo's longer strides closed the distance between us. I burst from the trees and smack into a divot in the ditch. My ankle twisted, I yelped, and my speed propelled me forward onto my hands and knees.

I flailed to right myself. Leo let loose another ear-splitting bellow, caught somewhere between a human scream and a canine howl. Someone was going to hear us. I rolled to my side and looked up. Backlit by the moon, the silhouette of his body loomed large in the air. He descended on me, claws extended and jaws open. I flipped onto my back and readied myself. Hopefully, I could stop him from crushing me.

Energy brushed along my body. The hair on my arms rose. From behind me, Ben's voice spoke the strange language of spell casting. A vibrant blue pane of light, like a sheet of glass, appeared above me.

Leo struck the barrier with an enormous thud. It crackled but remained intact. He snarled and slammed his fist against the barrier. It shuddered and spiderwebbed with thin cracks. The sound of shifting stones signaled Ben's descent from the railroad tracks.

I backpedaled away. Leo's attention snapped upward and focused behind me. His snarling suddenly ceased, and his head cocked to the side. His voice was low. I could barely parse the word from the growl. "George?"

Ben twisted his wrist, reciting words rhythmically like poetry. The sheet of blue light tilted upward toward Leo like a wall, driving the werewolf back.

Leo whined and tried to duck around the edge. "George!"

With splaying fingers, Ben sent the barrier's width to enlarge. Leo should have been able to tell it was Ben. He had the same heightened vision as me. I stood and limped back, watching Leo. "One last chance to be civil about this," I said. "Why are you following us?"

Leo looked at me, and his demeanor flipped back to rage. He threw his body against the barrier, seemingly not understanding why he couldn't get to us. His snarling increased. Pink-tinged foam appeared at the edges of his jaws. Muscles in his arms and legs bulged and slipped under his skin. Leo grasped his head and took a step back. Finally, he spun away and crashed off into the woods.

Ben and I stood in silence, puffs of steam coming from our mouths. When there was no sign of Leo returning, Ben lowered his hands. The barrier dissipated with an electric discharge. The energy harnessed for the spell rushed back over my sweaty skin.

"Holy shit, he's big." Ben's body intermittently trembled. "You know him?"

I limped to his side. "It's Leo . . . of George and Leo."

"Wait. The guys who jumped me in the alleyway last winter?" Ben swallowed and looked at me. "One was a big guy, but not that big or hairy."

I nodded and watched the woodline. "You should see him when he's fully shifted. He's huge. Nate took out the wizard, George, but Leo went MIA when we escaped the Mind Center warehouse."

"You said everyone has their own scent," Ben said. "Why weren't you able to recognize him before he was up close?"

"There's something wrong about the part of him that's lupine. I don't know how to explain it other than he doesn't smell right." I frowned. "And I'm not sure he understood me when I talked to him." I looked at Ben. "Or that you weren't his buddy, George."

"My magic is completely different than that guy's," Ben said. "So Leo has been following us since Detroit. Whoever or whatever launched the deer at us was definitely big. He must be the one killing livestock, too."

"But why?"

Ben shrugged. "To pin it on you?"

Leo was a violent criminal, but not the brightest crayon in the box. Would he have the foresight to plan something like that? "But what about the Dogman? And my grandfather's articles?"

"Coincidence?"

A low growl rumbled in my chest.

"Hey," Ben said, "no frustrated growling. We're going to figure this out." His hand slipped down my arm as he looked me over. "You okay? He didn't hurt you, did he?"

I shook my head. I'd managed to do more harm with my utter lack of grace. "My ankle and side are sore, but it's nothing serious. Thank you for running interference."

"Any time." He hesitated before adding. "I'm not a brawler like Trish or Nate, but I'm here for you. I can help you if you let me, Alex."

"Yeah, I know. But I'm anxious you'll get in trouble because of me." Ben served fifteen years with a tether, a punishment that blocked his ability to cast magic. The sentence severely impacted his mental health. Since the collapse of the Committee, discipline for breaking supernatural laws was still to be decided. Either way, I didn't want him taking the fall for my impulsive behavior.

"I appreciate that, but please let me be the one to make that choice," he said.

"Alright." But I knew if he were to get hurt because of my rash behavior, the guilt would destroy me.

I CALLED TRISH once we were safely back in the motel room. Ben sat by the window, his fingers hooked on the edge of the thick curtain, watching the parking lot for Leo.

"How was his scent different?" Trish asked.

"It smelled . . . rotten."

"Rotten?"

"Yeah." My nose wrinkled like the stench was still there. "I tried to talk him down to find out why he's following us, but he refused to have a conversation."

Trish blew out a breath. I worried I'd taken up too much of her time already. "Anger may be driving his actions. Leonard and George were promised their tethers would be removed if they completed the job for Mitch White. Leonard lost that chance when you and Nate exposed the Mind Center."

I'd experienced a tether firsthand, a punishment many werewolves didn't survive. It'd caused the rage to rebound around inside my skull with no outlet. My distress was nearly all-consuming.

Leo had made it so close to having his tether removed, to find relief from his anger and pain, and that freedom was yanked from his grasp at the last minute.

And I played a large role in why it happened. I thought of the car hood: YOUR FAULT.

"Why isn't he after Nate? Why me?"

"These are all hard questions to answer without Leonard speaking with you." There was a rare terseness to her tone. "It's fortunate we don't have to deal with him right now in Hopewell. Enough is happening here already."

"Trish, is now not a good time to talk? I'd been expecting an update, so I didn't think you'd mind me calling."

"To be frank, no. Are you in immediate danger?"

"No, we—"

"If Leonard is refusing to talk, put as much distance as possible between you and him," she said. "Don't engage him. We don't have anyone to spare right now to help you."

The conversation made me feel like a burden, but I wasn't sure who else to call about Leo. Trish was a mentor to me. "I'm sorry things are so stressful in Hope—"

"Good luck." The line clicked and the call ended.

I lowered the phone, staring at it. She'd never hung up on me.

"What'd she say?" Ben asked.

I crossed the room to sit next to him on the bed. "She doesn't have any guesses other than 'he's extremely pissed at you because you're why he still has the tether.'"

"Well, she has a point," Ben said. "What does she think we should do?"

"Run away. Which, after seeing how strange he was acting, is a suggestion I won't argue against." I put my head in my hands. "How did he follow us? Did we somehow not notice him?"

"Maybe he's tracking you through me," Ben suggested.

I sat up, confused. "What?"

"From the shows I'm playing," Ben continued. "The dates and locations would be listed online."

"I'm not sure he's smart enough to think of that." Between Leo and George, Leo was *not* the smart one. He was the extremely large, strong, and scary one.

"Did they ever find who altered George's and Leo's tethers?" Ben asked. "A complex spell would be needed for the tether to remain in place but allow those guys to access their abilities."

I shook my head. "When they tried to kidnap me last winter, Leo let it slip that a wizard altered the tether. We never found out who that was. Unless you heard something from Reginald about it?"

Ben didn't answer, which was all the answer I needed. He looked back out the window.

"Didn't think so." I drummed my fingers on the bedspread. "It sounds like it's a cluster at home. It makes me want to go and help."

"You're helping them by staying away and not adding a raging werewolf and pissed vampire to the mix," he said. "If you go back now, they'll have to worry about protecting you from not only Fillip, but Leo as well."

"This sitting still is getting to me. I want to leave."

"We've been here one extra day," Ben said.

"If the police won't release my car tomorrow, I'll ask for more money to rent a car." The thought wasn't pleasant, but between saving face with my parents and surviving a vengeful werewolf, I'd take survival. "I guess we're not done 'dealing with other shit,' are we?"

I meant for the question to be lighthearted, but Ben only sighed. His phone buzzed. He read the message. "It's Cathy. She says we need to be careful around that cop, Miller."

"Why?"

Ben passed me his phone. The words seemed to vibrate harshly on the screen as I read them. A deep dread swept over me.

Officer Miller is a Hunter.

11

I BARELY SLEPT a wink. Whenever I closed my eyes, Cathy's warning displayed on the backs of my eyelids. I left the room to pace outside, not wanting to rob Ben of any sleep. Over the past year, I'd tangled with Leo, one of the largest werewolves I'd met, and Fillip, a deadly vampire much more cunning than me.

Neither of them struck fear into my heart like a Hunter. A Hunter's sole purpose was to cleanse the world of what they believed were vile monsters. Supernatural beings. People like Ben and me.

And now I had to pick up my car keys from one.

Ben and I packed our things so we'd be ready to leave as soon as the car came back from the repair shop. Then we could put this town in the rearview. If the car wasn't ready, we'd leave it behind.

At the police station, Ben and I sat down in the same seats as the day before. My skin felt too tight. I kept my weight toward the front of the seat, my nose and ears working overtime to detect any move toward us by Miller. Ben sat rigidly beside me, the sharp odor of his fear hanging heavy around him.

If Miller noticed any change in our demeanor, she kept it to herself. She placed the car keys on the desk and pushed them toward me. "All fixed up with a full tank and ready to go."

I looked at Ben, who seemed equally puzzled. We thought *if* the car was returned to us, we'd have to spend time in the repair shop.

"We got what we needed, so we sent it to Dan's place for repairs," Miller said. "Yesterday it sounded like you wanted to leave as soon as possible."

"Yes, but . . ." I picked up the car keys, careful to avoid eye contact. "Do you have any suspects?" I didn't want to provoke a Hunter, but I wondered if she'd caught wind of Leo. If she had, he'd be in her crosshairs. I had mixed feelings about that.

"It's an open case, so I can't discuss that." Her tone wasn't hostile or even curt. My curiosity began to outweigh my caution. Maybe I could get info from her not directly related to the case.

"Don't we need to pay for the car repair?" I asked.

"Oh, thanks for reminding me." Miller retrieved an envelope from a drawer and slid it across the desk. The repair shop's logo was printed in the top left corner. "Here's the invoice. Dan threw the car wash in for free. He said to drop payment in the mail if you don't feel like swinging by on your way out of town."

There weren't any surgical scars on the tops of her hands. It was one of the places a Hunter could carry the key that gave them their special abilities.

"So that's it? We can leave?" I took a chance and looked straight at her. Oddly, the wolf in me didn't feel the agitation I'd felt the day before when Miller questioned us. Fear? Some. Anxiety, though? Not really.

"I told you yesterday you two can leave any time you'd like." Miller nodded toward the door.

Ben was already standing to make his escape. When I hesitated, he paused. "Alex, are you coming?"

"Go ahead. I'll be out in a minute."

"I can wait." His gaze shifted to Miller and back. He didn't want to leave me with her.

"I'll be okay. Can you get the car?" I passed him the car keys.

Ben's jawline tightened. He turned and pushed through the front doors of the station.

Miller's eyebrows raised. "Is there something else, Miss Steward?"

"My grandfather... You mentioned he'd visited here." I barreled forward before I could have second thoughts. "Did the case notes say *why* he was asking about the slaughtered livestock? I can't ask him. He's passed."

"I'm sorry for your loss." Miller leaned back in her chair and studied me for a moment. If I hadn't known she was a Hunter, I'd mark it up to her being a cop. My ex-friend Anne was a Hopewell PD officer and often wore the same expression. "I ran into Tammy at the pizzeria last night. She told me how she met a few charming out-of-towners at the fall festival who entertained her little boy by listening to his tales of the Dogman. That was you and your friend, wasn't it?"

After a twinge of impatience, it dawned on me why she was bringing it up. It aligned with what I'd already been suspecting. "My grandfather came here tracking a cryptid."

"Or at least that's what he said. Dad's evidence said otherwise." Miller held up a hand. "I don't mean to speak ill of the dead, but it looked like Alexander was suspect number one. He tried to pass the blame to an imaginary monster the locals made up."

An ugly slash of doubt filled my mind. My grandfather mentioned in his letter how his time overseas at war brought forth the darker part of his wolf. That he'd done things that haunted him long after he returned home to my grandmother and my father, a young child at the time. He'd given too much of his humanity to the wolf.

"Miss Steward, since you don't seem to be in a rush, I could use your help with a police report filed this morning." Miller reached forward and tapped her fingertip on her notepad. "We had a local, JD, spend last night in the sobering cell. He demanded we file a report about what he saw at the bar."

She watched me closely. A subtle sensation of unease came over me as Miller spoke. I shifted in my seat and focused on her desk, clear of items except for her computer, notepad, and the single photoframe.

"JD insists he saw a monster woman with sharp teeth and glowing eyes," she said. "This woman barked and growled at him like a dog or coyote."

Shit.

I licked my lips. Which was probably a tell.

Double shit.

"JD's stories are less than reliable." Her tone was casual even as my blood pressure was spiking. "But then we also got a lot of calls from people saying they heard an awful commotion over by the bar. They thought a pack of wild dogs had gotten a hold of someone."

People had heard our fight with Leo. Sweat trickled down my back. I cleared my throat so my voice wouldn't betray my nerves. "That's awful, but I'm not sure why you're telling me this."

Miller's chair squeaked as she leaned forward. "One of the wait staff described you and Mr. Sharpe as customers during that same time frame last night. Did you by any chance see or hear anything? Maybe you had your own Dogman sighting?"

The discomfort spiked, and the wolf in me pushed at the boundaries of my body. I couldn't voice an answer this time because a growl was ready in my throat. She knew I was the one to threaten this JD guy. Did she honestly think I'd admit to her, a Hunter, that I, a lupine, had hassled a Commoner? My jaw clenched tight, I shook my head.

"That's too bad. I was hoping we could puzzle that one out together." Miller sighed. The chair squeaked again, and the sense of being pressured lessened. "You have my card if you remember anything."

"Okay. Thank you." My voice was hoarse, and I fought an inkling of discomfort when turning my back to Miller to leave. I strode out of the cramped and hot office.

Once outside, I took solace in Ben's arms, burying my face in his jacket. Adrenaline coursed through my body. I focused on taking measured breaths to calm the wolf in me.

He held me in a hug. "What did she say?"

My words were muffled. "The guy I went after last night reported me."

We parted and Ben brushed his thumb across my cheek. "We'll be okay."

"You were right. What was I thinking?" I wiped impatiently at the tears of frustration in my eyes. I couldn't have a breakdown in front of the police station. "I was so pissed at that guy. I thought I was doing okay when I didn't slice him up."

"It's done." Ben slipped his arm around me and turned me toward the car. "We're leaving right now. We'll pick up our stuff and go."

I looked over my shoulder, torn between my instinctual fear of Officer Miller as a Hunter and my need to know more about my grandfather's involvement here.

"There's something else bothering you," Ben said.

My chest ached. "I don't think Grandpa was who I thought he was."

We returned to the motel, picked up our things, and drove to the repair shop. I paid the bill with a credit card, and we were on the road again. Ben offered to drive, but I didn't want to sit in the passenger seat with my thoughts. If my mind wasn't focused on driving, it would be drowning in doubt about my grandfather.

"WE HAVE A little over an hour," Ben said. "We head south for a bit, but most of the drive is a straight shot west on 20." He set his phone in the console between the seats. Our route led to the western lakeshore of the state.

"Do you think Miller will follow us?" I asked.

"I don't know," he said. "My only experience with Hunters was the extreme vigilante who chased us down in Hopewell. She doesn't seem as aggressive as him."

I scoffed. "She's a Hunter. She's trained to kill people like us."

"All we can do is stay alert," Ben said. "So, let's review our watch list. Number one, angry werewolf. Number two, a Hunter."

I bit my lip, caught between the anxiety and absurdity of the situation. When I glanced at Ben, he watched me, the corner of his mouth twitching. We both started laughing. If I didn't laugh, I'd have a panic attack.

"Can we still stop in Shelby, or should we drive straight through for your show?" I wanted to make the stop, but I was also prepared to wait so Ben wouldn't miss the scheduled concert.

"We have plenty of time. I don't need to be in Silver Lake until this evening. Where do you want to look first?"

"Their public library is right off the main street. We could park downtown and walk there."

He opened up the notebook he usually took notes in while I was driving. "I'm always up for burning a few hours in a library."

I knew this to be a sacred truth. "Does your obsession with books come with the wizard thing, or is that a you thing?"

Ben arched an eyebrow. "A wizard thing? Are you going to ask about my robes and wand next?"

His jab was good-humored, but I blushed anyway. "Sorry. I didn't mean to stereotype."

"I've always loved reading. The wizard thing exacerbated it. When my apprenticeship started, I devoured any book about magic I could get my hands on. I spent entire days studying in Reginald's library." The mention of his grandfather was followed by a grimace. Ben wasn't going to forgive Reginald's betrayal anytime soon. "My library card helped get me through my tethering sentence. Stories help us make sense of things, you know?"

"Yeah." I didn't have the patience or attention span for most books, but Ben introduced me to graphic novels. Once I started reading one, I couldn't put it down. Not only was the artwork enjoyable, but the stories of people not like me from situations unlike my own were intriguing. "They help you look at things differently."

"Yes." His hand settled on my thigh, his attention refocusing on the notebook opened across his lap. I waited a moment to see if he'd continue talking, but he'd slipped away into his thoughts.

As soon as we were on the highway south, we began passing signs for Hopewell. A wave of homesickness hit me. I debated giving Trish a call, especially with the news about a Hunter. Before our turn to the west, I pulled into a gas station and parked the car.

Ben looked up from a page covered in the strange symbols of spellwork. "Time to restock snacks? We're out of those peanut butter-filled pretzels."

I unbuckled my seatbelt and turned to face him.

Eyebrows raised, he slowly shut the notebook.

"Do you think we should go back to Hopewell?" I twisted my hands in my lap. "Would Leo actually follow us to Trish and Nate's doorstep? This time we're paying closer attention to cars following us, and I haven't seen any that may be his."

"Trish asked you not to go back there," he warned.

"Did she mean it though?" I knew the answer, but I still grasped for any possible excuse to return.

"Trish isn't someone who says stuff she doesn't mean. And I thought you were excited about solving the box puzzle." Ben's voice took on the *I'm-concerned-about-you* tone. "What's going on, Alex?"

Trish wouldn't tell me to stay away if she needed my help. And it wasn't simply homesickness. What *was* going on? We had to have lost Leo, I got to be with Ben, and I was free to track down whatever the hell it was my grandfather was up to.

I swallowed. It was the instinct that kept me safe for years after I'd learned I was a werewolf.

Run.

"I'm scared if I keep looking up stuff about my grandfather and that box, I'm going to find answers I won't like," I admitted. "Miller said her dad identified Grandpa as the main suspect in the livestock killings case."

Ben set his notebook aside and reached for my hand. It gave me the reassurance I needed to keep talking.

I held his hand in mine and absently ran my fingers along the lines of his palm. "But at the same time, I need to know. What was he doing when he ran away and left his family behind? I need it to make sense. Is that crazy?"

"Absolutely not." Ben never seemed to lose patience with my faltering attempts to share my emotions.

I lifted his open palm to my cheek, comforted by his skin against mine. He leaned toward me, slipped his fingers lightly to the back of my neck, and kissed me. Warmth spread throughout my body and the day seemed a bit less dreary. I rested my forehead against his and whispered, "Now I want a snack."

He chuckled. "Me too."

We grabbed snacks and drinks and spent five to ten minutes snickering like pre-teens while sharing a bag of Pirate Booty, a puffed corn flavored with white cheddar. Between the snack's name and our awful pirate impersonations, I had to pull the car over to wipe away my tears and regain enough composure to drive.

Our drive west brought us to Shelby, another sleepy and small town. The street through the block or two of the little downtown was lined with storefronts and a few restaurants. As seemed to be the trend, several stood vacant.

Ben and I left the car parked on the main street and walked a block to the public library. A sidewalk bordered by well-kept flowerbeds led from the sidewalk up to the pretty little building.

"Where would we even look for information about a local cryptid?" I asked.

Ben shrugged. "Ask the librarian."

"What? They're going to think I'm a conspiracy nutcase." I pulled open the front door for him. "They'll call security."

"I'm sure they've had stranger requests." Ben passed into the library. I followed him through an entryway posted with community fliers and business cards.

Steeling myself, I approached the circulation desk where a middle-aged woman sat at a computer. She looked up, her smile welcoming. "Hello. How can I help you?"

"I'm looking for information on the Dogman." I realized I sounded ridiculous, but there was no other way to ask. "We learned about him yesterday at a festival and thought it... uh, was neat."

She quirked an eyebrow. "And because there was a sighting here, you thought we'd have information about it."

"There was?" Ben asked.

She nodded and typed something into her computer. "We have a book on cryptids you could browse. Our wi-fi password is right up there." She pointed to a sign posted beside her desk. "Otherwise, I'd suggest looking through our local history room. Would you like to do that?"

A type of anxious excitement flickered inside me. "Yes, please."

She led Ben and me to a separate room off the main library. "The librarian who usually helps with our local history information is out to lunch." She walked around the room, pointing out resources that might help our search. "Local history of this part of the lakeshore is on the shelf. Clipped articles for this town specifically can be found in this filing cabinet. I'll go grab that book on cryptids while you two work."

We thanked her, and she left the room. Smiling, Ben nudged my shoulder. "Told you. Librarians are superheroes without capes."

"You weren't kidding." I grinned, impressed.

From browsing through various clippings and books, we sussed out Shelby took root at the western edge of the Manistee National Forest. The forest itself was huge, over 540,000 acres, and covered the western part of the state. Early logging decimated the trees around Shelby. Instead of replanting, the stumps were pulled and agriculture turned to asparagus and fruit orchards.

I pointed to a case of buttons made for town festivals over the years. "They're known nationally for their asparagus production." I wrinkled my nose.

"You don't like asparagus?" Ben asked.

"Blech, no."

He shook his head and went back to flipping through a file cabinet. "It's delicious." He stopped flipping through the folders, pulled one out, and brought it to the table where I'd been looking through old town photos.

"Company recognized for efforts to ensure trees for the future," I read the headline aloud. "How is this connected to the Dogman?"

Ben pulled a chair out and sat beside me. "So I was thinking a bit more about these Dogman sightings. Let's say it isn't a lupine, but purely a tall tale. If the sightings are only stories, is there someone benefiting from people being scared of this creature?"

"Like making money off it?"

"Maybe? Fear is used to sway opinions or distract people from what's going on," he said. "Many sightings involve forests, especially the Manistee Forest, in the state."

I considered the angle. "But why would someone have livestock killed to make a grab at lumber?"

"I don't know. To scare them away and buy up the land for some other use?"

I chewed at my thumbnail, turning the possibility over in my mind. "And why would Grandpa even care? I know he grew up on a farm northwest of Hopewell, but they moved to New York when he was a teenager."

There was a light rap on the doorframe of the room. The librarian entered with the book of cryptids. "Any luck?"

"Frustratingly slow." Even with plentiful info about the area at our fingertips, we were still making guesses.

"Maybe this will help." She handed me the book with the Dogman page bookmarked.

"Thank you." I opened the book, and Ben started browsing online. While only a section of the book was dedicated to the Dogman, Ben found pages and pages of information on cryptid websites, local news sites, and blogs.

"The woman I talked to at the bakery said he lives in the forest. There are white pine forests all over the northern half of the lower peninsula. Every county has had a sighting since . . ." I checked my notes. "The 1880s."

"Makes sense the reports would have started in the woods at that time," Ben said.

"Why?"

"The state industry was lumbering," he said. "There were lumber camps everywhere harvesting trees. Hopewell's river was one of the main shipping highways for lumber. That's why all the lumber barons lived up the hill from downtown and the river." He pushed his glasses up his nose. The gesture was a joke between us, but he also looked so damn adorable when he did it.

I grinned, leaned forward, and kissed him.

"What was that for?" he asked.

"I love you."

Ben's lips parted, and his blue eyes widened slightly.

I froze. For such a loaded phrase, it had unintentionally slipped out. I'd thought about it several times but never told him. Extreme heat surged from my collar through my face to my scalp. I cleared my throat loudly and stared a hole through my notes. "Anyway, reports of the Dogman's appearance are mixed, but most agree he's around seven to ten feet tall, has the head of a dog and torso of a man, and is covered in dark fur. He has sharp teeth and large, clawed hands and feet. So, very lupine in that way."

"Alex?" Ben placed a hand on my knee.

I jumped and looked up at him.

There was a pink flush to his cheeks. "I —"

Before he could finish, I forged on. "A lot of different eye colors: yellow, amber, blue . . . which is weird, right? But intelligent eyes and . . ." I scanned the page, not seeing it. "His howl sounds more like a human scream than a wolf."

My heartbeat rapidly hammered in my chest. Dark spots appeared in my vision. I realized I was hyperventilating and would soon pass out if I didn't do something about it. I stood and announced. "I need to pee."

Then I took off for the restrooms.

In the safety of the ladies' room, I paced. What the *hell* was going on with me? I wasn't a high school girl with a crush. I was a grown woman in my thirties. I splashed water on my face and focused on slowing my breathing.

I need to pee?

I groaned, closed my eyes, and leaned back against the bathroom wall. Maybe he'd forget about it? Probably not. I wished Emma was here to let me know how to fix what I'd done. The fact that the whole situation was getting me so riled up made me feel ridiculous, too. Ben and I had Leo following us, trying to frame us for heinous crimes, possibly a Hunter watching our every move, and I was blubbering like a damn teenager over a boy.

When I returned to the tables where we'd been researching, I sat down and opened my notepad.

"Alex?"

As soon as I met Ben's gaze, my face warmed again.

"Is everything okay?"

It wasn't okay. I'd botched a special moment with someone I cared deeply for. I was mortified.

I shrugged. "Yeah. Why wouldn't it be?"

His smile was shy. "It's nice outside. Do you want to get some food and find a park?"

"Sure." I gathered my notes. With new Dogman info fresh in my mind, I could sort through the box again. We packed up our few belongings and left the library.

Outside, Ben held his hand out for mine. "Can we talk? About what you said?"

My pulse jumped. I took hold of his hand, and we started walking. "Oh, it's okay. We don't have to have a huge discussion about it."

"I'd like to."

"No pressure. I mean, don't feel obligated to say anything. It kind of just came out—"

He stopped and squeezed my hand. I halted and looked up at him.

"I love you, too, Alex."

That embarrassing fluttering sensation danced in my stomach. Hearing him say those few words made me ridiculously happy. Was I going to swoon right now? I rested my hand on his chest, tipped onto my toes, and kissed him.

The wolf in me stirred. I wanted to be closer to him. Have his hands move over me. Breathe our mingled scents.

He's safe.

Ben pulled me to him and deepened our kiss. We were rapidly approaching swooning territory. A low rumble of a growl sounded in my chest.

Dammit.

I stepped back out of his arms, hoping to hell no one had been around to hear me.

"We're alone." Ben's voice was hoarse.

I kept my gaze lowered anyway. My eyes would be glowing like beacons.

"I'm sorry," he said. "That was stupid of me to do where someone could have noticed you."

"It's okay." I took a deep inhale and a slow exhale to bring my body back under control. He should be able to kiss his partner in public without worrying they'd turn into a hairy beast.

"Picnic, then?"

"Unless you see a cold shower, yes, a picnic sounds great."

12

AFTER A SIMPLE picnic in a township park, we started toward Silver Lake, a small resort town known for its inland lake, dunes, and state park. "How long are we stuck in the car?"

"About twenty minutes," Ben said.

"Good." Road trips could be fun, but I didn't enjoy all the time cooped up in the car.

"You find it difficult to sit still, don't you?" Ben teased.

"It doesn't make your skin crawl?" I tried to put into words how being sedentary made me feel. "Don't you feel trapped if you're stuck in one place too long?"

"You're asking this of a guy forced to spend fifteen years of his life in one place," Ben said dryly. "And you'd prefer to go back there instead of traveling with me?"

"No, not... It's not necessarily the location in that case. I guess I want to be a part of creating change instead of passively sitting by and watching. I've never really felt that need before landing in Hopewell. Am I making any sense?"

Ben looked out the window. "It makes sense for you."

An awkward silence settled between us. It rarely happened, and I didn't want it there.

"So tell me about tonight's show," I said maybe a bit too brightly. "It's outside? Isn't it getting a bit chilly for that?"

"Not everyone is a reptile that requires hot weather before they'll go outdoors."

I smirked. The love of summer weather wasn't something we shared. "I highly doubt I'm the only person who enjoys warm weather. The beach is somewhere to go when it's hot and sunny."

He shifted in his seat. "Maybe I should skip this show. We spent hours driving, but what if Leo tracked us?"

"How? This time we knew to watch for any cars following us."

"At least we'll be outside in an open area. It's not like he could sneak up on us."

"You sound like you're reassuring yourself more than me."

"I am." Ben grimaced. "The guy is a beast."

The main street into Silver Lake led through a traffic circle and toward the water. We stopped to get food at an ice cream parlor before continuing to the state park. Ben grabbed his laptop, and I carried the to-go bag of food. We started walking to the dunes where the show would be held. A young park ranger, stationed at the lot's entrance, gave us a nod as we passed by.

We were a few steps past him before I turned back. "Hi. Do you have a minute for a few questions?"

He straightened. "Sure. How can I help you?"

Ben stopped and waited. I blushed even as I asked the question. "Have you heard of the Dogman?"

"Wow, that brings back memories." The ranger chuckled and relaxed his posture. "Of course I have."

"Can you tell me what you know?" I motioned over my shoulder at Ben. "We're traveling around collecting stories of the Dogman."

"Well, I don't know all the official folklore, but I heard about him from my uncle."

"Your uncle saw him?" I pressed.

"No. I stayed with my uncle once in a while at his fishing cabin on the White River when I was younger. At night he'd say 'Don't go out or the Dogman will get you.' It kept me from playing in the woods after dark and getting lost."

Disappointment crept into my voice. "But you never saw the Dogman?"

The ranger gave me a quizzical look. "No. From what my uncle said, it's like a werewolf, only part man and part dog. It's just a folktale."

I thanked him for his time, and Ben and I continued down the short path to the dunes. Ben found and checked in with Mark, the concert organizer. The neon colors of Mark's bucket hat stood in high contrast to his shocks of sun-bleached hair and deeply tanned skin. He was Cathy's cousin and even younger than her, looking barely out of high school.

While Ben spoke to Mark, I left our food with Ben and wandered over the dune to the beach. Lake Michigan stretched far into the horizon while the wind whipped my hair around my head. I pulled my grandfather's jacket tighter and walked to the water's edge. My steps squeaked and slid in the loose sand. The sensation was unnerving since I was accustomed to passing quietly through a space on much surer footing.

I reached the damp sand of the waterline where the ground was more solid beneath my shoes. My stomach was uneasy. I realized I didn't like leaving Leo behind with a Hunter. Trish advised we not engage with him, especially since his behavior was so odd. Even though it was awful what he'd done to the farmer's sheep, Leo hadn't attacked or killed a person. But wasn't it my responsibility to stop him from running amok? He'd only been in the area causing problems because we were there. It was hard not to think of him as a mess I was running away from.

I inhaled deeply, my eyelids partially lowering as the scents of water and damp sand filled my nose. The fresh air traversed down into my lungs. My first attempt at flying solo as a werewolf found me in a resort town along the Atlantic shoreline. The body of water reaching for my shoes disappeared into the horizon like the ocean, but it smelled so different. Less fish and salt, and more damp sand and fresh water.

Did my grandfather ever stand beside the lake where I stood now? I wished he was with me. I could ask him about his time spent here, outside his days with his wife and child. What could he possibly be searching for that he didn't have with the family he loved? Did he find it?

My fingers closed around the metal key in my jacket pocket. What secrets was the key protecting?

The aroma of food attracted my attention. That odd squeaking noise of footsteps on fine sand sounded behind me. Ben's tall lean figure crossed the beach. He carried the brown paper bag with our food order and held it aloft when he saw me admiring him.

"Let's have something to eat and watch the sunset before the night gets started." He looked so happy. His eyes were bright and the tumultuous wind blew around his shaggy hair.

Warmth bloomed inside my chest. The tension in my shoulders eased. We backtracked to the top of the dune and sat shoulder-to-shoulder on the sand. Our closeness protected us against the cooling wind.

"What were you thinking about?" Ben took a huge bite of his sandwich.

"Not much." I didn't know how to talk to him about the emotions and thoughts ricocheting around inside me about my grandfather. Ben and Reginald were both wizards, as my grandfather and I were both werewolves, but Ben avoided his grandfather. How could Ben possibly relate?

"You sure?" His interest was genuine, but my fear he wouldn't fully understand kept my lips sealed. So I nodded, and he turned back to his sandwich. We ate our dinner together, this time comfortable in our shared silence. The small waves broke on the shore with a steady rhythm. The sun, a brilliant orange orb, sunk into the horizon line of the lake.

We walked back to the other side of the dune, an area protected from the wind. Three large bonfires were lit, their warmth already attracting people waiting for the concert. People hovered near the fires and each other. Laughter and conversation filled the air. A small stage with minimal lighting had been set up.

"Would you feel safer up there with me tonight?" Ben asked. I balked. "Hell no." Being in front of an audience, even tucked away at his side, sounded absolutely awful. I didn't thrive in front of groups of people like he did.

"Didn't think so, but thought I'd ask." Sharing his love of music outweighed any preshow jitters for Ben. Before I could say anything more, he gave me a quick kiss and left for the stage.

"Good luck!" I shouted after him.

He raised a hand without turning back.

I sighed and looked around at the people who'd arrived since we did. The crowd was sizable for the last-minute show and cooler weather. The music started, and the heat generated among the dancing bodies warmed me up. Other people lingered outside the glow of the stage's lights and even wandered over the dune to walk the beach.

I took a break from dancing to stow my jacket in the car. I made sure Ben noticed me leering at him before I sought out a drink. Not trusting the beer, I grabbed water.

"Having a good time?"

I turned toward the voice, recognizing Mark. "Yeah. The lake is beautiful, and I'm crazy about the performer." Since we were standing closer than earlier, a familiar scent tickled my nose. Mark was lupine like his cousin, Cathy.

"Alex, right?" His nostrils twitched. He was reading my scent.

"That's me."

Mark tilted his head toward the stage. "Ben knows about you?"

"He does."

"Cathy said you two are making your way across the state?" His arms were crossed, and he seemed to be sizing me up. Had Cathy told him about our run-in with the Hunter, Miller?

I kept my tone casual. "We're on a road trip, but live in Hopewell."

He snorted. His tone verged on derisive with all the confidence of youth to back it up. "Ah, city folk. And you plan to head deeper into the forest?"

"We'll leave right away or wait until morning. It depends on how tired we are." I hesitated before asking, "Do you live around here, or are you only here to help with the show?"

His eyes narrowed. "Yeah, I live here. Why?"

"This will probably sound ridiculous." I shifted my weight from one foot to another. "Have you heard of the Dogman?"

Mark laughed. "Of course I have! This area is known for dunes, fruit orchards, and that one winter a retired cop and her friend spotted the Dogman on US 31." His eyes grew wide. "Wait, are you like those people who track down paranormal occurrences and report them on TV? Or do you have a podcast?"

I choked on my water. "What? No! We know not to do that."

"Nah, I'm just kidding." He gave my shoulder a playful shove. I briefly entertained the idea of shoving him back. "But really, why are you asking about the Dogman?"

"The stories caught our curiosity, so today we researched the lore at the Shelby Public Library. No one can agree on what this cryptid looks like other than he's canine-like and walks on two legs."

"Like us." Mark smirked knowingly. "You want to know if he exists and is one of us."

The kid saw right through me. "All signs seem to point that way."

Mark pulled his hat from his head to scratch at the back of his head. "People are going to adapt him to fit the story they need at that point in time, especially Commoners." He shrugged. "It helps them make sense of something they don't fully understand. First the lumberjacks, then the farmers, the vans full of hippies, the sportsmen in their cabins, and on and on."

"So you don't think he's one of us?" My friend Nate assured me that lupine took care of each other by helping out whenever possible. I hoped Mark was being honest.

"I've never seen him. It's pure folklore." Mark twisted the cloth hat. Something about my questioning was making him uncomfortable. "You know, the area you two are heading into has the most sightings. Maybe you'll meet him."

The hair rose on the nape of my neck. Even with Mark's testimony, I wasn't convinced the Dogman was completely fictitious. "Uh, I don't think I'm ready for a private meeting."

Despite the thumping music, a long, spine-tingling scream reached our ears across the dunes. Mark and I ran to the top of the dune and looked down onto the moonlit beach. Two figures ran toward us, their feet slipping in the sand.

Wild-eyed, one of the guys shouted ahead. "There's something on the beach!"

An enormous form crouched at the waterline. Moonlight accented the hunched shoulders.

My heart skipped.

"Shit! Is that a bear?" Mark's face paled. "I hate bears."

"Clear people out of here." I moved to step down the hill.

Mark caught my sleeve. "Wait!"

I turned on him, baring my teeth and jerking my arm away.

"If you're going down there, make a bunch of noise. If it's a black bear it should run away." His round eyes were fixed on me. "Be careful."

Slinking away, I slipped and slid down the loose sand of the dune toward the water. The cold breeze quickly covered my arms in goosebumps. The moon's pale light made my skin tingle and my heart thump harder. The moon didn't affect us as it did Hollywood's werewolves, but her soft light did feel like a slow dose of adrenaline or a great cup of coffee.

As I drew closer to the water's edge, the massive figure became more recognizable. He stood, towering over the fallen heap on the sand. My stomach turned. The prone figure was a human and not a prey animal.

Despite my attempt at remaining quiet, the sand gave me away. Growling, the large creature swung his huge, shaggy head toward me. Red eyes met mine, and steam burst from the werewolf's nostrils.

I froze in place. "Leo."

13

THE WEREWOLF'S CHEST heaved. A rumbling growl reached my ears before being pulled away by the wind.

"You followed us? How?"

Leo stepped away from the still body on the sand. A strip of fabric was hooked around the broken canine in his maw. That injury should have healed by now for lupine. Leo took a lumbering step toward me. His balance wavered.

The wind danced and switched direction, bludgeoning my nose with the scent of water, fresh blood, and that rotten odor clinging to Leo. I stepped back with a glance up the dune. I couldn't run back to the crowd that may still be clearing out on the other side.

Leo took an unsure step and then another. With a lurch, he broke out into a loping run toward me. His breath came in bursts from his parted jaws.

Instead of trying to keep my footing in the loose sand, I sprinted down the beach toward the water. My ankle, sprained last night, barely twinged. When my shoes hit the damp sand, I put on speed.

Leo's heavy steps thumped over the packed sand close behind me. His clawed feet would act as cleats. I gritted my teeth, channeling my anxiety and fear, and reached deeper for that primal spark inside me.

The adrenaline masked the dull pain from the distortion and lengthening of my fingers. My claws pushed their way from my cuticles. My canines widened in my gumline and grew sharp.

Leo wasn't slowing, and his gait was longer. He'd eventually catch me.

The cold air burned in my lungs. I came to a sudden stop, spun, and dodged closer to the water, hoping to duck around him. Leo roared and dove for me. I tried another dodge out of the way. His massive hand closed around my upper arm even as his body moved past me into the water. I was pulled back off my feet. My body broke the water's surface. Cold water instantly soaked my clothes. I struggled to free myself.

Leo stood, growling, his claws puncturing my shirt and sinking into my arm. He pulled me into the deeper water. Instant fear flooded my consciousness. I was reduced to a snarling and flailing animal while the waves periodically dashed over my head.

Then I was underwater, viewing the moon through the rippling surface of the lake. I thrashed my feet, causing waves of sound, trying to twist loose from Leo's hold. I pried at his fingers, but I couldn't open the hand holding me underwater. Finally, I sunk my claws deep into his forearm. I hoped the pain would force him to release me.

No such luck.

He didn't even flinch. It was as if his nerve endings were dead.

A dark shape eclipsed the moon. Leo fell backward. His hold on me broke. A muffled splash sounded in the water beside me.

My feet planted below me, I burst through the water's surface. I sputtered and gasped for air. My lungs burned. A hurricane of snarls, water, and motion beside me threatened to pull me into it. I struggled to move through the water and distance myself from immediate danger.

Leo broke free and hurled himself at me. With a single swipe of his massive arm, he threw me aside. I fell below water again but was able to right myself. Soaked and trembling, I watched Leo lope away along the water line.

I spun back toward the lake. A smaller werewolf with a dark pelt stood in the water behind me. Was it Mark? My nose tried to pull their scent out of the mess of blood and lake water. They watched Leo escape before turning blue eyes back on me.

A growl sprung up in my throat. I narrowed my eyes, the hair on the nape of my neck and arms standing on end. I carefully backstepped toward the beach.

The unmistakable popping of cartilage sounded from the werewolf. They doubled over, holding their ribs with a whine, snout brushing the water. Muscles slid and bunched sickeningly beneath depleting fur. The dull crack of bones distorted their jaw and muzzle as the hybrid form slid back toward a man-like shape. The shift was horrifying but seamless.

An immediate stab of jealousy hit me. His shift didn't seem to faze him, where I usually vomited from the pain when I'd shifted back from wolf to woman.

Mark stood shivering in the water. "You alright?"

"Yeah. Thanks for the help." I looked away to give him privacy. "Did you call anyone?"

"Yes. The police and an ambulance." Water swished as he strode out of the lake to join me. His teeth began to chatter. Mark looked down at the still body on the sand. "He didn't kill the guy, did he?"

The body's upper arm was as tattered as its clothing. The aroma of blood swirled everywhere. My stomach clenched. I crouched beside the guy and held my hand under his nose. Faint exhales of warm air brushed my skin. "Not yet."

"Shit. I hope the ambulance gets here soon. We can't have a Commoner dying on us." The sharp scent of Mark's fear hit my nose. He looked down the length of the beach. "Who was the other wolf? He smelled terrible."

"His name is Leo. He's been following Ben and me. We thought we lost him, but he found us somehow." I looked up at Mark. He was shivering. His eyes still glowed an intense indigo. "I'm glad you noticed the weird scent, too. I started to think I was imagining it. There's also something weird going on with him. He's not healing and his mind seems cloudy. I don't know what he wants from us."

"I don't know your situation," Mark said, "but he seems to want you dead."

"Alex!"

I turned toward the dune. Ben quickly descended it, barely keeping his balance, his arms held out like airplane wings. He reached the bottom and jogged toward us. "What happened?" His brows drew together as he frowned. "Mark?"

My teeth started to chatter. "It was Leo. He tore up a guy who was here for the show."

Ben looked at the body on the sand. "He's not dead, is he?"

"Close, but no," I said. "Leo went after me when I tried to see what was happening."

Ben scowled. "You came down here alone?"

"He ran off when he found out there were two of us. Must not have liked his odds." Mark rubbed at his arms. "I need to get clothes on before I freeze my balls off." He started back toward the dune and the parking lot. "Come on. We need to get our stories straight for the cops."

I looked at Ben.

He was still scowling.

My voice lowered for his ears only. "I'm sorry."

Still with the scowling.

"You should change, too," he said. "Your lips are blue."

I started after Mark, trying to follow without having to look at his pale ass the whole way.

Ben muttered beside me. "How did Leo even find us again? We didn't see anyone following our car."

"I don't know." Guilt soured my stomach. If we hadn't been here, the guy on the beach wouldn't have been attacked.

"I don't want to be found near a mangled Commoner." Mark's nerves were audible in his voice. "But there were too many people here who saw us. Sooner or later, we'll be tracked down for questioning. It'd be better to get that out of the way instead of running and looking guilty."

Our recent visit with Officer Miller came to mind. Would she hear about this?

We reached the parking lot beside the fire pits, now low piles of glowing embers. Mark dug around in the bed of a beat-up truck for clothes. Ben draped a blanket around my shoulders. I stood huddled in the blanket, teeth chattering as he sorted through my bag for dry clothes.

"I'm worried about Miller finding out about this," I said. "She's already suspicious of us because of my grandfather and what Leo did to that farmer's sheep."

Ben handed me a sweater. "We'll be gone before she finds out. Once we get past talking to the cops, we head to our next stop."

"You don't think that'd look even more suspicious?" I shucked my wet clothing, pulled on the sweater, and then the pants Ben passed to me.

"Did the people on the beach see Leo?"

I zipped up my pants. "Yeah."

"Then we're good," he said. "The thing that attacked the person was a huge animal, not a 5'7" female tourist. They'll probably pin it on their Dogman."

"Maybe." I tossed the wet clothing in the trunk. I tried my best to dry my head full of curls. Ben wrapped me in his arms, holding me tight against his warm body. My teeth wouldn't stop chattering.

Mark, now in dry clothing, joined us. He talked fast, his gestures animated. "Okay, here's what I'm thinking. We stick to the truth because we didn't do anything wrong. Alex and I were talking and heard the screaming from the beach. When we looked down there, we saw a large animal standing over the guy. I cleared the crowd out to keep them safe—"

"But what about Hunters?" Dread tightened my chest.

Mark stopped. "What about them?"

Cathy *didn't* mention Miller to him. "We came into contact with a Hunter at our last stop. Will she hear about this?" Images of the Hunter in Hopewell flooded my mind. His bloody attack on Hell's Bells, our local werewolf hangout. His attempt to crush Ben and me with his truck. Because of my attack eight years ago on the man that triggered my werewolf gene, the Hunter had been contracted to kill me and didn't care who he took out in the process.

"Will Leo's attack be reported to a local Committee?" Ben's brows were pinched. We were worried about the same thing. How would this mess land with those who enforced laws written for us?

"The supernatural populations up here are too few and far between for a Committee." A thin ring of blue surfaced in Mark's irises, and I caught more traces of fear in the air. "As far as Hunters, we have an understanding with the knights of St. Hubertus. We don't harm Commoners, so the knights leave us alone. You and I should be fine."

An *understanding*? Had this kid ever dealt with a Hunter?

A growl crept into my voice. "There's a Commoner on the beach who was torn up by a werewolf. If any Hunter finds out, that's all they'll need to come after you and me, too."

Mark paled and the stench of fear thickened around him.

Flashing lights and a blip of a siren announced the police and ambulance's arrival. Oceana County Police was lettered across the sides of the dark cruiser.

"I don't like talking with cops." Ben shifted from one foot to another.

He'd been required to talk a lot with them lately. It pained me to know it was because of me. I squeezed his arm. "I'm sorry. Like you said, a few questions, and then we're gone."

A single officer took statements from all of us. The paramedics retrieved the injured man from the beach. He'd regained consciousness and was switching between moaning and incoherent yelling while they hauled him to the ambulance.

"Should we ask to stay with Mark?" I stood beside Ben and watched Mark nodding at the officer questioning him. "He might know lupine in the area we could talk to about Miller."

"Is he even going to want us around? This happened because of us."

"Because of me."

The police officer shook Mark's hand and walked back to the cruiser. Mark made his way over to us. He pulled bills from his pocket, counted out an amount, and handed it to Ben. "I know you didn't finish the show, but I also know you need to eat."

"Thanks." Ben took the bills and shook Mark's hand.

"Mark, can we stay with you tonight?" I asked. "We have a camping site reserved, but—"

"I don't think so." He swallowed and dropped his gaze.

Blindsided by his response, I blinked. Wolves took care of each other. I'd thought my question was only a formality. I didn't expect him to turn us away. "Why not?"

The stench of fear came off Mark in thick waves. He shook his head. "I need to distance myself from what happened here. I can't have my name in the knights' mouths." He took a step back, hesitated, and then added. "I'm sorry." With that, he turned and walked back to his truck.

Ben nudged my arm. "Alex, come on. I'll drive."

Clenching my teeth, I followed Ben back to the car. "We scared him by asking about Hunters. He didn't seem scared when he was helping run off Leo."

Ben watched Mark's truck leave the lot and started the car. "He's young. Maybe he leaped in without thinking it through."

"What does that have to do with being young?" I growled.

"He could be someone who helps when a situation smells rotten."

The corners of Ben's mouth turned up. "Imagine that."

"He and I are both wolves. What happened to us looking out for each other?" Nate had hammered that home in my mind. Lupine protected each other. What was different with the lupine in this part of the state that it didn't seem to apply? Was it only because I wasn't from here?

Then I remembered a definite difference. "Mark had blue eyes."

"So?"

"In his wolf form, he had blue eyes," I repeated. "Have you ever seen that before?"

"Not that I've noticed, but I haven't seen many fully shifted lupine. That's been discouraged in Hopewell for the majority of my life."

"I haven't seen it before, either." I leaned back in my seat. But out of the eight years I'd been a werewolf, I'd only befriended other lupine within the past ten months.

"You're thinking of those sightings reporting a blue-eyed Dogman," Ben said.

I nodded. "I mentioned the Dogman to Mark. He laughed it off, saying it was nothing but a folktale, but there was unease there."

"The Dogman is blamed for some grisly stuff. Maybe that makes Mark jumpy."

"Maybe."

WE DROVE NORTH for a little over a half hour, keeping ourselves awake by splitting a box of Bugles and singing select songs by Journey and Boston. A turn west on another highway took us back toward the lakeshore and the westernmost part of the Manistee forest. I was fading fast when we pulled into our camping spot. Ben and I took turns visiting the outhouse across the drive.

He returned to our site with his brow wrinkled. "That must have been awful for you."

"Be thankful you don't have better vision." I stifled a yawn. "Should we try sharing the backseat as a bed?"

"What about the tent?" Ben asked.

"I'm exhausted and don't want to lose a fight to a tent."

"Hammocks?" he suggested. "They're faster to set up."

"It'd be more comfortable than the car," I agreed. "Can you set any wards in case Leo shows up?"

"They won't stop him," Ben said. "The wards I know protect against magic, not a werewolf punching me in the face."

"What about that glowing shield thing you've made before?"

He smiled, no doubt at my mastery of magic terminology. "I can't sustain that while I'm sleeping. Mom had a ward in her spellbook that works like an alarm." He poked around the edge of the site and found a stick. "It'll wake us up if someone other than us crosses its boundaries."

"Perfect." I strung the hammocks between trees on our campsite and tossed blankets and pillows into them. Now distanced from the outhouse, the air in the woods smelled wonderful. I inhaled deeply, getting a nose full of pine and old wood ash.

Ben drew a symbol with the stick at four points around the site's perimeter. My ears picked up the soft words of his incantation. The energy he harnessed for his magic whispered gently over my skin as he wove it into the wards. His delicate and smooth gathering of energy to himself reminded me of his grandfather's spellcasting. At each symbol, Ben crouched and touched his fingertips to the lines drawn in the dirt. They momentarily glowed a bright blue before fading.

I sat on the picnic table, watching him work. "Now that you can use it again, is there anything you've been wanting to do with your magic?"

"I've thought of that since the day I was tethered."

"You didn't mention that to your mom when she asked."

"She didn't need to know." Brushing off his hands, he walked over to sit beside me on the picnic table. "It's changed a few times."

I leaned against him, my head on his shoulder. "What's the current plan?"

"I'm working on spell construction concepts. What I'll do with those, I'm not sure. I want to dig deeper into that book my mom gave me." He gestured to the closest symbol on the ground. "That's a fairly simple spell, but there's more complex spellwork in there."

"Have you found anything useful for dealing with Leo?"

"I was thinking the same thing while flipping through the book. There might be."

"When all the Leo stuff is behind us, and we can go home, do you want to help with the new setup in Hopewell?" I'd avoided asking because I was fairly certain of his answer. "From what Trish said, there's a lot to do."

"I don't think I'm going to, Alex," Ben said. "Hopewell doesn't mean the same thing to me as it does to you. It's great you found a home there, but for me, the city was a prison."

My heart fell. I wondered what our relationship would look like once we returned home. "It makes sense you'd prefer to be traveling." I sat up to look at him.

"Yeah." His smile wavered. "And you'll be in the thick of it, too busy in Hopewell to come with me."

I frowned, looked down at my hands, and nodded.

"I'm still going back with you, but I don't want to get trapped in supernatural politics while I'm there. We'll figure something out." Ben kissed me on the cheek and headed to his hammock. He sat on the hammock's edge, took off his shoes, and lay back into the sling-like bed. The ties creaked as the hammock swayed.

Something in Ben's demeanor was off, which worried me. I considered crawling into the hammock after him with the hope his embrace would squash any doubts about us. But tonight my body ached from my fight with Leo, and I was exhausted. I carefully balanced on the edge of my hammock, unlaced my boots, and tipped back. Thankfully I didn't flip the contraption.

Neither Ben nor I grew up with a family that went camping. We'd been looking forward to figuring out why people enjoyed it. Putting up a tent and roasting marshmallows may not be something others got worked up about missing, but it'd been something simple we wanted to share that didn't involve any of our baggage.

It would have to wait.

I turned and pulled the blanket up around me. Periodic calls of a type of night bird corkscrewed through the cold air. The pines and the strings of the hammock creaked. A hushed roar of tumbling waves drifted to us through the woods from the lake. The hammock's gentle swing and the soft song of the forest lulled me to sleep.

14

A SHRIEKING CAR alarm startled me awake. It took my mind a few beats to recall where I was, and that my car didn't have a functioning alarm. A distressed cry and the creaking of ropes from nearby reached my ears.

Ben. The wards.

Leo.

I tried to sit up quickly but was tangled in my blanket. The hammock swayed, threatening to spill me on the ground. Cursing, I overcorrected my balance. The hammock spun once and sealed me inside like a bean in a pod. The blaring alarm was a spike of pain driven between my eyes. The wolf in me leaped to the forefront, responding with a mix of panic and rage.

My hands shifted even as a bout of snarling erupted from my chest. I frantically slashed at the material trapping me. I couldn't gain leverage since my body was wrapped in a swinging sling. Struggling to focus, my mind buzzed within the aggressive haze of my wolf. I turned onto my stomach, pushed myself unsteadily back on my knees, and slashed at the bottom of the hammock, through the pillow and all.

The hammock tore with long ripping sounds. I fell to the ground on my stomach amidst a flurry of feathers and ribbons of material. Shouting voices from the dark accompanied the awful sound of the alarm. Scrambling to my hands and knees in the dirt, I saw Ben stumbling past with a light. He ran his shin into the edge of the picnic table, cursed, and fell to his knees. He leaned forward and swept his hand through the dirt.

The alarm ceased.

"Inconsiderate assholes! How long does it take—" The male voice shouting from several campsites away was shushed.

"Ben!" I got to my feet and ran to him.

"I'm okay! It's okay. It's not him." Ben was on his back in the dirt, his chest quickly rising and falling. He lifted his phone, blasting me with the flashlight. "Are you okay?"

I blinked against the bright light, shielding my eyes with a hand. "What the hell was that? I didn't know what was happening!"

He studied me, his brows drawing together.

"I ruined our hammock," I said.

"You have feathers in your hair."

"It's from a pillow. I ruined that, too."

He sat up and shook his head. "Sorry, I guess the parameters were too wide on the warding spell."

I offered him my hand to help him to his feet. "If it wasn't Leo, what set off the wards?"

"I'm not sure." He turned in place, shining the flashlight into the woods around our site.

I scanned the air with my nose and looked up at the pine tree beside the picnic table. A bulbous shadow perched on one of the branches. I pointed. "Try up there."

Ben swung the flashlight to shine into the tree's canopy. The beam wasn't strong, but a pair of beady eyes reflected the light at us from a quill-covered body. Ben narrowed his eyes at the intruder. "You. Little. Bastard."

I looked from the porcupine to Ben and started to giggle.

His gaze darted back to me, his brow smoothing as he chuckled.

"I said, shut the hell up!" bellowed the angry voice from the other campsite.

Which made us both laugh. We covered our mouths until our laughter petered out.

After such an extreme wake-up call, I didn't see myself getting any more sleep. "What time is it?"

He checked his phone. "A little after seven. The sun will be up soon. Want to find something to eat?"

It was a forty-minute round trip to find a gas station, refill the car, and grab food. When we returned to the campsite, the sun and a few campers had risen. I sat huddled in a blanket at the picnic table, sipped my gas station coffee, and watched Ben attempt to start a campfire. The coffee wasn't great, but it was caffeine.

"Why can't I meet a wizard who throws fireballs?" I said. "Why even *have* magic if you aren't able to throw fireballs?"

He looked up from his work, amused. "Didn't Leo's friend, George, do that?"

"Oh. Right." I revised my previous question. "Why can't I meet a wizard who throws fireballs and *isn't* trying to roast me with them?"

The fire smoked and then crackled to life. Ben joined me at the picnic table, putting one long leg over the bench and sliding close to face me. He picked something out of my hair and tossed it aside. "It might take a while to find all the feathers."

I shrugged and handed Ben his donut and coffee. "What did you find out about the area while I was getting gas?"

"Nothing in the local news feeds about mysterious livestock killings. A few ads here and there for farm supplies, but it looks like it's more of a lumbering community."

"The article in Grandpa's box was about a strange creature seen in the woods. It was reported in the sixties by a driver for a lumber company. The article said the creature was more than likely a bear."

"You think it was our Dogman?" Ben asked.

It could've been a bear, but Grandpa saved the article. He thought there was more to the story, so I was going to assume the same. "The description matches our library research."

"If the Dogman is a local legend, you'd think the article would have mentioned him," Ben mused aloud.

I sipped my coffee. It was already getting cold. "Maybe the local reporter didn't feel mentioning a cryptid would help her career."

"And you believe there's still a link between this career-sinking folk monster and your grandfather?" Ben finished his donut in several bites.

"I don't know what to think. If he was behind the livestock killings, sneaking away from Grandma to let his wolf run, why did he collect and keep the news articles? It's not too different from the Hunter keeping teeth from his victims as trophies." I gave up on the coffee and set it aside. "If it wasn't my grandfather, why did he care enough to draw the local police's attention to himself?"

"Why does anyone take risks like that?" Ben's hold tightened on his to-go cup. "Why would you?"

The answer was obvious. "To protect someone I love. I'd do it to protect you."

He leaned forward to place a soft kiss on my cheek, then on my jawline and my neck. His breath was a welcome warmth against my skin. I wanted to mentally check out and linger in the tender exchange with Ben.

But I couldn't.

I thought of my grandfather, wondering who he would care for enough to leave my grandmother and dad in New York and risk being discovered as a werewolf. I remembered the woman in the photograph. He'd had his arm around her waist. It gave me a sick feeling in my stomach and a resurgence of anger. Was any memory I had of him true? The way he pined over my grandmother, and the way he watched her like she was the only person in the room.

Footsteps drew my attention to the paved path running past our campsite. A park ranger raised her hand in greeting. "Good morning! I'm here to check you in since we missed each other last night."

She wrote down our license plate number and gave me a small slip of paper. "Tuck that in your windshield. It's your parking pass. Please be sure to review the campsite rules on the back."

I winced. "Did someone report us because of this morning?"

She snorted a type of half-laugh. It was goofy and friendly and immediately made me like her. "It's not crowded this time of year, but some people like to complain. Your neighbors down the way didn't appreciate the car alarm."

"It won't happen again," Ben said.

The park ranger hesitated before asking, "Are you Ben Sharpe?"

His eyes widened slightly, and he fumbled his words. "Uh, I . . . Yes. I am. Why?"

She beamed with excitement. "I thought so! I saw you perform this past spring with Derezzed."

"Oh, okay. Yeah." He rubbed at the back of his neck, his smile shy. "That was a great tour." Ben went through multiple hoops with the Committee before being granted permission to leave Hopewell. Even then, it was for a limited time, not outside the Midwest, and only because he'd served over ten years of his tethering sentence without causing problems.

People would chat with Ben after shows, but neither of us had experienced someone recognizing him outside a concert venue. I wasn't sure I cared for it.

"I read on your website about your voice being restored," she continued. "That's amazing. When I saw you on that tour I thought not speaking was part of your stage persona."

"Well, I could speak," Ben said. "But the general public doesn't understand ASL."

I stared at my clasped hands, feeling awkward as the two talked past me.

"Of course. Sorry. I'm Clare, by the way." She gave her forehead a tap. "I should have led with that. Anyway, every summer I help organize a weekend-long electronic music festival in the forest that—"

"Wait, you help organize the Electric Trees Festival?" The excitement in Ben's voice was palpable.

"Hell, yeah!" Clare beamed.

I felt stupid for not having heard of this event Ben was so thrilled about. "What is—"

He immediately launched into a rushed explanation. "It's a four-day festival packed full of musicians and artists in the middle of the woods. I was never able . . . The timing never worked out."

"Best EDM fest in Michigan," Clare said. "You should play it next year, Ben."

"Really? That would be amazing." He couldn't seem to stop grinning. "Who do I need to talk to?"

"My mom," she said. "If you two don't have plans tonight, you're welcome to stop by our cabin. It's right down the road from the park entrance. She can tell you more about the festival."

Ben looked at me, his eyes bright. "What do you think?"

I didn't like making split-second decisions in front of people. Irritation soured my stomach, but he was so excited I didn't want to ruin it. "Yeah, we can do that."

Clare gave Ben an address he noted in his phone.

"See you then!" She gave us a parting wave and continued on her rounds.

Since it was daylight and Leo had come after us in the evenings, Ben and I took turns napping for the remainder of the morning. Ben sacked out in his hammock, while I stretched out in the back seat of the car. There was no way I was getting in a hammock again.

In the early afternoon, we hiked along one of the many trails through the woods and found a picnic table to eat our sandwiches. The scent of damp soil was present, but overpowered by the sharp aroma of pine. The air had a chill that hadn't burned off with the sunshine. I lifted my chin to breathe a good lungful into my body.

"It must smell amazing to you." Ben unwrapped his sandwich.

"It does. I noticed it last night once I cleared the pit toilet. It's so clean. Even the parks in Hopewell have exhaust, chimney smoke, or other odors from people living nearby."

Because it was late in the camping season, we had the trail and picnic area to ourselves. The wolf in me drew forward. I allowed my hands to shift, followed by my teeth and ears. The change felt like I could exhale the past days' stress. My vision, hearing, and sense of smell heightened further. The birds and other small mammals moving among the trees competed for my attention. My muscles twitched, and something inside wanted my body to be in motion.

I looked at Ben. "Would you mind if I went for a quick run?"

His only reply was a goofy smile, which made me self-conscious. "What? Is there something in my teeth?"

"You're beautiful."

Heat rushed from my neckline up through my face. "You're ridiculous." I looked away but couldn't help but smile. "Thank you."

"You're welcome. And of course I don't mind if you go for a run, just be sure to—"

"Be careful." I shrugged out of my jacket, folded it over, and set it on the table. "Can I leave this here? You'll wait with it?"

Ben placed a hand lightly on the fabric. "It's safe with me. Have fun."

Warmth spread from my chest through my body.

He's safe.

I started down the path at a steady jog. I used to run all the time in the parks and woods when I lived in New York with my parents before I was a werewolf. Even then my body responded to the natural environment, the sounds and smells soothing any anxious thoughts trapped in my head. But ever since the day my werewolf gene was triggered, runs outside hadn't been the same. I often relied on the noisy, exhaust-filled streets of Hopewell to repel the dark memories from that awful day.

The wolf in me was on high alert. My nostrils continued to twitch, and I constantly scanned the area for threats. But something was different among these trees. I lengthened my stride, stretching my muscles to their full potential. The burn in my legs made me smile. My shoes pounded the packed dirt as I dashed along the trail.

The woods opened up and the pines formed tidy rows with sparse undergrowth, allowing me to look through them into the distance. I smelled something small and warm. A cottontail rabbit was flushed from the trailside by my movement. It darted off along the row of pines. The wolf in me noticed. Without blinking an eye, I gave chase.

The sharp scent of the animal's fear struck me. My mind swirled with wild excitement. I dashed between the trees after the rabbit. The space between me and my prey continued to shrink. Before thinking of the consequences, I dove at the rabbit, claws outstretched. It disappeared into a burrow. I crashed to the ground and slid along my front. As I lay panting in the cold and damp, the reality of the situation slammed back into focus.

What was I doing?

Trembling, I pushed myself up onto my hands and knees. I sat back on my heels. My shoes were tight. The front of my shirt and pants were smeared with dirt and covered in pine needles. My palms were scratched from fallen twigs. I raised a shaking hand. A fine layer of gray fur had begun to sprout from the back of my hand and my arm. I hadn't intended to shift form that far.

I stood and brushed off what I could from my shirt and pants. Turning, I realized I didn't know where the hell I was. Did I run in a straight line from the path? Zigged and zagged in pursuit?

I patted down my pockets. I'd left my phone in my jacket. "Shit." I tried to follow the scent of the rabbit back to the trail but was soon turned around, confused by the crisscrossing scents of multiple rabbits. If I hadn't worn my shoes, I could've traced my scent back. I walked the treeline for several minutes but still didn't find the hiking trail. Lifting my nose into the air, I tried to find Ben's scent. No luck.

"Shit!"

I sat at the base of a pine tree to wait. My conversation with Ben already played in my head. "You left the path to do what?" he'd ask. I covered my face and groaned. How embarrassing.

I dropped my hands to my side. My fingers brushed one of the many pine cones littering the forest floor. I picked it up, the end sticky with sap. It was curved and looked similar to the pine cone in my grandfather's box. I leaned back against the shaggy bark to look up the height of the pine tree. During our visit to the Shelby library, Ben and I read about pine trees growing everywhere in the northern part of the state. Finding a similar pine cone didn't mean we were retracing the exact steps of my grandfather.

It seemed like forever before the crunching of pine needles underfoot caused me to look down the line of trees. The park ranger, Clare, was walking toward me. I stood, already feeling foolish for getting myself lost.

"There you are." She gave a friendly wave. "Ben is worried about you. Did you get turned around?"

"It's really beautiful out here, and I didn't keep track of where I was running."

"That's why we suggest inexperienced hikers stay on the trails."

"Noted," I said. "You probably never get lost out here, do you?"

"Nope. I know these woods inside and out. I grew up here." She patted a compact radio at her hip. "Plus, I have this guy."

"How far off am I?" I asked.

"About a half-hour." Clare waved me toward her. "Follow me."

Now that we were closer, I got a better sampling of the woman's scent. Most people had a natural and unique scent. Layered on top of that were additional odors hinting at their homes, foods they liked, or perfumes or colognes.

Clare had none of those multiple layers, which was odd. The scent of her bronze skin and spiky hair was almost a duplicate of the sandy soil and sharp pine sap surrounding us.

We walked several minutes in silence before she glanced at my hand. "What do you have there?"

I still carried the pine cone. "Oh, I was looking at this while I was waiting." I used it to motion to the trees. "What type of pine trees are these?"

Clare's smile was warm with affection. "White pine. They're harvested for lumber and pulp to make paper." Her fingers brushed over one's rough bark as we passed. The bark briefly shimmered. Or maybe it was the way the afternoon light filtered into the area.

"Even in the parks?" For some reason, I'd thought the trees in parks were protected.

She nodded. "There are only a few remaining areas in the state protected from lumber companies. Among those, there's a single stand of old-growth forest left. Doesn't stop the lumber companies from trying, though. They've been pining for the old growth for decades."

I winced at the pun, chuckling. "Ouch."

Clare gave the snort laugh from before. "Conservation is hard. Without humor, I'd be in trouble." She stepped onto the wide trail I'd veered from. "I'll walk you back to your site. Ben is waiting there for you."

If Clare grew up around the forest... I hesitated before asking, "This might sound odd, but have you heard of the Dogman?"

She tucked her hands in her pocket as if discussing cryptids was everyday conversation. "Of course. Why do you ask? Are you one of those paranormal hunters who tries to capture proof of the supernatural on film?"

"No. Not at all. I think my grandfather passed through this area investigating the Dogman."

"That's kind of fun. What's his name?"

"Alexander Steward."

Clare stopped. Her eyes flashed a brilliant green before turning back to dark brown. That definitely wasn't a trick of lighting.

"You've met him?" Excitement overtook any curiosity I had about Clare.

"Yeah!" Her gaze darted over my body and ended at my eyes. "Alexander used to travel through this forest often."

"Do you know why?" She must have been a teen when my grandfather traveled here.

Clare started walking again. Instead of answering, she asked, "He won't tell you?"

"He's passed." A sharp ache pinged in my chest. Every day since I'd left my parents' house with the box, I'd been reminded of his loss.

"Oh, I'm so sorry to hear that. We wondered when suddenly he stopped visiting," she said. "And now your question about the Dogman seems less random."

My heart stuttered. "So, Grandpa was trying to track him?"

"He was trying to understand the legend."

"Alex!" The trail opened into a path wide enough for a car. Ben jogged toward us, his forehead creased. He seized me into a tight hug. "Are you okay? Where've you been?"

"Sorry." I inhaled his scent, and my tightened muscles relaxed. "I wandered off the trail and got turned around. I didn't mean to make you worry."

Ben parted from me. "Thank you, Clare."

"You're welcome! See you two this evening."

Ben frowned as he looked back at me. "I thought Leo got you. What really happened?"

My face heated. "No, seriously. I got lost."

"What? How didn't you notice you were leaving the trail?"

I hesitated before admitting. "There was a rabbit."

Ben's eyes widened slightly. His head tilted. He took in the dirty state of my clothing. One corner of his mouth began to curve. "I'm sorry, a rabb—"

"Yes!" I growled and wiggled out of his hold. "I was running . . . and it felt so good . . . and everything smelled wonderful . . . and then there was this rabbit." I motioned at the ground as if the creature were there. "Everything inside of me wanted to go after it. So I did. And when I realized what was happening, I was too far off the trail and couldn't find my way back."

"I'm glad you're okay," he said, which was nice, but he was full-on grinning.

"I knew you would do this." I turned to walk back to our campsite. "Thanks for making me feel stupid."

"Wait." He chuckled and followed me. "I'm sorry. I didn't mean to make you feel stupid." I allowed him to slip his hand into mine. We walked a few steps in silence before he asked, "So, you'll be handling dinner from now on?"

"You ass." Smiling, I yanked my hand from his and gave him a hefty shove. It was enough to knock him off his feet. He lay on the ground laughing.

15

SINCE LEARNING THAT Clare had met my grandfather, I looked forward to our evening visit. Hopefully, I could ask more questions about what Grandpa was doing and why he was interested in learning about the Dogman.

"You're surprisingly okay with this," Ben said while we waited outside the cabin door. "You're usually anxious about spending time with new people."

"We chatted on our walk back to the campground. She's met my grandfather."

Ben's eyebrows rose. "Really?"

"Oh," I remembered. "And I think she might be gifted like us."

His eyes widened. "Wait, what? Why didn't you say some—"

The door opened and Clare greeted us. "Hello! Welcome." The aromas of a log fire and cooking spices rolled out on waves of warm air. She seemed less rigid without the uniform. Her hair lay smoothly over her skull but still had the spiked ends, reminding me of the porcupine. She wore a chunky knit sweater in different hues of green, a pair of jeans, and thick wool socks.

We were immediately enveloped by the warmth of their home. Across the cozy cabin was a small kitchen where an older woman about my mother's age stood tending to pots on the stove. The woman's silver-streaked dark hair fell to her waist and swayed like a curtain as she moved around the kitchen.

Clare offered, "Hot tea? It's our homemade herbal mix."

I answered, "Sure. Thank you."

The petite woman at the stove, dressed in draping layers of fabric, approached. I tried to catch her scent, curious if it was similar to Clare's, but all the pleasant aromas in the cabin muddied the air. Clare introduced us. "This is my mom, Betty."

Betty extended her hand to each of us. Her firm grip was strong despite her delicate build. Her eyes were the same brown as Clare's, but her greeting was more reserved than her daughter's. "Nice to meet you."

Clare returned with two steaming cups of tea. "Have a seat by the fire."

Ben and I claimed a love seat among the furniture gathered near the fireplace. The cabin looked old, with plenty of love evident in the scuffed floors, resident spiderwebs, and worn furniture. "How long have you lived here?" I asked.

Clare chuckled and handed us the tea. "I've lived here my whole life. This was Mom's childhood home, too."

"So many years." Betty sat next to Clare and passed her daughter one of the two steaming tea cups she held. She looked at Ben. "Clare says she saw you perform this past spring, and you're interested in the Electric Trees festival."

He sat at the front edge of his chair. I wasn't sure if it was his excitement about the festival or his puzzling out what kind of supernatural being Clare was. "I'm trying to book as many gigs as possible, and a festival is a great place to meet other artists."

"This is an EDM festival like no other. We started it in 2011 and it's been happening every June since," Betty said. "The forest is a natural place to gather and connect."

Ben grinned, his eyes bright. "Where do I sign up?" It was the festival on his mind.

I sipped at my tea, struggling with letting Ben have this moment. The fact Clare could have answers about my grandfather made me impatient. I focused on the tea. It was slightly spicy on my tongue before creating a comforting warmth in my chest and stomach.

Betty leaned forward and handed Ben a business card. "We'll need to hear a sample of your work. Our contact info and where to send the demo is on the card."

"Thank you." Ben scanned over the card before he pocketed it.

"You're welcome." Betty settled back in her chair. "This festival is a safe space we provide, so if you want to participate, we'd like your guarantee that no trouble will be finding you there."

"Mom!" Clare chided. "Don't be rude."

"I'm not being rude," Betty said. "I'm being prudent."

Ben's brows drew together. He looked between the women. "I don't understand."

I set aside my tea, muscles tensing.

"I saw your tether this past spring," Clare explained. "Then I noticed it was gone when I met you two at the campground. And then there was the whole thing with your voice returning."

The color left Ben's face.

"Wizard?" Betty asked.

Ben swallowed and nodded. He gave me a sideward glance.

Clare noticed. "We know about Alex, too. The trees said she's the same as Alexander. Lupine."

My heart skipped. "I'm sorry? The trees—"

"The trees saw you on your run." Ben puzzled thru the words.

"What." Great. Hopefully, the trees didn't mention the rabbit.

Ben studied the women. "You're dryads."

"Hamadryads," Betty said.

Yet more supernatural beings I knew nothing about. I kept my mouth shut, saving any questions to ask Ben later. It was too embarrassing to let these strangers know how far behind I was in *Supernatural 101*.

"This forest is our life. Its safety is our safety." Betty's fingertip tapped the arm of her chair for emphasis. "If we invite you to perform at the festival, you can't bring trouble along with you."

"We've had problems with wizards before," Clare explained. The pair reminded me of a good cop, bad cop duo.

"And you've been tethered." Betty's statement sounded too similar to an accusation for my liking.

Spots of color appeared high in Ben's cheeks. I set my hand on his knee, hoping to offer some comfort. He lowered his gaze to the teacup in his hands. "Okay. I understand."

The room fell silent except for the crackling fire and soft ticking of a wall clock.

Clare pushed past the tense exchange, declaring brightly, "Alex is on a quest to find the Dogman, just like Alexander!"

Ben choked on his tea. I rushed to explain. "I know it sounds silly, but the Dogman description is very lupine-like. My grandfather saved newspaper articles about strange attacks on livestock around the state. Now I'm trying to puzzle out what he was doing and why. I wondered if there was a connection to the Dogman."

"Why do you need to know?" Betty asked.

Because I needed to know if my grandfather was the man I grew up believing he was. But I didn't want to voice my doubt of Grandpa's character in front of strangers, supernatural or not. "It was something I was curious about."

Betty took a sip of tea before starting, "He often passed through this forest—"

I interrupted, "Yes, trying to understand the Dogman legend ... But why?"

"Alexander said he arrived home from the war as a different man than when he left. Part of him had turned dark. He feared he'd harm his wife and child. Since he was raised on a farm in this state, he returned to travel the woods, lakes, and dunes of his childhood. He fell in love with them. The trip kept his family safe and provided him a reprieve."

"But the Dogman, all those articles—"

"It was a simple curiosity at first. Not long after he started making his trips, he learned of the sightings and the attacks. He suspected the Dogman was someone like himself." Betty paused, watching me.

"Another lupine," I said, my voice quiet. "But why would he endanger himself to help a stranger?" And abandon his wife and child to do so.

Clare chimed in. "Not only lupine, but someone who'd lost too much of themselves to their wolf. Alexander wanted to find the person and guide them like someone did for him."

I sat back on the love seat, the new information percolating in my mind. Grandfather saw himself and his sickness in someone else and wanted to help. Shared struggles can bind us to people we wouldn't otherwise spend time with.

There was a knock on the cabin door.

"Excuse me." Clare stood to answer it. Betty sipped her tea.

I looked at Ben. His gaze was unfocused as he stared into the fire. I nudged him. "You feeling okay?"

His consciousness swam sluggishly to the surface. He blinked slowly at me and gave a single nod. His tea cup slipped from his hand. I caught it before it could tumble off his lap onto the floor.

My pulse leaped. I seized his arm. "Ben?"

His eyes rolled upward and his eyelids closed. His chin fell forward to rest on his chest.

"Ben!" I looked at Betty in a panic. "Help! There's something—"

"He'll be okay." Betty remained calm as if people passing out in her living room was common.

I looked from Ben to his near-empty tea cup. As a werewolf, my body fought off the side effects of almost everything I ingested. Ben's would react like any other Commoner's. A growl sprang into my throat. I glared at Betty. "What did you do to him?"

Clare returned with a bearded man, at least ten years my senior, in tow. He looked vaguely familiar. The strong musky scent of a fellow werewolf crept up my nose. The man was dressed in jeans and a flannel shirt with a camo vest and hat. Clare hadn't mentioned expecting additional guests.

I pressed my side against Ben, my attention switching between the three strangers. "What's happening?"

"I'm Steven Hall," the man said. "And we need your help."

"My help?" The wolf in me strained to take the lead. To wield my anxiety and concern for Ben in the form of fangs and claws. "You're not getting anything from me until you tell me what you did to Ben."

"It's okay, Alex. I slipped a sedative into his tea. He's only sleeping." Clare reached for my shoulder, but I leaned into Ben and snarled at her. She jerked her hand back. "Mom was afraid he'd complicate things for us."

"Wizards usually do," Betty added.

Who the *hell* were these people? Steven stepped forward and extended a hand. A warning growl rumbled in my chest. His hand dropped back to his side. "We won't hurt you."

I narrowed my eyes. "Start explaining or we're leaving."

"There's someone following you who's a risk to us," he said. "Cathy said you brought him from Detroit to her area. Mark told us you led this person to the dunes where he severely injured a Commoner. Since this person is following you, we need your help learning about him so we know how to best deal with him."

He was talking about Leo. "How do you know Cathy and Mark? Are you all part of some lupine spy network?"

"Cathy is my niece. Mark is my son. I count on them to be my eyes and ears." Steven crossed his arms over his chest, his stance wide. "They're the reason I could travel down here and intercept you before the guy you brought with you did any more damage."

I scowled, his comment inflaming the guilt I already felt about Leo. "We didn't purposely bring him with us. I didn't expect him to—"

"That doesn't matter right now," Steven snarled, impatient. "If we don't take care of him, he'll draw unwanted attention or, even worse, kill a Commoner. Then every Hunter in the Midwest will be tracking us down."

"I asked Mark about Hunters!" My chest tightened. "He said there was an understanding—"

Steven's laugh was short and sharp. "He's young, selfish, and doesn't know half the shit he should know by now to survive as lupine. He shouldn't have contacted you."

Clare frowned at Steven but didn't speak. I wondered if there was a difference of opinion between the generations.

"Mark told us you don't have a Committee. Is that not true?" I asked.

"He's correct," Betty explained. "We don't have an established governing body in this area of the state. The services you have access to in larger cities aren't available here. There are fewer of us spread over a larger area, so we're not considered worth the effort."

"Not having that in place is dangerous," Steven added. "Unfortunately, my son believes the truce with the Hunters means something. The reality is, if Hunters decided the terms were violated, whether they were or not, they'd do whatever they wanted to us. Committees may skew in the Commoners' favor, but at least most don't allow hunting."

I thought of Hopewell, the fall of our Committee, and the work ahead for us. From my calls with Trish, I sensed uncertainty. It made me all the more anxious to get back to my friends.

Betty interrupted my thoughts. "Tell us about this dangerous man following you."

"Leo is a tethered lupine from Chicago." I felt defensive. It's not like I wanted to put anyone in danger. "I don't even know what he wants from me. I've tried talking to him, but he either doesn't want to listen or isn't understanding me."

Steven shook his head, clearly skeptical. "He's not tethered if he can shift."

"He took a job in Hopewell, and his tether was altered to temporarily restore his lupine abilities," I explained. "When the job went south, his partner-in-crime was arrested and shipped back to Chicago, but Leo disappeared."

"And now you've brought him to our home," Betty said, her tone heavy with judgment.

I threw up my hands, growing increasingly frustrated. "I told you, we didn't purposely lead him here! We've tried to lose him a few times, but Leo somehow follows us." Why couldn't these people understand I was on their side?

Steven began to pace. "What else do you know? There's something strange about him that threw off my nose."

"Yes! I noticed that, too." The fact that two other werewolves confirmed I wasn't imagining the odd scent provided some relief. "I don't know why his scent is so strange, but Leo is extremely strong and really angry."

Clare waited for Steven to respond. When he didn't, she spoke up. "Alex, if you returned to Hopewell, would Leo leave this area to follow you?"

My hand found Ben's. "Right now Hopewell isn't safe for Ben and me, but we're leaving tomorrow to travel farther north. You guys won't have to worry about Leo anymore."

"Not an option," Steven growled. "My family protects the entire northern part of the lower peninsula and the entirety of the upper peninsula. If you're going north, he's still a problem for us. We'll stick to the original plan."

Betty nodded and stood.

"What original plan?" The whole situation, the confusion, guilt, and anger, didn't help to keep the wolf in me in check.

"The three of us are going to put Leo down and be done with it." Steven stopped his pacing. His eyes were the same intense blue as Mark's. It must've been a family trait. "Since he's been tethered, he's fair game."

Steven seemed to loom over me. I stood and growled a warning. *Back off.*

He retreated a step out of my space but bared his teeth.

"I don't want to cause more trouble for all of you, so tell me how Ben and I fit into this plan," I said. "Should we wait here while you go after Leo? Or should we leave?"

"I'm staying here with Ben," Clare said.

I blinked. "I'm sorry, what?" I looked from her to Steven, realizing I had a larger part to play. "You're counting *me* as one of the three to grab Leo."

Steven gave a derisive laugh. "You're the reason he's here. You should help get rid of him."

"When do we go?" I preferred to take Trish's advice, carry Ben to the car, and run. But that wasn't going to happen.

"Now," Steven started toward the door. "I caught traces of him around the campground."

16

MY GUILTY CONSCIENCE agreed with Steven. Leo was here because of me. The mess he was making was my fault. And finally, the three refused to let me leave with Ben until I helped. I knew nothing about hamadryads' abilities, so I wasn't sure I could fight my way out of the cabin and to the car.

I folded my jacket and tucked it into the crook of Ben's arm as if it could protect him like he'd watched over it during my run. I admired his features, feeling that familiar flutter in my stomach. Leaning down, I kissed him lightly on the cheek. He'd be pissed when he woke up and found me gone. Ben wasn't a guy who rushed into a fight. It's one of the things that attracted me to him. But he struggled to let me take on anything dangerous without offering his help.

Clare spoke from behind me. "He'll be safer here."

I narrowed my eyes. It wasn't comforting coming from the person who slipped him a knockout tea. "He better be okay when we get back."

Steven, Betty, and I stepped out of the cabin into the brisk night. The scent of winter laced the air. Our breath lingered in clouds of steam. Hamadryads must not need a lot of light to see because Betty, like Steven and me, wasn't hindered by the dark.

I rubbed my hands briskly along my upper arms, even though I wore a sweater. "What do you plan to do with Leo once we subdue him? Send him back to Chicago?"

"We put an end to the threat." Steven clapped his hands together like a gunshot.

"I'm not doing that," I growled. "I've never taken someone's life, and I don't plan to start now."

He dismissed my objection with a wave. "Don't worry, you won't have to. I'll do it."

Agreeing with him and forfeiting Leo's life would be the quick solution. It'd be the most simple. The easiest. Leo was a convict. I swallowed. "Give him a chance to leave."

"He's attacking Commoners," Betty said. "He's not going to leave because we ask."

"Let me try to convince him." I'd failed twice already, but if Steven planned to kill Leo, I had to try one last time.

Steven blew a burst of steam from his nose, compromising. "You get one try."

Betty muttered beneath her breath and turned to face a pine tree. She settled her fingertips on the bark and closed her eyes. The bark shimmered. Her hand changed form. Betty's fingers elongated, branched, and fused with the bark. Her eyes twitched beneath her eyelids. "He's left the campground and is moving toward us."

"Perfect," Steven said. "Come with me, Alex."

"I thought—" I looked back at Betty and stifled a gasp. Her entire body, clothing and all, sunk into the tree's trunk with the noise of creaking wood and cracking branches. Then she was gone. When I turned to ask Steven what the hell just happened, he was already on the move. There was no time for a lesson in *Alex-learns-about-the-supernatural*.

Steven broke into a loping run. I pulled up to keep pace with him, my nose filling with his scent and the crisp aromas of the night. My senses hummed with information as we ran along the road to intercept Leo. Steven glanced at me, grinned, and lengthened his stride. I couldn't help mirroring his grin, my body firing with more heat as the wolf in me delighted in the lupine companionship and the chase.

Up the road, Betty's slim figure stepped from the woodline. She pointed back into the trees. Without breaking his stride, Steven curved toward the woodline and leaped over a fallen tree into the woods. I pulled up short of the log, my chest rising and falling rapidly. Steven continued, unhindered by the undergrowth.

I paced once in front of the log, growling, before awkwardly hopping over it and impatiently wading into the woods. Branches reached for my hair and clothing. I cringed at the amount of noise I was creating. A charging elephant would have made less.

Light laughter surrounded me. Betty's voice sounded from the air. "I suppose the city lupine don't let their wolves run, do they?"

A sapling swatted me in the head. I cursed under my breath. "It's not encouraged, no."

"Do you believe you're too refined for that?" she asked. "That's unfortunate. What a stifled life you must live there."

"You're not making me want to help you right now," I growled. Another branch clawed at my face. "I could be warm and curled up next to Ben instead of tromping around the woods in the cold night, with people I barely know, looking for a raging werewolf."

"You're not in the city here," Betty said. "Be your wolf."

My stomach immediately twisted at the thought. The last time I fully shifted, I managed to remain coherent. But it wasn't an obstacle to overcome once and suddenly I was the master of my abilities. It would take practice, and it might backfire on me if I tried again. Would now be a time to take that chance?

A howl that wrapped around my core and squeezed echoed through the woods. My first thought was to respond, and my body began to shift form, unbidden. I clenched my sharpening teeth together and focused. The transformation of my body slowed to a stop. My hands were clawed with a light covering of gray fur. Having learned a lesson from my earlier run, I'd left my shoes at the cabin so my feet could change freely if needed. The partial shift left me with tougher soles, protecting my feet as I moved more deftly through the woods.

I came upon a hiking path, free of underbrush. It led to and passed through a small clearing. Steven's scent filled my nose but was quickly overtaken by a waft of the strange odor Leo carried. I crouched where the path met the clearing's edge, scanning the dark woods to detect any movement. A bulky shadow, facing away from me, waited off the path at the base of a large tree.

My body shaking, I swallowed and crept forward. The wind blew past me and carried my scent toward the shadow. Steven turned blue glowing eyes in my direction. His werewolf form, with brown fur so dark it looked black, was nearly as large as Leo's.

Roaring sounded from ahead. Leo had caught a whiff of me as well. He charged across the clearing in my direction, his eyes glowing red. Leo leaped and was met mid-air by Steven. The werewolves rolled onto the forest floor, a snarling mess of flashing teeth and swiping claws.

Like on the beach, Leo was fully shifted into his werewolf form. He jumped atop Steven. His jaws clamped onto the other werewolf's hide. With a jerk of his head, Leo pulled fur, skin, and muscle loose with a rough tearing noise.

Steven yelped and threw his body into a roll. The motion separated him from Leo.

My mind spun. How could I help without being in the way? Leo was so much stronger than me in his current form. My body, however, longed to shift further and allow the part of me that was wolf to leap into the fray. Constant snarling pushed its way past my lips. I dashed forward and landed a brutal swipe of my claws into Leo's flank, sending fur flying.

That did the trick of getting his attention.

Leo turned a foam-filled maw on me. The pungent odor clinging to him made me sick to my stomach. His attack, a lunge and snapping of his jaws, was clumsy. I dodged easily to the side and slashed him across the side of his muzzle. Leo shook his head and wiped at his face. Steven's claws opened up a wound across Leo's shoulder blades. Leo stumbled forward.

With a tremendous chorus of snapping and creaking wood, the roots of the large pines around us broke the surface. The rich odor of damp earth filled the air. The roots curled around Leo's ankles and wrist to restrain him. He severed the one at his wrist with his massive jaws and tried to pull loose from the others. The roots at his ankles retracted into the ground. Leo fell with a crash. More roots swiftly looped over him and buried themselves back into the soil.

Steven waited, ears forward and nostrils flaring. He watched the raging Leo struggle, then turned his blue eyes on me. I stepped closer to the bound werewolf's back and raised my voice. "Leo, it's time to stop. You're disturbing the locals."

At the sound of my voice, Leo fell still. His eyes widened and his pointed ears swiveled toward me.

"They're willing to let you go with a warning, but you have to leave the area," I said. "Go back down state. Stop making trouble for everyone here."

Leo's ears flattened to his skull, and his lips pulled back from his teeth. The broken canine I'd seen at the beach was still there. Leo snarled, and Steven responded with a rumbling growl.

"If you don't, they're going to kill you." My gut twisted. "Tell me how we can settle this so no one else gets hurt." I was close enough to see the whites of Leo's bloodshot eyes. At his throat where the tether would be branded, patches of thick fur were missing as if scratched bare. The skin was raw and covered in boils or blisters.

"What happened? Who did this to you?" I inched closer to get a better look at the broken skin. "Please, shift so we can talk."

His bloodshot eyes rolled back. Body shuddering, he whined.

The sound pulled at something inside of me. My need to protect. I entered his field of vision. "Are you not able to shift?"

Leo saw me and immediately doubled down on efforts to free himself. His snarling and thrashing verged on incoherent. I sprung back, barely avoiding his snapping jaws.

Steven lifted his shaggy head to look at me.

"No. I can't." I shook my head. "I'm not making the decision." I didn't want the weight of someone else's death on my shoulders. I'd seen what it'd done to Ben.

Steven suddenly sat upright, ears pointed forward and nose working. I'd heard it, too. Conversation and occasional laughter came from back along the hiking trail.

Betty's voice sounded near us. "Hikers."

"Shit! We have to let him go, Steven," I said. "He's making too much noise, and we can't have Commoners stumbling in on us."

Steven's eyes narrowed and he growled.

The cracking and snapping of tree limbs led my gaze to a stand of pines. A woman's form emerged from the trunk as if a sculpture in relief. Bark slid over her skin, bunching and stretching into forms that became Betty's features, limbs, and clothing.

"We can't let them see us, Steven. Are you ready for me to release him?" she asked.

He growled again but didn't make any aggressive move toward me. Nodding, I said, "We're ready."

Betty's eyes flashed the brilliant green I'd noticed in Clare's. The roots binding Leo loosened and retracted into the ground. Steven and I crouched, ready to tackle Leo if he decided to attack us or the hikers. Leo rolled to his knees with a whine, his head lowered. He crawled a few feet away from us, stumbled to his feet, and fled.

Steven's massive hand clamped over his shoulder. His body sagged, and the odor of fresh blood hung around him. His head swung toward me.

I lowered my hand toward his other shoulder but paused and withdrew it. I despised people touching me without my permission. "I can help you to the road while Betty redirects the Commoners."

Betty nodded and started down the path to intercept the hikers. Steven held on to his werewolf form and slowly walked with me from the path and through the woods. When we reached the road, a rattling, rusted pickup was waiting. At the steering wheel was Clare.

Steven climbed into the bed of the truck. I joined Clare in the cab. "Your mom is down the trail with some over-adventurous hikers." I buckled my seat belt. "How did you know—"

"Mom called me. She'll meet us at home."

We drove to the cabin. Ben's silhouette stood in the doorway. Clare parked the rumbling truck and switched off the engine. "It took convincing to keep him here when he woke up."

Ben stepped outside as we walked to the door. He opened up his arms despite the fact he was frowning and my sweater and hands were dirty with blood and tufts of fur. I hugged him tight and inhaled deeply of his warm and spicy scent.

"I'd like to talk about this later," he said against my curls.

"I know," I said. "We will."

"Is this over with? Is Leo dead?"

I spoke my answer against his shirt. "No. We had to let him go."

Inside the cabin, the familiar sounds of grinding bone, shifting muscles, and contracting cartilage signaled Steven's change in shape. His transition from werewolf to man didn't appear painful. It reminded me of Mark's fairly smooth shift back to his human form at the lake.

I'd only shifted three times to my full lupine form, a hybrid of woman and wolf, in the eight years I'd been a werewolf. I couldn't remember the first transformation. The other two had been extremely painful and caused me to vomit. Was there something different about the lupine up here that young and old alike could smoothly transition from one form to the other? Even Trish and Nate, skilled at wielding their shifting and other werewolf abilities, didn't stray too close to a full shift.

Ben paled when he saw the extent of Steven's wound. He dropped his gaze, and his hold on my hand tightened.

Clare waited with clean bandaging and a compress of poultice she must have concocted in the kitchen while we were out. The aroma was sharply herbal. She patiently applied both to Steven's wrecked shoulder.

"Alex, what the hell were you doing out there?" Steven winced and cursed. "Why didn't you shift once we found him?"

"Stop wiggling," Clare muttered. She secured the bandage.

Ben's hand flexed in mine. I lifted my hand and rested it on Ben's arm, letting him know I could handle Steven. "I did what I could." I reminded myself that becoming a master of my shifting, without being scared of eating someone in the process, would take time.

"I sent the hikers home, telling them a bear was in the area." Betty nursed a steaming cup of tea. "They weren't happy, but packed their tent and left."

"I could've helped if you hadn't spiked my tea." Ben scowled, his cheeks flushed. He looked irritated and still a bit disoriented.

Steven ignored him and spoke to me. "What aren't you telling us about Leo?" His nose wrinkled. "His scent changed."

He was right. Leo had smelled even worse than at the lake. I turned to Ben. "Has a tethering spell ever had side effects on lupine? I didn't see a tether, but that area of Leo's throat was almost... infected."

"Not that I know of," Ben said. "But if the spell altering his tether had a time constraint, it could be expiring with bad consequences."

I drummed my fingers on my leg. "What about a spell that traps a lupine in their wolf form?"

The question drew a snarl from Steven. The control of our shifting was a deeply personal relationship between our mind, emotions, and body. Manipulation of that by a third party would set any werewolf's teeth on edge.

Ben grimaced. "It's an awful thing to do, but it's possible. Is that what happened tonight?"

"When we ran into Leo outside the restaurant, he could still shift between man and wolf." I recalled Leo's pained whimpers from tonight and shuddered. "I think he tried shifting back while we were out there but couldn't."

"And we're sure this wizard isn't in on it?" Steven growled, eyeing Ben.

Clare placed her hand lightly on Steven's arm.

I returned his growl. "Hey, Ben has nothing to do with Leo being here."

"You need to go back to where you came from." Steven pointed an accusing finger at me and then at the door. "Take your pet wizard and leave. You're endangering all of us with shit you brought up here from the city."

My anger burned hot in my cheeks. I looked at Betty and Clare. Both women remained silent.

Steven's eyes narrowed. "And if you don't leave, we'll be forced to remove the reason Leo is here."

Ben released my hand and strode outside. I gave Clare and Betty one more glance to see if they would come to my defense. When they didn't, I slunk from the cabin.

Ben waited, shivering either from the crisp air or anger. His eyebrows were drawn together, his eyes stormy. "Would that guy really try to take you out if we don't leave?"

"I've been tethered before, so I'm fair game. And as lupine, we're allowed to settle our differences amongst each other." I shook my head. "But I can't see him killing me to get rid of Leo. There'd be too many consequences for him with the Hopewell wolves."

The cabin door opened, and Clare walked outside. "I'm sorry for Steven's behavior. He's the elder of his family, so he's responsible for everyone's safety. Not only the lupine, but the hamadryads, too. He's scared."

"I understand." I did. It didn't make being kicked out by other werewolves any easier. "It's my mess and I should take care of it. We aren't sure how to do it with only the two of us, but we'll try."

"Alexander had a friend who lives in Manistee," Clare said. "It's a town north of here beside the lake."

Her words caused a sudden flurry of excitement inside my chest. "Do you know the person's name?"

She nodded. "Theodore Grenham. The two served in the Army together. When Alexander traveled through this way, he'd go there after visiting us. Maybe Theodore will have answers for you."

I gave her a pass on not standing up for me inside. Something had stopped her then, but she was helping now. "Thanks, Clare. I appreciate it."

"You're welcome. Good luck." She tightened her arms around herself and headed back into the cabin.

"Maybe your grandfather's friend was lupine, too," Ben said as we walked to the car. "We'd have the extra help we need to wrestle with Leo."

"Yeah. Let's hope." Even though we'd just been talking about Leo, when Clare mentioned Grandpa had a friend, I immediately forgot about stopping Leo. Selfishly, my priority was the box.

And that damn key.

17

IN THE PASSENGER seat, Ben's face was underlit by the glow of his phone screen. "We have to drive east a bit, then it'll be north again until Manistee. Are you sure you're not worried about Steven?"

"He'll have to deal with it." I wasn't going to let Steven's warning keep me from talking to my grandfather's friend. I watched the road's shoulders for reflective eyes. "Any news in the area about the Dogman or people losing livestock?"

"There's a town an hour east of here, Luther, where there was another Dogman encounter," Ben said. "Someone reported a break-in at their cabin. No slaughtered livestock, but scratches at the doors and windows from a large animal."

"An hour is too far out of the way. I want to track down Grandpa's friend first." I tried to soothe the bit of guilt I was feeling by reminding myself it might be a multipurpose visit. "We need help dealing with Leo."

We pulled into a rest area to use the restrooms and forage for vending machines. The lot was empty save a semi-truck and trailer. My nose revolted at the scent of the restrooms, a combination of waste and cleaning products.

When I returned to the car, Ben was crouched down beside one of the tires. My heart immediately sank. The last thing we needed was more car trouble. "What's going on?"

Ben shined the flashlight from his phone into the wheel well of the car. Stuck to the car's body was a fluorescent green dot sticker. A symbol, mathematical in appearance, was written in marker on the sticker.

My chest tightened. "I saw those at the antique store. They were used for pricing on the albums you wanted to buy. What is it?"

"It's a tracking spell. I recognize the symbol from my mom's book. This has been broadcasting our location."

"Why the hell would a dragon be tracking us?" Anxiety squeezed my chest even tighter. "Do you think she's pissed I didn't give her the jacket?"

"No. We're nothing to her." Ben's expression was grim. "I think this is how Leo is tracking us."

"That doesn't make any sense. Why would she help him and not us?"

"Maybe he agreed to trade something valuable to her." Ben gestured to the symbol. "What do you want to do about this?"

I chewed at my thumbnail, debating. "Leave it. If if enables him to follow the car, we know where he's going."

"But you chased him off at our last stop. He's the one running right now."

Ben was right. We were on the offense for the first time in the whole Leo fiasco. "Which means we finally have the chance to surprise Leo instead of waiting for him to find us. Can you replicate your mom's spell to track him?"

"Yeah, I can try," Ben stood. "I'll read up on it in the car."

We'd solve the puzzle of the box and figure out how to detain Leo. Hopefully, Grandpa's friend Theodore would be the key to both.

MANISTEE DEVELOPED AS a port town on Lake Michigan. After grabbing food and coffee at a gas station, we drove to the harbor to watch the large ships while having our makeshift breakfast. We sat bundled up, our sides pressed together for warmth.

"What if we contain Leo first and then call for help?" Ben suggested. "I have a spell I could alter for that."

It sounded straightforward enough, but doubt nagged me. "I hope whoever helps us will give Leo a chance to explain himself."

"Leo doesn't seem interested in doing that."

"I'd like to try again." To an outsider, I understood how it didn't make sense. Leo acted violently toward us, and I'd failed to reach him multiple times.

How could I help Ben understand why I wanted to try again? Betty and Clare told us how my grandfather lost pieces of himself to the darker part of his wolf. He'd shared the same in his letter.

I tried to be a good father and a good husband, but my spirit was sick from what I'd experienced during my tour. I no longer fit into civilian life. I'd given too much to the wolf and had lost pieces of the man I was.

Grandpa struggled, frightened and alone, until he found help. Then he helped others like him.

Should I tell Ben of my fear that the same would happen to me someday? Over time I'd give in to that fragment of rage lodged inside me, the parts of the wolf that made me dangerous.

I tried a different approach. "You and I know how it feels to be tethered. No one, no matter what they've done, should experience that. And then this messed up tether seems to be rotting away his ability to communicate, to hold a coherent thought, to shift, to—"

"Yes, but he's trying to *kill* you, Alex. I don't want to keep running from this guy, hoping to hell we stay ahead of him so you aren't hurt." Ben gave a short laugh. "It's not really how I imagined our road trip playing out, you know?"

My mouth went dry, and my pulse thudded in my ears. Did he find my mess *inconvenient* to his travel plans? My words came out in quick succession. "Would you rather I follow you around and stand quiet in the wings while you entertain your adoring fans?"

Ben flinched. "What?"

Shit.

"No, I didn't mean that." My mind hurried to fix my reckless reply. "I'm frustrated and scared. I don't know how to handle Leo, and I don't want you to be in danger, either."

"Do you really feel that way?" He studied my features, trying to catch my gaze. "That I'm only interested in playing shows during our time together? That I forget you're there?"

Sort of. I shrugged and looked down at my hands. "Let's forget I opened my mouth. I say stupid shit when I'm scared."

"But some part of you must be feeling that way," Ben insisted. "I'm confused. You'd said before you're happy for me to be booking these shows and growing a fan base."

"I am. I love seeing you on stage in your element." Watching how happy it made him gave me warm fuzzy feelings. But it brought along a host of other emotions, too. "It's also hard. You're making it work, and I'm still a screw-up. I have no idea what I'm supposed to be doing right now."

Ben was silent a moment before he offered in a more gentle voice, "Alex, it's *your* life. You're not *supposed* to be doing anything. What do you *want* to do?"

To be home in Hopewell helping my community rebuild. But that wasn't an option at the moment.

I reached for his hand, and because he's a bigger person than me, he didn't pull away. I gave his hand a gentle squeeze. "I know what I don't want to do. I don't want to run anymore. I've spent too many years doing that. I want to help Leo so you and I can be safe, but I don't know how to make that happen."

Ben put his arm around me, reassuring me I wasn't alone in figuring it out, whether it be the Leo situation or anything else. "Let's think this through. What's standing in our way?"

He was so patient with me.

He's safe.

It made me want to try harder to be a better partner for him.

"Leo doesn't seem to understand us," I said. "If his altered tether is causing weird side effects that are scrambling his brains, we get rid of the tether. It isn't blocking him from using his abilities anyway. With the tether gone, the side effects are gone, and he can communicate with us."

"So he can more clearly state why he wants you dead?"

I found myself already practicing that "being better" bit. I paused, tamped down the irritation his comment triggered, and explained, "It gives me a chance to reason with him, wolf to wolf. But I obviously can't be the one to remove the tether. I can't wield magic."

"I'd be willing to do it, but I haven't successfully puzzled out the spellwork for removing a tether. My attempts only managed to weaken them," Ben objected.

Another possibility was Sebastian, Ben's ex, but the two would still be stuck puzzling out the spell. We didn't have the time to spare. There was only one person I was positive knew the spell, and Ben wasn't going to like it. "Reginald removed our tethers. He was your teacher, right? Could you ask him how to cast the spell?"

Ben's expression darkened. His fingers tightened on mine. "There's no way he'd tell me."

"Because of Committee rules?" I asked. "The Committee doesn't exist anymore."

The struggle inside Ben played out across his features. He stared down at our entwined fingers, the gathering of his eyebrows like storm clouds. A tic pulsed at his jawline. I was asking him to contact someone he carried a deep dislike for, if not hated, and request their help.

"If you can't ask him, I can call Em. Maybe her dad knows someone who knows someone who knows the spell," I said, even though that would be a shot in the dark.

"It's not a spell that . . ." Ben shook his head. "I'll call him."

"Why not right now?" I knew I was pushing, but if Ben didn't ask Reginald very soon, I might. I hoped it wouldn't come to that because Ben's patience with me wouldn't help us through that breach of trust.

Ben blew out a sigh and cursed for good measure. He tapped a number on his phone. His tight grip on my hand twitched, and his heel bounced impatiently. The pungent odor of his fear thickened the air.

I lifted his hand and lightly kissed his knuckles, a quiet gesture of support. The faint ringing ceased, and a voice answered from the other end of the line.

Ben's body went rigid. His mouth opened and closed. He swallowed, then tried again. "Hello. It's Benjamin."

I rubbed my hand along his back. Reginald's voice was loud enough for me to hear his exclamation of surprise and happiness.

Ben released my hand, stood, and started walking to the car. "I need help removing a tether." He got into the car's passenger seat. The notebook he'd been scribbling spellwork in was stowed up there.

The following ten to fifteen minutes passed with me fighting every urge to follow Ben and make sure he was okay, and him talking on the phone too far away for me to eavesdrop. He wasn't even facing my direction so I could fabricate the conversation solely from his expressions and my anxiety. I watched his silhouette, on the lookout for any wild gesturing, but there wasn't even a raised voice.

Ben got out of the car and waved me over. When I reached him, his mouth was pressed into a thin line and his eyes were glassy. He'd been crying.

My heart fell. "What can I do for you right now?"

He opened his arms. I stepped into his embrace and we hugged each other tightly.

"I have it," Ben said. "He told me the spell."

"Thank you!" I hugged him tighter, lifted him from his feet, and spun once.

"Nope. Not a fan of this." He tapped my shoulder.

"Sorry." I set him back down. "Do you want to talk about your phone call?"

"No." He sniffled and cleared his throat. "We'll track down Leo, trap him, and remove the tether. With the tether gone, there'll be no more side effects, and you can find out what he wants and reason with him."

"Yes. First, we'll meet this friend of my grandfather's, though," I said. "Because if he's another wolf or some other supernatural being, he might be willing to help us with Leo."

With the dreaded phone call finished, Ben's mood lightened a bit. "Hey, I know we just met, but I'm the granddaughter of your friend and I wondered if you could help me contain a furious werewolf that has tried multiple times to kill me," he joked.

I grimaced. "Okay, it sounds stupid when you put it that way."

Back in the car, I looked up the surname Grenham in the Manistee directory. Two names with two different addresses in the town came up.

We parked along the road at the first address belonging to a "T. Grenham." Ben followed me up the walkway to a small home. A For Sale sign was posted on the lawn. I raised my hand to knock and noticed a large lock, the kind used by realtors, on the front door. "Looks like no one is living here. Next address?"

We followed the GPS across a bridge and to the northern end of town. It was another small house, but the lot was longer. We parked in the driveway and walked to the door together.

Ben pressed the button for the doorbell. He stepped back and motioned at the decorative gourds on the stoop. "At least someone is living here."

"This was a woman's name in the listing, wasn't it?" I knocked, the screen door rattling in its frame.

"Yeah. Dorothy Grenham."

"Hopefully she's a relative who can tell us where Theodore is. If he moved out of town, I hope it's not far." I raised my fist to knock again when the sound of a car engine made me pause.

A sedan moved up the drive and parked. An older woman got out of the car and looked over the roof at us. "Can I help you?"

Her hair was gray and bound back from her face in a braid, but I recognized her.

I lowered my voice so only Ben could hear me. "It's the woman from the photos in Grandpa's box." The wolf in me immediately reached for the anger and disappointment, having seen my grandfather's arm around the woman. She was a stranger. She didn't belong in a photo with him. I swallowed back a growl, trying to parse through the whirlwind in my head.

"Hello!" Ben smiled and took only a few steps toward the car. "Are you Dorothy?"

Her gaze darted to me and back to him, her tone wary. "I am."

"I'm Ben. This is Alex," he said. "We're looking for Theodore. Does he live here?"

"No, he doesn't," Dorothy said.

Ben tucked his hands in his pockets. "Do you know where we could find him?"

"I'm sorry," she said, "but Theo is dead."

18

MY HEART CRATERED. I thought we'd finally located someone who knew Grandpa and would have answers. What kind of man was my grandfather? What was he doing here? Sudden tears itched the corners of my eyes.

"We're sorry for your loss," Ben said.

"Thank you." Dorothy hesitated before asking, "Why are you looking for him?"

"My grandfather was Alexander Steward," I said. "We were told Theo was a friend of his."

Dorothy's eyes widened. She smiled and her posture relaxed. "Alexander's little Alex?"

I gave a nod and walked up beside Ben. When I clenched his hand, he winced and wiggled his fingers.

I loosened my grip.

Dorothy chuckled. "Oh my, I can't believe I'm finally meeting you after all this time!" She retrieved a canvas sack of groceries from the car and walked toward the house's side door. "Come inside out of the cold, kids. And please, call me Dottie."

Ben looked at me, eyebrows lifted. I nodded. We followed her into a small kitchen with daisy wallpaper, white appliances, lace curtains, and a simple wooden table.

"Have a seat." She offered us drinks. We declined.

Ben pulled out a chair for me. I squeezed his hand, thankful for his support. He sat beside me at the end of the table. I scented the air of the place for any hints about Dottie. Flowers, candles, a cleaning product. Nothing indicated the woman was lupine.

Dottie set her bag on the counter and filled an electric kettle with water. "I need some tea. We're having such a frigid autumn." She put away the groceries as the water heated. "The man you're looking for, Theo, was my older brother. He and Alexander served in the army together and remained friends afterward." She finally sat down in the seat across from me. "Theo passed away in the spring."

Solving the mystery of Grandpa's box and the key evaded me again. My fingers found the metal object, warm from riding in my pocket. I picked my words carefully, keeping my tone neutral. "Were you friends with my grandfather, too?"

"All three of us were good friends. Alexander owned a cabin north of here. Other guests would come and go, but Theo, Alex, and I spent a lot of time there." Dottie's eyes brightened. Her smile emphasized the lines at the corners of her eyes. "The two would go hunting together, and I'd make my way through a pile of books."

I pulled the photo of my grandfather and her from my pocket, the corners now bent from my constant handling. I set it on the tabletop and pushed it toward her. My jaw was clenched so hard it ached. I focused on keeping my breathing even.

She picked up the photo. Wistful sadness touched her smile. "I can barely remember being that young." Dottie looked across the table from my tight fists up to my eyes. "It's so obvious in this photo, isn't it? I was naive and smitten. But Alexander was married, and he adored your grandmother, so we were never more than friends." She pushed the photo back to me. "You and your grandmother held the entirety of his heart."

I swallowed and my eyes grew glassy. It was the answer I'd hoped for, so why did it still hurt? Why did his leaving us behind bother me so much?

"You miss him," she stated in a soft tone.

I nodded, sniffed, and wiped impatiently at my eyes with the heel of my hand. Ben's hand settled lightly on my shoulder.

"You didn't turn before he died, did you?" she asked.

My pulse jumped. "How could you tell—"

"Your eyes. They're the same gold as his." Her smile was kind. "He was so sure your wolf would eventually surface."

My heart told me the wolf was just beneath your skin.

Grandpa's letter to me admitted as much. But why? Did he fear I would someday struggle with the part of me that was wolf like he did?

"Was your brother lupine?" Ben asked.

Dottie nodded. "When I was fifteen and he was seventeen. It passed me by."

"Do you know why Grandpa left his family at home when he went to the cabin?" I asked.

The kettle whistled. She stood and prepared herself a cup of tea. "There were horrendous acts the men experienced when they were sent overseas. My brother didn't talk to me about them when he returned. All he would say is the line between him and the wolf was blurred. His heart darkened while away—"

"And the darkness followed him home." Another admission of my grandfather's in the letter he left me before his death.

"Yes. The cabin was a type of reprieve for Alexander and Theo. They spent time there recentering themselves." She sat down again. The cup of tea steamed in front of her.

"Then why were you there?" Even though she'd reassured me of her friendship-only relationship with my grandfather, the question still sounded hostile.

Dottie looked down at her tea. "I didn't travel to the cabin with them every year." She looked up. "Some years they were scared for my safety, especially when guests were expected. They asked me to stay behind."

I blinked. Guests?

"When your grandfather first purchased the cabin, the land around it was mostly state forest," she said. "The uninhabited woods allowed the two freedom to run without anyone noticing."

"And no Commoners getting hurt," I said.

She nodded.

To my knowledge, a cabin wasn't in my grandfather's will. My parents and grandmother never mentioned it, and I wondered if they knew he'd owned it. I withdrew the tarnished key from my pocket, its chain wrapped around my fingers and the tags grasped in my palm. "I found this in a box of Grandpa's things. Is it for the cabin?"

Dottie gave another sad smile. "Yes. It's his copy of the key. Theo had one, too."

My heart leaped. "Who has ownership of the cabin now?"

"Alexander left it to my brother, and my brother left it to me. I plan to gift it to my daughter if she'll have it."

"I'd like to see it," I said. "Would you be okay with that?"

"Of course." She wrote an address down on a scrap of paper and handed it to me. "This is where you'll find it. The cabin should be in good shape. Even after Alexander passed away, my brother traveled there to make sure it was kept up."

I tucked the paper and key safely into my jacket pocket. "Is there anything else you can tell me about my grandfather?"

Dottie sipped her tea. "I can only tell you about the part of Alexander he shared with us. He was a kind and stubborn man. If he sensed someone was being wronged, he tried to help them. He credited your grandmother for that." She looked down at her tea. "My brother believed Alexander also feared the anger he brought back. He thought of it as a burden to his family."

Or maybe he worried they wouldn't fully understand. I stared hard at the wooden tabletop, withholding tears. I wished more than ever that my grandfather was alive. We could share our worries and talk about that darker side of ourselves. How it came to be and how to coexist with it. Because no matter how hard I tried to overcome it, my rage was a part of who I was. It was written into my story. Even as the years wore it down, making the edges less sharp and painful, I would carry it within me for the rest of my days.

Seek help. Don't let it fester.

The words of my grandfather's letter took on a new tone of urgency. He must have felt so alone at first. The trips to the cabin, the chance to safely let his wolf run, were a pressure release so he wasn't constantly struggling with the darker part of himself at home around his family.

I cleared my throat so my voice wouldn't quaver. "I'm glad Grandpa had Theo to talk to."

"And I'm glad Theo had Alexander."

"Did my grandfather ever mention the Dogman?"

She blinked, probably surprised at the abrupt turn in conversation. "I beg your pardon?"

"The state cryptid," Ben provided. "Seven feet tall, glowing eyes, half man half dog?"

Dottie looked between the two of us with a hesitant smile. "I've heard of the Dogman, but no, Alexander never spoke of it with me. It's a folktale people tell so their children don't wander alone in the forest at night."

My grandfather's secret cabin in the woods made more sense now, but not the trail of newspaper clippings. Was he following someone he was trying to help like Clare said? Or was he keeping trophies of kills for the darker part of his wolf?

"You mentioned guests at the cabin. Do you know if they were other lupine?" I asked. "Maybe someone who was struggling to contain their wolf?"

"It sounds like something he would do, to try to help others, but they never spoke to me about the guests they invited to stay."

"Thank you for all your time, Dottie," I said, standing. "Finding out what that key goes to is beyond helpful."

She shook both of our hands, seeming pleased. "Are you off to the cabin next?"

"Yeah." Excitement buzzed inside me as I imagined what the cabin would smell and look like. "If Grandpa found it so relaxing, I can't wait to see it."

"Having only lost Theo this year, I couldn't bring myself to close it yet for the season, so you'll have electricity and water. There isn't a cell signal up there in the woods, and it's a bit of a drive for groceries, so be sure you're prepared," she said.

I looked at Ben. "Can you remind me to stop on the way?"

He wore a slight frown, lost in thought, as he stared past my shoulder at the wall. The question caused his attention to jump to me. "Uh, yeah. Sure."

Dottie walked to the door to see us out.

I mouthed the question to Ben. *"What's wrong?"*

He pointed behind me. On the wall was the same photo of Officer Miller and her parents that we'd seen on her desk at the police station. I realized now why the older woman in Miller's photo had looked familiar. It was Dottie. Hanging beside the family picture was a photo of Miller in her late teens, a younger version of Miller's father, and a man I recognized as Grandpa's friend, Theo.

My muscles tensed, and my mind raced to draw connections. How could Miller be a Hunter if her mother, Dottie, descended from a line of wolves? Dottie walked back to us, and I withheld the growl brewing in my chest.

Ben settled his fingers lightly on the small of my back. He pointed with his other hand at the photos on the wall. "Is this your family, Dottie?"

"Yes, it is." Warmth and a hint of sadness colored her voice. "My husband Ed passed away several years ago. The young woman is my daughter, Lucy. That's when she graduated from the police academy. The man in the other photo with Ed and Lucy is my brother Theo."

Did she lie? Were Dottie and Theo Hunters? Was this a trap?

"Alex, I met my Ed because of your grandfather," Dottie said. "Ed would periodically visit Alexander and Theo at the cabin. I was lucky that one such summer our stays overlapped, and we were introduced."

"Need. Air." It's all I could manage. I turned and focused on making it to the back door and outside.

"Are you okay?" Dottie followed and stopped in the doorway.

"I'm fine. Thank you!" I started toward my car without looking back.

"She's alright," Ben said. "Thanks again for talking with us."

"You're welcome," Dottie said. "Have a safe drive."

I closed the driver's side car door. Ben tapped on the window. I shook my head. He opened the door. "You're upset. I'm driving."

I sat in the passenger seat instead. The rumbling in my chest cleared my throat as low growling. "She's lying."

"About what?" Ben backed the car out of the drive and started down the road.

"Why would a wolf marry a Hunter?" I snarled.

His tone was frustratingly calm. "Dottie never became a werewolf. Her brother did."

I threw up my hands. "But if she supposedly cared so much about her brother, why the hell would she marry a Hunter?"

"We don't know if Miller studied under her dad to become a Hunter. The Hunter could be someone else. It's not genetic like it is for us."

I sank my claws into the cushion of my seat. "Miller's dad, Ed, was a cop during those livestock killings. As a Hunter, Ed would have been able to see that Grandpa was lupine. It's one of their superpowers. Why else would Ed name Grandpa as his main suspect?"

"Why would your grandfather invite a Hunter to stay at his cabin?" Ben asked. "Was he working with a Hunter?"

"No! Of course, he wasn't." The mere suggestion caused my gut to burn with anger. "She has to be lying about that. Grandpa wouldn't endanger everyone else by having a Hunter there."

He was a protector. He would never aid someone whose goal was to eliminate people like me.

"But you said yourself you're not sure your grandfath—"

"He wouldn't do that!" I shouted.

"Okay." Ben's tone lowered and softened. "I need to cast that tracking spell if we're going to find Leo. You could use the time to decompress. Can you please look up some out-of-the-way place for us to do that?"

His voice acted as a soothing agent. I focused on steadying my erratic breathing. The wolf in me was difficult to mask when I felt anger. "I'm sorry. I know you're only trying to help." I brought up the map on my phone. "I'm scared."

"I know." He gave me a sideward glance. "Where to?"

"There's a little park near the river," I suggested. "Doesn't look like any houses are around it."

WE DROVE INTO the countryside until we crossed a narrow bridge with wooden railings. Immediately over the river, an entryway on the right led to a small gravel lot. What I thought was a park on the map was an access point to the water for fishermen and recreationists. It was late in the season, so the lot was empty.

Ben parked the car. "For this tracking spell, I'll need your sweater from last night."

"My sweater?" I dug around in the back of the car until I found the crumpled piece of clothing. "Ah, you need Leo's blood to track him."

Ben took the sweater from me and laid it on the hood to look it over. "Unless you know whose blood is whose, his hair will work better." He picked a tuft of fur from the fibers.

I waited at his elbow. "What else do you need?"

"Luck?" He opened his notebook and flipped the pages.

"You're kidding, right?"

"No." His mouth bent in concentration. "The nature of the spell falls into my type of magic, but I've never used material components in my spellwork."

Anxiety tightened my shoulders. I wanted to locate Leo, remove the tether, and find out why he was on such a rampage. We needed the spell to work. "So what can I do to help?"

Ben looked up, his forehead wrinkled. "Give me space and be patient."

Dammit.

I was awful at being patient.

"Okay." I stepped out of his space and wandered to where the river tumbled and flowed beneath the bridge. Odors of damp earth and water-logged vegetation hung in the air. A sign on a wooden post at the edge of the lot read Old Stronach Bridge in white lettering on red. An autumn flower released a sweet scent into the cool air. Large stones lined the riverbank.

A flicker of a shadow moved beneath the wooden supports of the bridge. My muscles tensed. I scented the air again, searching out any threat. Nothing. My nerves were strung tight between puzzling out Grandpa's box and dealing with Leo.

Was I overcomplicating matters by not simply turning Leo in to Officer Miller or whatever Hunters were lurking in this part of the state? My experience with a Hunter didn't lead me to believe they were selective about which supernatural beings they tracked down. In the end, they wanted all of us gone. A Hunter would get rid of Leo, but Ben and I could become the next targets. And I wanted to give Leo another chance, especially after seeing the state he was in during our last fight.

A familiar, gentle brush of energy tickled my exposed skin. I softly padded back to where Ben was crouched. My car's defunct air freshener, a piece of cardboard shaped like a tree, was at the center of a symbol he'd drawn in the dirt. The tuft of Leo's fur sat atop the air freshener. The intensity of Ben's stare as he concentrated on the spell had me imagining everything I'd like to do to him later. His soft murmuring of the strange language wizards used for spellcasting intensified the attraction even more.

"Do you realize how incredibly hot you look?" I asked.

A corner of his mouth lifted. "Alex."

"Sorry." I covered my smile.

The glyph emanated the bluish light characteristic of Ben's spellcasting. The tuft of fur melted away like it was absorbed into the cardboard. He picked up the air freshener, the cutout having taken on the blue glow. Ben inhaled, hesitated, and spoke a single word. A sudden pulse of light lit up the area, collapsed into a beam, and vanished. Holding the air freshener by its string loop, he stood and scuffed his shoe over the symbol to erase it. "Ready?"

I looked around us. "Did it work?"

"What? You can't see that?" Ben held up the cardboard tree and pointed back toward the river and the direction we came from. "He's that way."

"Must be your wizard vision."

"Huh." Ben consulted the notebook again.

I crept closer to get a better look at the air freshener. "What does it look like?"

"Like . . . a lighthouse beam."

We got into the car, and Ben hung the air freshener on the rearview mirror. He picked up his phone and consulted the map. "It looks like the general direction is northeast. Are we still going to look for him today?"

"Yeah. Let's see if we can find him."

"Turn left here," he said. "We'll eventually need to sleep, Alex."

"I know." A growl rumbled in my chest. "We should probably sing Bon Jovi at the top of our lungs to stay alert."

Ben chuckled and the sound eased the tension in my body. "You're probably right. Let's do it." He flipped through my road trip playlist, turned up the volume, and the iconic intro started.

Things were upside down, but Ben was riding it out beside me. I'm not sure I could have asked for a better copilot.

19

WE FOLLOWED A combination of directions between Ben's tracking spell and the map he watched on his phone. After almost an hour, the beam of light led us to the area of Benzonia and Crystal Lake.

"Wasn't there a Dogman sighting around here?" I asked.

"Correct," he said. "An inn owner reported seeing the Dogman when he was getting boats ready in the morning."

"Have you noticed that in all the Dogman sightings we've heard or read, not once does he attack someone? He scares people away from places." I chewed at my lip. "There's only one encounter where an elderly farmer 'dies from fright.'"

"Didn't one of those kids at the festival tell you the Dogman doesn't eat people, he only eats animals?" Ben asked.

"Yeah, but in those articles about the livestock killings, no one reports seeing the Dogman. He's blamed for the act because the wounds look like they're from a canine."

"Turn here," Ben said. "This light beam is getting brighter."

We turned at a roadside market and followed the road into the countryside. The property lots grew, which would be to our advantage if we found Leo. More space between neighbors would mean less of a chance we'd be interrupted by a curious Commoner.

"Also, there's the timing," I continued. "The Dogman lore seems to have started a long time before my Grandpa took trips to this cabin. The articles in his box reporting the livestock killings were from the mid-seventies to the early nineties."

Ben looked from his phone out the windshield. "Start slowing down after the road bends."

An abandoned house came into view and my skin immediately wanted to vacate the scene. Wood siding, bleached from the sun, made the slouching building appear like a specter lurking in the overgrown field. Even in daylight it creeped me out.

Please don't let this be—

"Right here." Ben pointed. "He's around this old house."

I pulled the car off to the shoulder. We peered at the house from the safety of the car. "Goddammit. This place is so haunted," I muttered.

The windows of the two-story building were boarded over. A bedraggled wreath was tacked up beside the front door. The steps and part of the porch were missing. I pulled the car slowly down the uneven drive. Tall yellow wildflowers were in bloom, scratching at the car's body and undercarriage as we passed.

"Is he inside?" I parked behind the house so the car wouldn't be noticed from the road.

Ben shielded his eyes from the cardboard tree hanging off the rearview mirror. "I can't tell. This whole place, the house, the field, the woods . . . Everything is lit up. Either I messed up the parameters of the spell, or Leo has been circling here."

"How do we shut off the magic light beam so you can see?"

He squinted at me. "If we're done using it, I can destroy it b—"

I tugged the air freshener from the mirror and tore it in half.

He lowered his hands. "Or you can do that."

Outside the car my senses went on high alert, continuously scanning for any scent, sound, or movement that indicated Leo was nearby. The strange odor clinging to him was barely noticeable beneath rotting wood and mildew. Ben and I waded through the wildflowers and grasses, trying to find a way inside the house.

"When I looked for a tracking spell in my mom's notebook, I found a few different ones we could use on Leo," he said.

I sneezed. "What do they do?"

"One is a straightforward barrier spell to contain him. It requires some preparation." Ben waved away a flying insect. "But there's another more complex one that would immobilize him in space. He wouldn't be able to fight his way free."

"I've experienced both. That second one wasn't fun," I said. "When I lost my temper with Stone at a Committee meeting and leaped across the table, Reginald used a spell that froze me in place."

"You'd told me about that." Ben attempted to hide his amusement. "In the middle of a Committee meeting, right?"

"Listen," I growled. "Stone *really* pissed me off. He . . ." I shuddered. "Smiled at me."

"His mistake." Ben gave me a sideward glance. "I hope Leo isn't here right now. I want to practice that spell first."

I sneezed. Scrunching my nose, I brushed at it with my hand. "I think I'm allergic to these flowers."

"Any signs of Leo?" He scanned the woods behind the house.

"His scent is here but pretty faint."

Ben pointed at the side of the house. "There's our way in." The board covering a window had split. Part of it was pried loose and lay in the grass. Long gouges marred the siding beneath the window and along the frame.

He hoisted me onto his shoulders. The scent of age intensified. Through ungraceful maneuvering and colorful swearing, I made it up onto the ledge. Tufts of fur were wedged in the jagged bits of the window frame. I hopped down lightly into the house.

Whenever I entered an abandoned building, which honestly was too often, I noticed a certain type of odor that clung to its guts. It was like a carcass emanating a scent of decay. This house's insides had deteriorated so much that nature was reclaiming them. Moss lined the edges of the floorboards near the broken window. A seedling grew from a crevice in the floor. Several paths of large, clawed footprints wove back and forth across the dusty floor of the room.

Ben's voice from outside startled me. "Everything okay?"

I slowly exhaled and leaned out the window. "Yeah. He's been in here. I'm going to take a look around."

"Be careful not to fall through the floor."

At that moment, his concern made me smile. "Will do."

I followed the large tracks through rooms on the first floor and found the stairs to the cellar. The door had recently been ripped from its hinges. Leo's strange scent lingered there stronger than outside, but it still seemed diluted. My vision adjusted as I crept down the creaking stairs into the darkness. I tried to keep my breathing even and not focus on the fact I was willingly entering a more-than-likely haunted basement alone and oh there may be a rage-filled werewolf waiting for me.

I paused at the bottom of the stairs, straining to detect any sign of Leo. A mantle of dust draped wood shelves and long-forgotten canning jars. The footprints crisscrossed everywhere on the dirt floor. His scent was stronger and mixed with damp stone. A pile of tattered fabric, possibly the remains of Leo's clothes, was in a heap against one of the walls.

Across the room, I spotted another door. Cellars like this usually had a second door leading back outside. I'd be lying if I said I didn't dash across the dark room. The corroded padlock broke easily when I wrenched it open. I climbed stone stairs up to a wide door above me, unhooked a metal latch, and opened the door up into the sunlight of the backyard.

"Back here," I shouted.

Ben jogged around the corner of the house. He peered down the stairs. "No Leo?"

"No, but his scent is strongest in the cellar. It looks like he's staying in there," I said. "If you go down there now, you'll have light to draw your spell symbols."

"Sigils." He smiled, gave me a peck on the cheek, and headed down into the cellar. Ben re-emerged from the dim basement later, blinking in the daylight. "Done."

"Do you want to practice that spell while we wait?"

"Sure." He scuffed in the dirt with the toe of his shoe before picking up a stone and handing it to me.

I looked around. "Where do you want me?"

He cocked his head. "Anywhere you'll let me have you."

His casual delivery and the images it conjured made my cheeks burn. "Keep that up and it'll be right here in the backyard."

Ben arched an eyebrow. "Is that supposed to deter me?"

"No one wants grass stains on their knees." Though it'd be worth it.

"If you say so." He backed away. "Can you toss that at me—"

I threw the stone at him.

He ducked, eyes wide. "Not yet! And I said toss, not pitch like a baseball."

"Sorry." I picked up another stone, turning it over in my hand. "Tell me when."

Ben put a good ten feet between us, faced me, and got that familiar wrinkle between his eyebrows as he focused on the stone. "Okay. Go."

I underhand lobbed the stone. His energy pull was more sudden than usual, and the telltale blue light of his magic coated the stone like a skin. The stone didn't halt its movement, but it slowed as if the air was viscous.

Ben shook his head and stepped to the side. The spell's energy discharged and the rock completed its path at normal speed. He faced me a second time. "Can you do that again?"

I selected a second rock and wound up like how I imagined a major league baseball pitcher would. My reference was cartoons, but it couldn't be that far off.

He smirked. "Go."

I lobbed the second stone. This time it slowed to a stop at the peak of its arc. It remained suspended for a few moments, then gradually sank. Ben muttered to himself. The rock fell to the ground. "I'm worried his mass is going to be a problem. He's a huge guy."

"Do you want me to jump at you?"

"Leo is three times your size."

"But at least I'm larger than a rock," I said.

"Alex, it'll trigger your Shield," he protested. "Even if my magic isn't strong enough to get through, you'll still feel your Shield's feedback."

"I know." I swallowed. "Can you end the spell as soon as you know if the spell worked?"

Ben's jaw clenched.

"Can you?" I repeated.

He blew out a sigh. "Yeah. I can."

"Okay. Go!" I took off from my spot, the wolf in me charging my leg muscles for a burst of speed. I leaped toward Ben with a snarl, my claws outstretched. Wide-eyed, he crouched, ripped the energy from the air, and shouted an incantation. My body immediately halted, my fingers a foot from his figure. Breath still moved in my chest, but every other part of me was caught in limbo. The Shield over my breastbone lit up with a burning sensation in response to the magic.

Ben quickly braced his knee on the ground and reached up to put his hands under my arms. With one whispered word from him, the space around us exhaled and I fell into his hold. I wrapped my arms around his neck, grinning despite the lingering sting of my Shield.

He sat back with me in his lap and rested his forehead against mine. "You startled me."

"It worked, didn't it? No time to overthink what to do or doubt yourself," I said. "Leo isn't going to wait for us to be ready."

Ben kissed the tip of my nose. "I love you, Alex."

His words caused a ridiculous giddy sensation throughout my body. I could almost forget we had an enraged werewolf to confront. "I love you, too."

20

AS SOON AS the sun set, the temperature plummeted. The cars passing on the road were few and far between. Ben and I sat huddled together with a blanket on the car's hood.

"I wonder if Leo is even coming back here," I said. "Maybe he already moved."

"We left the sigil on the car," Ben said. "If he's pissed enough to follow you across the state, I don't think he'll pass on you coming to him."

"When I catch his scent, you'll go into the cellar and sit at the top of the stairs into the house," I said. "I'll wait out here, try to stay unnoticed, and sneak in after him."

Ben nodded, blowing in his cupped hands and rubbing them together briskly. His nose and the tips of his ears were red. "I need to touch his throat to break the tether."

I chewed at my thumbnail, my leg bouncing as I scanned the backyard and woodline. Our whole plan rested on the hunch that removing Leo's tether would clear his mind.

A sudden yipping noise sounded in the woods behind the house, followed by short howls and cries. The hair rose on the nape of my neck. I slid off the car, wildly scenting the air.

Ben sat stone still, his voice low and his pale complexion glowing in the dark. "What the *hell* is that?"

The series of rapid yips multiplied and overlapped with the howls. "It sounds like coyotes." I couldn't smell anything, but the pack sounded as if it lurked along the treeline. "I've heard them in other places I've lived. They always sound closer than they are."

Ben slowly slid off the hood and stepped behind the car, placing it between him and the woods. His gaze darted among the shadows of the trees. The sharp scent of his fear filled my nose.

A cracking or falling branch sounded from the woodline. Two red orbs peered at us from the dark. I tried to scent the air again, but the breeze blew against my back. Whoever was in the woods would be getting a noseful of us. So much for me remaining hidden.

The howling sounded like the pack of coyotes was on top of us now. My pulse quickened as I slunk beside Ben. "I think he's here." I reached out to the wolf in me and my vision improved.

Leo's large, bulky body waited among the trunks of the pines. Steam escaped his nostrils. His red eyes, locked on Ben and me, finally blinked.

"I'll distract him so you can sneak downstairs," I whispered.

Ben's voice quavered. "Okay. Be careful."

I brushed my fingertips against his palm. "Good luck." I jogged away from the car and along the side of the house. Leo tracked me with his eyes. He moved within the treeline, mirroring me. In my peripheral vision, Ben turned and ran for the open cellar door. When he passed out of sight, I curved my path toward the woods.

Leo's enormous, fur-covered mass bursting from the darkness of the trees was terrifying. He dropped to all fours, lumbering after me in that disturbing, lurching gait werewolves have.

I reached deeper and prompted my body to shift, gaining my claws. His stride was longer, so I needed the increased speed to stay ahead of him. I circled sharply back around the house and ducked behind the car. Leo turned the corner and halted. His nose snuffled along the ground and through the air, searching for me.

A loud clunk came from the cellar. Leo stood at his full height, his attention drawn to the open door. The fur of his flank was matted with blood from long gashes in his hide. Leo growled, his nostrils twitching. His ears swiveled. He stepped toward the stairs.

I sneezed.

Leo spun toward the car. I tried to stand but ducked when his large body passed over top of me. He'd leaped to my side of the car. I crawled out of reach, stumbled to my feet, and almost bit it dashing around the car. I bolted for the cellar stairs. Leo was right at my heels. He shoved me toward the open door.

My body flew forward into the void above the stairs.

I'm going to break my neck.

I closed my eyes and curled my body, trying to protect my head. Energy raced along my skin, and Ben shouted the words of a spell. My body struck a semi-pliable surface hovering above the stone steps three quarters of the way down the stairs. The surface crackled with blue light and dissipated. I dropped a few inches onto a step and tumbled down the few remaining stairs to the floor.

From the top of the stairs, Leo bellowed a rage-filled scream. The horrific sound echoed into the confined space and set every hair on my body on end. He crashed down the cellar stairs after me, snapping and snarling. I scrambled to get on my feet.

Leo's body struck me off balance. We rolled and thrashed on the floor, kicking up dirt and snarling. I strained to hold him at arm's length. His jaws snapped at my face and throat.

My skin prickled. Ben's spellcasting reached my ears.

Leo pulled up short at Ben's voice and released me. His ears swiveled. Forgotten, I backed away.

Four of the five sigils on the floor lit up. The fifth had been wiped clear by Leo and me. The magical barrier shimmered into existence and immediately started to crackle and flicker. It collapsed in a burst of blue light and returned energy.

A brief look was exchanged between Ben and me.

My heart seized.

"No! Ben, wait!"

He jumped from the stairs and dashed across the room. Leo zeroed in on Ben. A nasty wound stretched over Leo's shoulder blades. I leaped forward and sunk my claws into the old wound.

Another ear-splitting scream left Leo. He reached back over his shoulder and grabbed my wrist. With little effort, Leo hauled me over his shoulder, and I fell flat on my back in front of him. All the air was expelled from my lungs.

I rolled to my side gasping. Ben kneeled, frantically scribbling in the dirt to redraw the ruined sigil. Leo lunged at him. I tried to yell a warning but didn't have the air to speak.

Ben looked up and his eyes rounded. I winced at the sudden ripping sensation of the energy from the space around me. Ben shouted the spell command and Leo's body froze in place. The soft blue glow coating Leo's figure crackled but held.

Panting, eyes still wide, Ben fell back on his hands. He looked over at me. "Alex, are you okay?"

I lifted my blood-covered thumb.

Ben got up and helped me to my feet. We cautiously approached Leo. Long, oozing scratches ran down the side of his muzzle. Rumbling growls vibrated in his massive chest.

"He hasn't been able to heal," I said. "Some of these wounds are from Steven and me. They should have at least closed up by now."

Leo's breath expelled through his nose in ragged bursts. It sounded almost congested. The scent clinging to him was so putrid, I covered my nose. The blue light coating his body vibrated.

"We want to help you, Leo," I said. "Ben can try to remove what's left of your tether. We think the remnants are preventing you from shifting."

"I need to touch you to do it," Ben said, his voice unsteady.

Leo whined. The muscles in his upper arms and chest spasmed as if something were living beneath his skin and trying to escape. The crackling noise from the spell sounded again.

Ben tentatively reached out. The light shimmered as his fingers passed through it. His fingertips brushed the muddy and blood-caked fur of Leo's scruff.

My pulse pounded in my ears. I watched for any minute change in Leo's behavior or the solidity of the blue light.

Leo's entire throat was absent of his thick fur. Long slashes ran the length of the bare area. Like before, the area was covered in boils and lesions, but there were more of them. The marks of the altered tether were still there on the bare patches of skin, but they burned a deep red like Leo's eyes. The light pulsed as if it were synced to his heartbeat.

Ben paled. He looked at Leo. "I'm going to cast the spell now."

I twisted my hands. Tethers had lashed out at Emma and Sebastian when they tried to tamper with them. Ben's eyebrows gathered and more energy swirled past me. He recited the words of the spell. As he curled his fingers back into his palm, the tether's mark lifted from Leo's skin.

I'd watched Reginald remove Ben's tether, and the brand was lifted in a similar way. But with Leo's tether a harsh crackling noise, accompanied by a brightening of the red light, occurred. Hairline fissures split over the surface of the blue light containing Leo. The edges of Ben's mouth dipped. His tone of voice grew harsher and more urgent.

My stomach clenched as my focus darted between Ben, the tether, and Leo. Muscles twitching, a canine-like whine slipped through my teeth. I felt useless.

Ben braced his free hand on Leo's shoulder and closed his fingers around the tether's mark. With a grunt of effort, Ben yanked his hand back. Arcs of red light leaped up Ben's arm and across Leo's body. Ben cried out in pain. His fingers convulsed open, and the mark of the tether evaporated into oily smoke.

The shell of light encasing Leo shattered.

Leo seized Ben's wrist.

"No!" I moved toward Leo but stopped when he pulled Ben back against him. "Let go of him!"

Leo clasped Ben's shoulder in his other clawed hand. He slowly ran his muzzle and twitching nose along Ben's neck and hair.

"Are you okay?" My words sounded strangled.

Ben stood rigid except for his rapid breathing.

Leo's red eyes narrowed. A low rumbling resonated in his chest. His body shifted, realigning itself from wolf to man. He stopped his transformation at a point where he still had claws and sharp teeth. The brand of the altered tether was gone, but his throat, neck, and top of his chest were still covered in the angry lesions.

Leo stared at Ben. His eyes were having difficulty focusing. His deep voice was husky with disuse. "Why don't you smell like yourself, George? Did she hurt you, too?"

"George is in Chicago." I tried to keep my tone calm. "Let Ben go, Leo. He helped you."

"Don't lie," Leo snarled. "George wouldn't leave me behind. He's my pal. We had a plan." His gaze moved back to Ben. "Tell her, George. Tell her the truth and then we'll kill her together."

"I'm sorry." Ben swallowed. "We were told George was sent back to Chicago."

Leo released Ben's wrist and pressed his hand to the side of his head. He squeezed his eyes shut. "Lies!" When his eyes opened, they glowed red again. He glared at me. "You're making George lie to me! We were pals. We wanted to go back home. You ruined everything for us!" The red pulsing light flared along his neck. His muscles spasmed and he started to shift back toward wolf.

Ben attempted to twist away, but Leo's grip tightened and his claws punctured Ben's shoulder. A strangled cry came from Ben. Leo yanked Ben to his muzzle. A string of blood-streaked saliva fell from his parted jaws.

"Stop!" I screamed. "Leo, stop! Don't hurt George!"

Leo flinched. His bleary gaze slid toward me.

I leaped at Leo, snarling and slashing at his face. My claws cut across his snout. He tossed Ben to cover his face. His other arm swung around, his club-like fist colliding with the side of my body. I stumbled sideways, nearly tripping over Ben on the floor. Leo charged after me. His movements remained unusually clumsy.

Ben pulled me back. Leo's jaw snapped closed around empty space. With a tug of energy and his palm open toward Leo, Ben shouted a word. A blast of force struck Leo square in the chest. He was thrown off his feet and slid back across the cellar floor.

Wincing, Ben clenched his injured shoulder with bloody fingers. "I can't keep casting like this. We need to run."

Could I take Leo if I fully shifted my body? What would happen if I fought Leo and got lost in the frenzy of the fight? Especially in such close quarters? I couldn't take the chance of hurting Ben.

I nodded. "Let's go."

We ran across the cellar and up the stone steps to the backyard. Leo's roar reverberated after us. The scrabbling of claws signaled his pursuit. Ben and I dashed to the car. I fumbled with the door handle. My claws and larger hands made the simple task difficult.

Leo snarled behind me. A shadow passed overhead. I yanked open the door. Leo landed with a crunch on the roof of the car. The metal groaned as the frame bent. Leo leaned over to swipe at me. I smashed him in the nose with my fist. He yelped and pulled back.

I ducked into the driver's seat and fumbled with the keys. They dropped on the floor of the car.

"Alex!" From the passenger seat, Ben reached for me.

I was yanked out of the driver's seat and dropped in the grass on my back. Leo sprang from the car's roof. I rolled out of the way and onto my feet. Leo landed, stumbled, and fell to his knee.

Ben had recovered the keys. He slid into the driver's seat and started the car. Powering my muscles, I dove over Leo and through the still-open driver's side door. It was far from flawless, but at least I was inside the car.

Ben threw the car in reverse and stomped on the accelerator. The car sped backward while I crawled across Ben's lap and fell into the passenger seat. He spun the steering wheel. The car swung to face the road. My body tipped against the door as I struggled to find my balance.

We slid to a stop. The driver's side door slammed against the car's body and bounced open again. I managed to sit up and look through the passenger window.

Leo was back on his feet and running at us. Ben shifted the car into drive. I screamed as Leo struck the passenger side door. The car rocked. My window shattered.

Leo reached through the broken window and tried to grab me. I slashed at his arm while trying to flatten myself to the seat.

Ben hit the gas. The car kicked up turf as it lurched forward. Leo lost his hold. The car bounced over the uneven ground. We finally hit the shoulder of the road and then the pavement.

An oncoming car blared its horn and swerved around us. I rushed to sit upright and look in the passenger side mirror. The overgrown drive of the abandoned house was empty.

21

BEN'S SHIRT WAS tattered and soggy with blood. He held the driver's door shut with one hand while, white-knuckled, he kept the car on the road with his other.

My hands stung. I was bracing myself in my seat, now covered in shattered glass. The icy autumn wind whistled in through the broken window, making a maelstrom of my hair.

"We have to pull over." My voice was hoarse, and I shook from all the adrenaline in my system.

"The hell we do!" Ben glanced with wild eyes up to the rearview and back to the road.

"We can't drive the car like this, and we need to check your shoulder. You're bleeding pretty bad."

His jawline twitched.

"Ben, please."

"Ten minutes. I'll stop in ten minutes."

I swallowed and nodded. It would get us a good distance from Leo since he was moving on foot. At least we thought he was.

It was ten very long minutes.

We pulled over. Ben slammed the car into park, shoved open the ruined door, and left the car. I turned the engine off but left the keys in the ignition. I joined him where he paced near the trunk.

I leaned against the car, my hand pressed against my aching ribs. "Hey, you alright?"

He gave a manic laugh and ran a shaking hand through his hair. "How the *hell* are we supposed to stop this guy? He almost killed us!"

"You removed the tether. The spell worked."

He scoffed. "A lot of fucking good that did."

"He can shift back now," I explained. "He's not trapped anymore. That's a big deal."

Ben shook his head. "Alex, we can't do this alone. We tried, but we don't know what we're up against. Something else is going on with him. Without a Shield, my arm would've been toast."

"I don't know who to contact," I said. "Our people are busy dealing with their shit in Hopewell, and the lupine up here don't want to help us."

"We need a healer." Ben made a face like he'd seen something foul. "His throat . . . That busted tether caused some sort of infection to take hold."

Whatever had festered inside Leo was eating him alive. The look in his eyes, even after Ben freed him from the tether, was pure rage. He couldn't focus. He struggled to control his actions. He lashed out.

But tied up in all of that, I'd also seen pain and grief.

"What about Clare? She was mixing up those teas and made a salve for Steven's wounds." And there was the tension I'd sensed between her and Steven.

Ben finally settled beside me. "You think she'd help us?"

"She told me about my grandfather's friend. Maybe she'll see the benefit of helping us," I reasoned. "You have a card with their contact info, right? For the festival?"

He nodded.

"It's early, so I'll call her later." I touched my fingers to his arm. "Can I see your shoulder?"

I helped him out of his ruined shirt. Leo's claws had punctured the fabric, skin, and muscle around Ben's collarbone. The wounds looked deep and were still bleeding. I searched through the first aid kit in the car for gauze and a bandage. Ben rested his hand on my hip and monitored the roadside shadows as I dressed the wound.

After caring for Ben's injury, we tried to make the car drivable. I wrapped my hand in a towel and brushed the glass off the seats and dash. We bundled up in jackets, hats, and gloves to deal with the breeze since we had nothing to cover the missing window. Ben tied the driver's door shut as best he could with a bungee cord despite the bent frame. Bloodied, dirty, and exhausted, we drove north.

IT WAS ANOTHER hour before we pulled off at a roadside park. The state of our car received a few second glances. We ate a breakfast of apples and granola bars while sitting on a bench at an overlook. The sun peeked over a small lake. Exhaustion was hitting us hard, and my body ached from my latest encounter with Leo.

"We could make it to the cabin today." Ben tossed his apple core into the underbrush. "Or do you want to find a different place to lure Leo?"

"The cabin," I said. "I'm done playing this cat-and-mouse game with him."

"How do you feel knowing you're this close to the place?"

"I have mixed feelings," I said. "I've been waiting to get answers ever since I found that damn key in my Grandpa's stuff. For some reason, I feel the cabin will have them. But what if it doesn't?"

Ben took my hand in his. "Then it doesn't, and it might be best if you let it go."

I frowned and pulled my hand away. I didn't appreciate the suggestion. It enforced my belief that he couldn't understand what I was feeling.

He tilted his head and reached out to touch my cheek, but I leaned away and stood.

He let his hand fall back to his lap. "Alex."

"I know you're trying to be comforting, but telling me to 'get over it' if I don't find answers doesn't help," I said.

"I'm worried if we don't find anything at this cabin, you're going to carry that disappointment around with you long after we leave the place."

I bit my lip and looked over the lake. He didn't seem to understand why I found this all so upsetting. How could a seemingly kind and caring grandfather be a man who'd abandon his wife and kid to run off to the woods and do who knows what with strangers and possibly a Hunter?

I blinked back tears.

Could anyone be trusted to be who they say they are?

And if my grandfather eventually lost parts of himself to the darker parts of his wolf, what did that mean for me? Who would I become?

Ben stood and wrapped his arms around me. I turned into him, closed my eyes, and inhaled. His scent and the steady beat of his heart soothed the anger jackhammering in my mind.

I was so tired.

Everything hurt.

He rested his cheek against my head and rubbed a hand lightly over my back. "We have all day to get there. Do you want to find somewhere to take a shower and get some sleep? I wouldn't mind changing out of these clothes."

"What about Leo? He's going to hurt more people."

"Right now we need rest or we're going to be worthless when we have to face him again," Ben said. "Don't you think?"

I nodded and sniffled.

"Let me drive. You can close your eyes and nap," he said.

Anxiety about the cabin lurked at the edges of my consciousness. There was no expressway to our destination, so we coasted at a casual fifty-five miles per hour through patches of woods, fields, and one-stoplight towns. It was for the best since a chilly breeze whistled through our messed-up car.

My mind fell to cataloging all the scents my nose caught in the autumn air. The landscape was beautiful, with trees full of colorful leaves interspersed between the pines. I leaned back in the passenger seat, pulled a blanket around me, and watched the scenery pass.

I AWOKE TO find us driving along a body of water. Rubbing my eyes, I looked over at Ben. "Where are we?"

"Traverse City." Shadows were beneath his eyes. "There was a Dogman sighting called in to a radio show, but it was proven to be a hoax."

I looked out at the water again before checking the map. "Why don't we stop for a few? We'll check your bandages and stretch our legs. There's a roadside park up on the left. I could try giving Clare a call, too."

We pulled over at a little park with an outhouse and picnic tables. The body of water was a bay, and the wind made the surface choppy. A windsurfer was preparing his gear to go out.

I stretched my legs and arms, my body protesting the movements. I admired Ben's wide wingspan as he stretched and the way the wind tossed his hair around. He caught me staring. His chin dipped, and those stunning eyes disappeared behind dark lashes.

"What?" I smiled. "I like what I see."

He chuckled and shook his head. He held his hand out to me, and I went to him.

"The car wasn't sounding good on the drive here," he said. "Should we take it to a repair shop? Maybe they have a better way to secure the door so it doesn't completely fall off."

I snapped my fingers and pointed at him. "Jessie's Auto Repair."

His forehead wrinkled. "What?"

"In Detroit," I said. "I met Jessica at your show. She was visiting family, but she owns a car repair place here."

"Oh, okay. You hadn't mentioned that."

"We can stop by her shop and try to squeeze into today's schedule." I motioned to the picnic tables. "But first let me look at your shoulder."

He sat down, and I helped him out of his sweatshirt. The fabric of his t-shirt was bloodied.

I didn't like it. "I wonder if you should get stitches."

"I'd rather not go to urgent care. Too expensive and we wouldn't know the doctor." He handed me clean gauze and fresh bandaging.

"Have you stitched someone up before?"

"I've only seen Trish do it. I haven't tried it myself."

He looked from his wounded shoulder up at me. "Do you want to give it a go?"

"Let's try another bandage first." I redressed the wound. His cheeks were flushed. I pressed the back of my hand to his forehead. His skin was hot to the touch. "Do you feel sick?"

He shrugged, then winced. "I'm not feeling the best, but we haven't slept or had a decent meal in a while."

I looked from Ben to our wrecked car and back. He was right. We needed to stop and regroup if we were going to have any chance against Leo. While he pulled his sweatshirt back on, I got out my phone and asked for Clare's card. When she didn't pick up, I left a message asking for her help and included the cabin's address.

Leo was my problem, and I wasn't sure Clare would help. A part of me believed she wasn't like Betty or Steven. Hopefully, she didn't view the danger Leo posed as being the responsibility of one person to remedy.

Helping Leo would help all of us.

22

BEN AND I walked into the cramped and dirty front room of the repair shop. My ears were greeted by Black Sabbath and my nose by oil and gasoline. Ozzy's vocals were accompanied by the loud whirring and clanking noises from the shop floor to our right.

I poked my head through the open doorway, scanning the room full of lifts, tools, and mechanics. "Hello?"

Jessica approached and stepped through the doorway, wiping her hands on a greasy rag. "What can I do for—" She stopped. "You're the lady from Detroit. Alex. And you're Ben Sharpe." She tucked the rag in the back pocket of her overalls and eyed our disheveled appearance. "You two look like shit."

"We need your help with our car," I said. "It's the Camry over there. Can you fit us in today?"

Jessica walked to the window. "Your car looks like shit, too. I'll get it on a lift to see what's broken." She held out her hand, palm up. "Keys?"

I surrendered the keys. Ten minutes later she was back in the front room with us. "I can fix it completely, but it'll be finished tomorrow. Or I can fix it kind of, and it'll be ready in a few hours."

"Just enough that it's safe to drive, and we don't lose the door," I said.

Jessica nodded. "Did you know about the sigil by the wheel?"

My pulse stuttered and Ben shifted from one foot to another. She recognized the magic sigil on the sticker? Was she a wizard?

She looked between the two of us, expectant.

"Yeah," Ben said. "We'd like to leave that."

"You're wordweavers," she said.

It confirmed she was familiar with supernatural beings. The term was slang for a wizard.

"That's okay. Wordweavers can be dicks, but I don't mind fixing their cars." Her tone wasn't unfriendly, just matter-of-fact.

I snorted, glancing at Ben. Wizards considered themselves at the top of the social ladder in Hopewell. I found any opinions suggesting otherwise a bit humorous.

Jessica looked at me with a slight frown, apparently confused by my reaction.

"Sorry," I lowered my voice. "He is, but I'm lupine."

She gave a curt nod. "Having met you, that makes sense."

What exactly was that supposed to mean? I blushed, chagrined, and Ben chuckled.

"I need to fix your car now if you want it back today," Jessica said. "Give me your number. When I'm done, I'll message you."

"Is there a doctor or medic Ben could see while you're working on the car?" I wrote down my phone number. "Someone discreet. And a cheap motel nearby where we can shower and sleep?"

"The motel is three blocks away. Here's the guy I know who can repair the wordweaver." Jessica flipped over a flyer from the counter and scribbled a name, phone number, and hotel chain on the paper. Despite her annoyance, she lowered the car from the lift so Ben and I could get our bags. I also grabbed my grandfather's box.

"So what's your guess?" I asked Ben as we walked to the motel. "For Jessica. She referred to herself as a maker when we met."

"A maker? Mechanic. Seems comfortable in cities. From Detroit." He shrugged. "More than likely a gremlin. A lot of them settled on the east side of the state during the automotive boom. They're incredibly intelligent and savvy with anything electrical or mechanical."

I sighed. "Is there like an extended family directory?"

Ben winked and pushed his glasses up his nose. "I have books you can borrow when we get back to Hopewell." I liked hearing him say that. Going back to Hopewell. Together.

"Another thing for me to accomplish when we get home."

Once we had the room, Ben called Jessica's medical contact. He was a volunteer clinic doctor and agreed to meet Ben at the motel. I dropped my bag to the floor, set the box on the bed, and looked at Ben. "Shower or bed?"

He set his bag down. "Shower."

I grinned and pulled Ben by the belt loops of his jeans into the bathroom. His smile was a flicker, his cheeks more rosy than before. I released him and touched the back of my hand to his forehead. His skin was still hot. "Are you feeling worse?"

"I'm tired, that's all," he said with none of his usual playfulness.

I'd hoped for a shared shower and a romp in bed before falling asleep wrapped in his arms, but that could wait. He wasn't well, and we were injured and exhausted. Plus, as soon as the car was done, I wanted to get to the cabin.

I helped Ben out of his sweatshirt, t-shirt, and bloody bandaging. The wound was looking angry, with the skin around it a purplish red. When my fingers found the button of his jeans, he placed his hands over mine. He kissed my forehead. "I got it, thanks."

Definitely not in the mood. I removed my hands. "Okay. Yell if you need anything." I exited the bathroom and perched on the edge of the bed, holding my hands in my lap. My heel bounced as I scanned the room for something to keep me occupied. If I laid down now, I wouldn't be getting back up anytime soon. I gave the collar of my shirt a sniff and grimaced. I also didn't want to get the bed filthy before we slept in it.

I pulled my grandfather's box over to me and removed the lid. Why had the box been kept at my parents' house and not the cabin? I flipped through the articles for what felt like the hundredth time, rereading the headlines. Dottie said Grandpa and Theo went to the cabin to help mitigate the dark parts of their wolves. Was my grandfather the one who killed the livestock during the years he fled to the cabin? Or was it another werewolf who he saw his past self in and wanted to help?

And did the Dogman have anything to do with this? Or was he a cryptid who made a convenient scapegoat for an out-of-control werewolf? Maybe the Dogman was used to scare others as Ben suspected. But to whose benefit?

The shower turned off and soon Ben emerged from the bathroom, trailing steam. He wore only a towel slung low around his waist. The wolf in me immediately noticed, and that achy hunger I got around him gnawed low in my navel.

He smiled at me as if reading my mind. "Your turn."

He'd more than likely noticed my eyes. They shifted color whenever I lusted after him. I made sure to sigh wistfully as I entered the bathroom. The sound of his chuckle warmed me as much as the hot water. If only the shower could wash away all the dread of dealing with Leo.

As expected, I was covered in bruises and minor cuts from our fight at the abandoned house. The cuts would close by tomorrow morning, and the bruises would disappear within a few days.

When I finished my shower, I towel-dried my hair the best I could and got dressed. I paused, hearing voices in the room. My immediate thought was to rush into room to protect Ben. Instead, I took a calming breath and quietly left the bathroom. A man two-thirds Ben's height, presumably the doctor, was finishing work on stitches in his injured shoulder.

"All patched up." He repacked a small medical bag. "Remember the medication for the fever."

Ben stood and shook his hand. "Thanks."

"Thank you," I said.

After the doctor left, Ben and I crawled into the bed. If my muscles could audibly sigh, they would. Ben curved his body behind mine, his hand resting at the dip of my waist.

"Ben?"

"Hmm?"

"I'm sorry this isn't the fun road trip we'd thought it would be." He didn't respond.

"And I'm sorry you were hurt. If you want to bail, I understand." Unlike my injuries, Ben's would take the usual time to heal.

He briefly tightened his hold and kissed the back of my neck. "Like I told my mom, we're in this together."

I brought his hand from my waist to my lips and kissed his knuckles. "Thank you."

"YOU LOOK BETTER." Jessica held out the car keys to me. "And you don't smell as bad."

"Thank you," I said. "And thanks for the medical contact."

"Here's your bill." She set the slip of paper on the counter.

My eyes widened at seeing the number. Ben picked up a pen and the invoice. "Can I borrow this for a minute?"

"Borrow it?" Jessica shrugged. "As long as it's paid before you leave."

Ben pulled his phone out of his pocket and stepped outside. The door swung shut, leaving Jessica and me in awkward silence.

"I used a sledgehammer to bend the frame on the driver's side back into shape," she said. "It's not precise, but the door closes again."

"Thanks."

"There was fur in the passenger door assembly near the broken window," she stated.

"Yup."

"Yours?"

"Nope."

"So whose is it?" If Jessica was picking up on my social cues to 'drop it,' she was ignoring them.

I folded my arms across my chest. "I'd rather not talk about it."

"Oh." She shrugged. "Okay."

Ben returned and set the invoice and pen back on the counter. "I wrote down credit card info on there. You can use that for payment."

Jessica ran the transaction and handed us the receipt. "Thank you for your business. If you're nearby when you wreck your car again, you can bring it here."

Ben chuckled and I grinned. "We'll be sure to do that. Thanks for your help."

We hauled our bags and my grandpa's box back out to the car. "Who paid for the repairs?" I asked.

He winced. "My parents. I know I'll eventually regret it, but we can't put all our fuckups on your parents' tab."

"That couldn't have been easy for you. Thanks."

Ben reaching out for help to anyone in his family other than his sister was a big deal. I was glad he took that step. Hopefully he could build toward the closer relationship with them he seemed to want.

WE DROVE TWO more hours, stopping briefly for groceries, before arriving at the address Dottie gave us. Pine needles and pine cones littered the dirt driveway winding into the woods. Broad bands of sunlight reached between the pine trees, emphasizing the orderly pattern in which they were planted. The drive ended in a small clearing of struggling grass and wildflowers. A single-story wood cabin, windows dark, awaited us.

My pulse hammered. This was it . . . the end of the road in my search for who my grandfather was, and what I might expect for my future surviving as a werewolf.

23

EVEN THOUGH THE thought of entering the cabin made me uncomfortable, I had to do it. I might not get the answers I preferred, but at least there would be answers about the man who played such a pivotal role in my childhood. The grandfather I adored. The person who guided me first with spoken words and then through handwritten words on a now crumpled and worn letter.

I jumped when Ben broke the silence. "Ready to go inside?"

"Um, yeah. I'm ready." We exited the car and my sweaty fingers closed around the key in my pocket. My nose picked up the sharp scent of the pines, along with the overgrown wildflowers and aging wood of the cabin. Ben held the squeaky screen door open while I fumbled with the key in the door. The lock opened with a solid thunk.

The heavy door creaked as I pushed it open. I remained in the doorway, letting the scents of the new space come to me. Moist wood and molding tile. Damp and deserted. As I stepped into a long narrow kitchen, I imagined my grandfather doing the same in years past. It was dark inside the cabin and as cold as it was outside.

This place brought him peace when the wolf in him became unmanageable and longed to run.

A clicking noise startled me out of my thoughts. Ben flipped on the light switch inside the entrance. The kitchen lit up. "How're you feeling?"

I swallowed, my throat suddenly dry. "I'm not sure yet."

"We're staying, right?"

"Definitely. I want to search for answers about what Grandpa was doing here."

"I'll bring in our bags." He kissed my cheek.

"If it's too much for your shoulder, I can grab them later." I passed cautiously through the living room, steps light, my nose searching for anything left behind. Dust, ash, and damp fabric. I strained to catch the aroma of my grandfather's aftershave, a scent imprinted on my mind from childhood. His lingering presence in the letter he'd left me.

Nothing. Not even hints of his friends who'd more recently been here.

A fine layer of dust covered most surfaces, except for the few pieces of furniture draped in fraying sheets. The cabin's walls were built from logs, reminding me of a building playset I had as a little girl. Had it been Grandpa's? Sparse decorations adorned the walls. Everything in the room seemed scavenged, like it had been abandoned but found a second home here. A set of bookshelves caught my attention. I had to make a concentrated effort to continue my initial sweep of the cabin instead of stopping and getting lost in whatever was on those shelves.

I slunk from the living room out into an enclosed sitting room. The damp odors in my nose thickened. Large screens covered the majority of the walls where there would usually be windows. Noise from Ben closing the car door sounded to my right. The sound of running water came from my left, more than likely a river or creek where the cabin backed into the woods.

The sitting room contained the same odds-and-ends furniture as the living room. Shelving held board games and puzzles. An atlas and a deck of cards were on a coffee table. I grabbed the cards, something for Ben and me to do during a research break, but noticed it was incomplete. The deck only contained nines, tens, aces, and face cards.

I tossed the deck back on the table and returned to the living room. A hallway, enclosed like the porch, led off the kitchen and had several doors. Ben came back inside with our bags. "That's the last of it. Do you want to sleep in front of the fireplace?"

"Hmm?" I looked from the hall to him.

"Instead of the bedrooms, we could sleep in front of the fire," he said. "Or are we risking burning the place down if something is living in the chimney?"

"Maybe shine a light up it and check?"

Ben's lips quirked. "I'm going to get a raccoon in the face, aren't I?"

I laughed. "Maybe not, then."

He hauled the bags to the living room. "I'll drop them here for now."

My attention returned to the breezy hallway. Daylight was fading fast. The setting sun shone onto the cabin's walls, turning them a golden brown. Each of the three doors in the hallway opened into a small bedroom with a window facing the back of the cabin and the river. Every room had a small dresser and bed frame with a bare mattress.

Which one had my grandfather used? I couldn't find his elusive scent in the bedrooms either.

A bathroom was at the end of the hall. Rust and mildew filled my nose. The cracked tile was cold against my fingers as I felt for a light switch and turned it on. The room held a sink, mirror, toilet, and shower.

The floor creaked out in the hallway. "Alex?"

"Back here," I called.

Ben appeared in the doorway. "I wanted to set wards on the front door and windows, then do you want to eat?"

"Sure. I can make the sandwiches."

I found a closet in the living room with blankets and uncovered a broken-in sofa. By the time Ben came back inside, I had sandwiches made, and we sat together to eat.

"Your grandma and parents didn't know about this place?" Ben asked.

"I think my grandma did," I said. "But she never came here or knew what he was doing."

"That didn't piss her off?"

"I think I'm more upset about it than she is. My grandma told me once, 'I was married to your grandfather long enough to know the support he needed.' Maybe part of supporting him was allowing him this private part of his life."

"And trusting him," Ben said.

I glanced at him, wondering if his comment was meant for more than my grandparents' relationship. "Yeah, maybe." I brushed the sandwich crumbs off my lap, got up from our nest of blankets, and started for the nearest set of wooden cupboards and bookshelves.

Ben watched me from the couch. "Whatever you find here doesn't determine who you are or will be. You know that, right?"

My gut twisted and a growl sprung into my throat. "How could you understand how messed up this whole situation has me?" I strained on my tiptoes to reach the photo albums on the top shelf. "You despise your grandfather. I adored mine."

Ben stood and joined me at the bookshelf. "You've told me how important he was to you. I get it. I see how close you are to your family." He reached past my fingertips to pull down the albums and hand them to me. "I wasn't born hating Reginald. I used to idolize him."

I hugged the large albums, smelling of dust and leather. "What was it like? Your apprenticeship with him."

"It was amazing. I thought I was the luckiest kid alive. I mean, having the ability to cast magic? And your teacher being one of the best wizards around?" The memory lit up his features with happiness. "I couldn't get enough. Magic became my life. My identity."

My heart sank for him.

"And Reginald took that away." The brightness faded, but the anger his grandfather's name usually brought to his eyes was more subdued.

"So, can you say you knew the real him?"

"I didn't know *all* of him," Ben said. "Or maybe part of me did, but my love and respect for him kept me from seeing those faults."

"That's what I'm worried about. I *thought* I knew Grandpa. What if the man I'd cherished and trusted was lying to us? What if he lost his battle with the darker part of his wolf and hurt people? What if eventually that happens to me?" Ben opened his mouth, but I didn't let him speak. "Don't say it won't because there's no way for you to know that."

"No, you're right. There isn't." He took more books down for himself, and we sat back on the couch. "But knowing how Reginald operates has me watching for those behaviors in myself. It helps me be a better person. I'm a wizard because I descended from Reginald's line, but I'm not him."

But Ben also wasn't lupine. Wizards didn't have a primal beast in their blood and bones who could effortlessly inflict harm.

He opened a book. "So, what are we looking for in these?"

"Anything. What was this place to him? Who was here with him?" I opened an album across my lap. "What was he doing?"

The album's pages were yellowed with age. A younger version of my grandfather smiled at me from a photo, his arms around two other people I recognized now. The handwritten caption beneath the photo read: Dottie, Alex, Theo.

Flipping through the pages, I glimpsed my grandfather's life at the cabin. There were photos of the three friends hiking, fishing, and sitting by a campfire. Seeing his smile made me smile, and I missed him even more. I studied one of the photos more closely. Both my grandfather and Theo wore dog tags.

I took out my phone before remembering there was no cell signal available. I looked over at Ben. "Did you notice how far away the town is where we got groceries?"

"About twenty minutes." He closed the small hardbound book he was browsing. "Check this out, it's a handbook for The Civilian Conservation Corps."

"The what?"

"They worked with the Michigan Department of Conservation to replant the state after lumbering wiped out the majority of the forests."

"Is that why the pine trees we've seen are growing in lines?" I asked.

Ben nodded and handed me the book.

I flipped to the back of the title page. "What year was the first Dogman sighting?"

"1887," he said. "In Wexford county by some lumberjacks."

"1937 is the publication date on this." I flipped through the pages until I reached a few blank pages near the end. "There's an unlabeled list of names and dates written here." My grandfather's name was near the bottom of the list.

Ben grinned. "Maybe your granddad was part of Roosevelt's Tree Army."

I shook my head. "He wasn't born until 1945. Is the tree army still around?"

"No, the program ended when the funding was funneled into World War II. The Michigan Department of Conservation became the DNR, though. That's still around."

"How do you know all this stuff?"

"I was stuck in Hopewell for a while, remember? I read a lot of books." He shrugged. "I picked up a few things."

I kissed him. "It's pretty handy having a book nerd around."

Ben pushed his glasses up his nose and winked.

I ran my finger down the list of names. "There's a surname in here, Strobus. Why does that sound familiar?"

"It's Clare's and her mom's last name," he said. "You probably noticed it on their business card."

"And the surname of Hall. That's Steven's last name."

"And Cathy's and Mark's."

I pointed to the first name on the list. "Robert Hall." I moved my finger to the date. "1887." I set the book aside, stood, and started pacing. "When I met Steven, he said his family 'watches over' the northern part of the state. And remember, Clare told us he's in charge of everyone's safety. He shuts down anything that may bring the supernatural citizens unwanted attention and tosses a bit of fear in the mix to keep Commoners hesitant to muck around too much in the woods. What if Steven is the current Dogman?"

Ben was nodding. "Makes sense. Both the lupine and hamadryads would benefit from forested lands being replanted and preserved. The hamadryads can't exist without the trees."

"And the lupine have large areas of semi-secluded land to run free as their wolves." I pointed at the book. "Maybe that list is a record of the forest caretakers over the years. That could explain why the Dogman sightings don't happen every year. Some years the hamadryads take on the responsibility."

"And why the descriptions of the Dogman vary. The Dogman is not a single person, but more than one lupine. There are multiple werewolves throughout the years that act as the Dogman," Ben said. "But isn't your grandfather's name on the list?"

"No. Way." I jumped back on the couch with Ben and grabbed the next photo album. "What if Grandpa wasn't killing livestock, but was instead protecting the forests, and the supernatural citizens who lived here, as the Dogman?"

The next album was older. Many photos were of natural landscapes familiar from our drive to the cabin. Every several photos, my grandfather would be in the frame as well. His smile was small. Quiet. It didn't radiate happiness like the previous album, but instead a type of relief. Peace.

Toward the end of the album, another man appeared. The photos would suggest the two were friends. Like my grandfather, the man appeared younger. He wasn't wearing his police uniform, but I recognized Ed Miller, Dottie's husband.

A Hunter.

My chest momentarily seized. All the relief I'd felt minutes before was replaced by an anxious dread. Then came growling. I shut the photo album and pushed it aside.

"That's your frustrated growl." Ben looked up from another book. "What's going on?"

I shook my head. "If Grandpa was coming up here to protect people, there's no way he'd be working with a Hunter. It doesn't make sense. I'm still missing part of the story."

"It's getting late. Why don't we go to bed and start again tomorrow morning?" he said. "I can build us that fire. The damper was shut, so we should be okay."

There were more photo albums to go through, but he was right. We needed to stay rested and ready for when Leo arrived. "I'm not sure I'll be able to sleep, but I'll try."

Within five minutes of curling up beside Ben, I was out.

I WOKE TO embers glowing in the hearth, but the room hadn't chilled. Careful not to disturb Ben, I slipped from beneath the covers. I checked the time. It would still be several hours before the sun made an appearance. Stifling a yawn, I padded toward the bathroom in my bare feet. When I approached the long hallway, the scents of the night hit my nose. I paused, inhaling. The temperature was warmer. The air was pure and unblemished by anything man-made.

The wolf in me stirred, and warmth bloomed throughout my body. I closed my eyes and took a large lungful of air. Pines, water, and soil. I opened my eyes and the landscape outside the cabin sharpened. The lazy breeze rustled the pine needles and branches. I suddenly wanted to be enveloped in the unseasonably warm air.

After using the bathroom, I slunk out the front, wincing at the squeaky screen door. Outside, the breeze picked up. I shivered as it lifted my hair and tickled my skin. Looking up through the trees, the inky sky was splattered with stars, making me feel both very small and a part of something larger.

The underbrush announced the presence of a small woodland animal. My nostrils flared and my attention immediately snapped to it. The water in the creek was louder, as well as the call of a nighttime bird and insects.

I stretched my arms at my sides, wiggled my fingers, and dug my toes into the loose soil. A low rumble like an approaching thunderstorm sounded in my chest. I wondered what it would feel like to let my wolf fully surface here. Even though the whole rabbit thing had been mortifying, shifting even that far and darting through the woods had been thrilling. Every bit of my body was hooked into something larger. It felt so natural, not something disturbing I should lock away and hide.

And why wouldn't it be? It's who I was. I leaned into the feeling, allowing my hands to shift. My gums burned as my teeth lengthened. The points of my ears were tickled by my curls as they pushed up through my hair. The environment became more vivid: scent, sound, and sight.

What about control? Could I remain clearheaded enough so no one would be in danger? I sent a fleeting glance over my shoulder. Ben should be safe from my wolf. My body recognized him as someone who wouldn't harm me. The wards would alert him to intruders, and I'd hear them since I'd stick to the woods around the cabin.

The warm autumn breeze caught me in a sudden swirl of scents. The tree branches creaked and rustled. Another growl surfaced and my muscles twitched. I wanted to run.

No. I *needed* to run.

Without another thought, I pulled my nightshirt off over my head and let it drop onto the ground. I stepped out of my underwear. I felt so light and alive that I couldn't stop grinning. Finally, I let go of the last bit of restraint holding back the wolf inside me. Adrenaline flooded my system, curbing the pain of grinding bone, slipping muscle, and popping cartilage. A pelt of gray fur emerged to cover my body.

I parted my jaws, letting my tongue loll out, and took even more scent in through the roof of my mouth. My mind exploded into a multitude of colors. I snapped my jaws shut, and I was off at a loping run. In this balanced hybrid of woman and wolf, I deftly navigated the woods. The knowledge to do so had been programmed into my muscles generations ago. Why hadn't I done it sooner?

I cut through the woods, around the cabin, and down toward the smell of water. My stride didn't break as I crashed into a river. I shook the water from my fur and continued along the riverbed. My ears and nose were in overdrive, flooding my mind with shapes and colors to accompany the sounds and scents of the nocturnal world around me.

The odor of something large and warm caught my attention. I broke away from the creek and dashed between the trees to the peak of the bank. When I reached the edge of the woods, several white flags bounded away from me. Without hesitation, I gave chase, dashing after the deer into a large field.

My pulse thundered in my ears, mixed with the frightened heartbeat of the animals ahead of me. The stink of their fear blew back into my face. A growling bark left my body. All I wanted at that moment was to draw up beside one, sink my teeth into the warm flesh of its throat, and pull it down to the earth with me.

Something in me balked.

No.

I slowed to a stop. A whine slipped past my lips as the deer bounded away. I'd strayed too far from the cabin and Ben. Would I be able to find my way back, or was I lost like before?

I shook the chase from my body. A loud crack sounded and a chunk of soil and plant matter was erased from the ground near my feet. My gaze jerked to the opposite woodline. Movement part way up the trunk of a tree. A neon splash of unnatural orange in the murky light of the approaching dawn.

Another crack and the side of my neck exploded in hot pain. I yelped and pressed my fingers to the spot. The scent of my blood flooded my nose. Someone was shooting at me. Sudden rage scorched my veins.

Go back. Run.

My body lowered itself closer to the ground, among the cover of the tall grasses, and charged toward the movement in the trees.

Go back!

My vision grew hazy at the edges. The prey was huddled atop a wooden platform in the tree. A figure in camo with a neon orange hat.

I burst from the tall grasses and crashed my body into the tree. A startled cry was shaken from the platform above. The tree shuddered up the length of its trunk, and a rain of needles and pine cones fell to the forest floor. Slamming my shoulder against the tree again caused a rifle to fall from the platform. I snatched up the object that'd caused me pain and smashed it into pieces against the ground and trunk of the tree.

Stop! Go back to the cabin!

But the wolf in me awoke to protect me. Someone inflicted pain on my body, and with that came a fury I couldn't ignore. As with the first time I shifted into a werewolf, my consciousness became detached. The snarling noises filling the air couldn't be from me, could they?

The screaming didn't stop from the platform above. Cries for help. Another swirl of autumn air wrapped around me. The sharp scent of fear was irresistible. My claws sank into the mangled bark of the tree. I'd climb. I'd leap atop the prey. I'd sink my teeth into his throat and pull him down to the earth with me.

24

I LURCHED AWAKE, panting, my hands clenching the blankets. Sweat covered my face and chest, and trickled down my back. Surrounding me were the scents of the cabin and Ben. My flesh broke into goosebumps. It'd been months since I dealt with nightmares related to my shifting.

My body ached, probably from the hard floor. We should have hauled one of the bed mattresses into the living room. Sinking back down to the covers, I turned to face Ben. He lay asleep, his lips slightly parted, his breath even and unbothered. He appeared at peace. I wanted to bury my nose in the crook of his neck and take him into my lungs.

I smiled, raised a hand, and gently brushed his dark shaggy hair away from his face. My touch marred his skin with a dark smear. The scent of blood filled my nose.

My stomach twisted. I yanked my hand away. My palm and fingers were sticky and dark. I sat up again, my breath quickening. I raised my other hand to find the same, but my arm was darkened to the elbow. I seized hold of Ben's shoulder and shook him. "Ben!"

He groaned and lifted his arm, his eyelids fluttering open. "What's . . ." His eyes flew open wide. "Alex? What's wrong? Is it Leo?"

Relief flooded me, and I started to cry. "I thought I—"

"Hey, it's alright. I'm here." He sat up and fumbled for his phone. Bright, electric light blinded me.

I raised my hand, blinking, to shield my eyes.

"Alex, where are your clothes?"

I looked down at my bare skin. "I don't know. I had this nightmare..." I threw the covers aside. The odor of water and decaying vegetation wafted into the air. My feet and lower legs were covered in mud. "No. This isn't real." I shook my head. "I'm still dreaming."

Ben stood and offered me a hand to help me to my feet. "Are you hurt?"

"I don't know." My neck throbbed with pain. "Am I *not* dreaming? I must be dreaming." I stumbled away and rushed to the bathroom.

The only mirror was a partially clouded one tacked above the sink. I flinched away from the image of my face. My mouth and chin were also darkened by blood. Leaves were caught up in the snarls of my hair.

My heart was going to pound its way through my ribcage.

"Alex, talk to me," Ben demanded. "Tell me what happened."

I turned on him, snarling and baring my sharp teeth. "I said I don't know!"

He frowned, raised his hands in defense, and stepped back. The acidic scent of his fear crept up my nose.

"No, I'm sorry. I don't remember everything." My mind raced, trying to recover the past several hours. I turned on the shower and ducked into the spray. "I went for a run." When Ben didn't respond, I continued. "It felt so good to run at the campground, I wanted to feel it again. The wind, the trees, everything... I wanted to be a part of it."

His voice was unsure. "You shifted? Fully?"

"Yes. I thought I understood that part of myself better." I scrubbed at the stains on my body, trying to rid myself of them. "But there was a hunter."

"What!" Ben's voice rose sharply. "A Hunter is out there? Is it Miller?"

"No. A regular hunter. I think he was hunting deer. I'm a different shape and color, but he shot at me anyway!" Hot angry tears mixed with the water. "It hurt. I wanted him to stop."

"Did he hit you?"

My fingers found where the bullet tore the skin at the side of my neck. "Yes." I knew his next question and answered it before he could ask. "I don't know if he's alive." I clenched my teeth against the rising panic and rubbed at my stinging arms harder.

Ben reached forward and caught my wrist and held it away from my body. "Stop."

Panting, I froze. My claws were red with fresh blood. When had my claws appeared? A strange moan left me.

"Shh. Slow down." Ben ran his fingers lightly down my arm under the spray of the water. "Please, let me help you."

I leaned against him, allowing him to brush his hands over my face, my limbs, and the curve of my neck and shoulders. The blood, dirt, and leaves swirled into the drain at my feet. Ben bundled me in a towel and ransacked the bathroom cabinet for a first aid kit. He wrapped my forearm from wrist to elbow and dressed the wound near my neck.

Dazed, I let him guide me back to the living room. I sat on the sofa and tried to modulate my breathing while he dug clothing out of my duffel bag.

"What am I going to do, Ben?"

He handed me the clothing. "We're not sure what happened, right? We have to figure that out first. Do you remember where you found him?"

"It was a field." I sorted through the memory, clear until I reached the tree where the hunter was perched. Until the part of me that was wolf took over. "Across the river." I dressed. "I need to know what happened to the guy."

Ben frowned but nodded. "Is it somewhere we could drive?"

"I only know the way through the woods."

He pulled on his jacket. I shook my head. "Stay here."

"What? No." Ben scowled. "Stop discarding me. I told you I can help."

"I'll bring my phone and call you if I run into trouble." I started toward the front door.

He followed me, his voice rising. "We don't have a cell signal out here!"

"I'll be okay," I said. "It's light out now, and I won't look like an animal."

"Does that make a difference?" he asked. "Don't these guys accidentally shoot each other?"

I pushed open the screen door. "If you come along, you'll—" The overpowering odor of blood assaulted my nose. My stomach twisted, and I felt I was going to get sick.

Ben stopped beside me. His voice turned hoarse. "Shit."

Laying in a heap beside the front door was the mangled body of a deer.

Adrenaline coursed through me, causing me to tremble. I crept closer to the corpse. Suppressing the urge to gag, I crouched beside it. I tapped into my wolf senses, amplifying the scents around us. The bright coppery odor of blood was the same Ben washed from my body.

Shaking with relief, I looked up at Ben. "This is where the blood came from. I must have spared the deer hunter."

He watched me closely, uncertainty creasing his forehead.

My heart ached. Ben's caution was linked to me. I would never willingly hurt him, but I couldn't be upset over his reaction. I'd woken up covered in blood and dirt beside him, not being able to remember the night before.

Ben glanced around the clearing of the cabin. "What do we do with the deer?"

"I'll move it into the woods away from the cabin." Nausea threatened as I pulled the carcass from in front of the cabin deeper into the trees so the forest could reclaim it. I touched my fingertips to the deer's neck and felt a pang of guilt. "I'm sorry."

When I left the woods and rejoined Ben, he was standing near the car, cursing.

My heart stuttered. "Holy. Hell."

The front tires of the car had been wrenched off and discarded on the ground. Ben and I turned, scanning the woodline. I scented the air. I got a noseful of Ben's fear and lingering traces of Leo.

WE WERE STILL brainstorming on how to contain Leo until we found a healer when an engine sounded from down the drive. A green jeep emerged from the shadows of the pine trees. Through the windshield, Clare smiled and held up a hand in greeting.

Hope flickered in my chest. I met her in the driveway.

She shut the jeep door. Her posture relaxed when I smiled.

"Hey," I said. "You got my message. Thank you for coming."

"This has to end," she said. "We already had an officer stop by the cabin. Steven said she's from a line of Hunters."

"Officer Miller." My skin broke out in goosebumps.

"She asked about you and Ben. The report of the animal attack on the beach brought her to the western lakeshore. She's been following you."

The memory of the Hunter in Hopewell was fresh in my mind. It'd been several months since the man with an active contract to kill me shot up Hell's Bells and tried to come after me. The thought of Miller tracking us caused me to shiver.

Ben appeared behind me. "What did you tell her?"

"Betty told her you two passed through, but she didn't know where you were going," she said. "She wanted Officer Miller gone."

"The three of us need to solve this Leo mess before that cop turns up," Ben said.

We went into the cabin and sat in the living room. Clare's eyes widened when she saw the mess of blankets, mud, and blood on the floor. Her complexion paled. "What happened here?"

Ben cleared the blankets away.

I hesitated, but like Ben, Clare was someone who understood the challenges involved in being different. "Last night I went for a run as my wolf. I couldn't help it. Outside, it was so..." I physically reached for the words with my hands.

Clare provided, "Welcoming."

"Yes! And it felt so—"

"Natural." She smiled.

"I ran. I thought I'd improved, synced with my wolf, so no one would get hurt. But then I came across a field where a deer hunter was in a tree. I'm not the same color as the deer, but he shot at me."

Clare's smile faded. "Deer hunters shoot dogs that run deer."

"But I'm so much larger than a dog in my wolf form, and most of the time I walk on two legs," I said. "Once I realized someone was shooting at me, the anger took over. I wrestled to get control again, but woke up, covered in mud and blood, and not remembering what happened."

"She didn't kill the guy," Ben said. "The blood was from a deer."

Clare hesitated. "How do you know that?"

"We found a carcass outside the cabin," I said, "and the blood smelled the same."

"What about the werewolf you tracked with Steven and Mom?" Clare asked. "Do you know where he is?"

"He's here," Ben said. "Leo wrecked our car last night."

I wrinkled my nose. "Leo has that awful odor of what seems like a lingering infection—"

"Like a hex," Ben said.

"—that's affecting his thoughts. Ben removed the tether, but Leo is still confused, pissed, and after us."

"And you think I can help treat this hex-like infection?" Clare looked and sounded doubtful.

"You healed Steven from his more serious wounds," I said.

"My healing is more gradual." She gave Ben a sideward glance. "It's not like a wizard's magic."

"We don't have access to a wizard with healing magic right now," I said. "And time is running short on our Leo problem. Either he's going to kill us, or Miller will catch up and take us all out."

"Have you thought of leaving a lead for the Hunter?" Clare asked. "Maybe she's the solution to Leo."

I bit my lip. It was a quick and easy fix, but was it the correct one? Was it Leo who was trying to harm us? Who was Leo without his mind clouded? Who was he without George? I thought of my grandfather and his supposed attempts to use the cabin as a place where wolves could rest and reset themselves. To gain inner peace. Balance.

"I'm not sure this hex or whatever it is within his body isn't what's driving his bloodlust," I said. "If we decide to turn Leo over to Miller, I want to make sure it's actually Leo. He shouldn't be punished for being sick. Am I making sense?"

Ben must have heard the doubt in my voice. He rubbed his hand comfortingly along the back of my upper arm.

"You sound like Alexander," Clare answered.

I swallowed, my eyes threatening tears. Her tone was too neutral to tell if it was praise or condemnation, but the mention of my grandfather prodded that hurt in my chest I felt when thinking of him.

"I'll help in any way I can," Clare said. "Mom told me Leo is incredibly strong. How will we hold him while I work?"

Ben lifted his hand. "I'm working on that. It's a new spell for me."

"New?" She looked nervous. "As in you haven't used it before?"

"The spell will contain Leo," I said. "Can you make something like the knockout tea you gave Ben? But faster-acting and more potent so it would affect a lupine's system?"

"Yes. It's all a matter of dosage."

"I can give it to Leo," I said. "Then he'll be asleep for your healing magic."

"How much time do we have?" Clare asked.

"He's been laying low during the day, and if he comes after us, it's at night," Ben said.

"So, we have today," I said.

Clare brought in an overnight bag and a few canvas totes with bundles of plants. She set up shop on the kitchen counter, and the cabin was soon filled with scents of boiling sap, flowers, and the green of chopped herbs.

I made us sandwiches as she worked. "Thank you for helping us. Ben and I knew we couldn't do it by ourselves."

"You're welcome." She stirred a thickening substance in one of the pots on the stovetop.

"We were looking through my Grandpa's books and albums last night. We found one with your family's name noted in it. Why didn't you tell us more when I asked about the Dogman?"

"It's complicated," Clare said. "For generations, the lupine and hamadryads in the area have kept each other safe. We have to. We don't have the resources other supernatural citizens have in the city." She transferred the concoction to a bowl. "Then one year Alexander visited us and it all changed."

"Why?" I set a plate with a sandwich beside her. "What did he do?"

"He brought a Hunter to our doorstep," Clare said.

"Ed Miller."

Clare nodded. "Your grandfather discovered our families' practice of using the Dogman legend to protect the forests and the supernatural citizens within it. He proposed we expand with lupine he counseled at this cabin."

"But why did he involve a Hunter?" I tried to keep a growl from my voice. The thought that my grandfather would knowingly endanger other lupine angered me.

Clare glanced at me. "Mom said that the lupine your grandfather invited here were troubled. Many weren't from this area. He found them through news reports of mass animal slaughterings. The unsolved events were chalked up to the Dogman, but the threat the offending lupine posed was serious. Ed Miller, the Hunter Alexander befriended, came here in case those lupine could no longer be reached."

I wondered if Grandpa ever gave up on someone and released them to the Hunter. I didn't ask because I didn't believe my heart could handle the answer.

Clare turned her attention to chopping a fine-leafed herb. "My family and the Halls didn't want to rely on lupine outsiders to keep us and the forests safe, especially lupine unstable enough they had to be monitored by a Hunter."

"They must have eventually made a deal," I said.

"Steven's grandmother, the Halls' matriarch at the time, made an agreement with Alexander and Ed," Claire said. "Our families allowed the recovering lupine into our ongoing Dogman charade. Ed made sure it was understood by any Hunters who wandered through that the Manistee forest was his territory to monitor."

"Why didn't you tell me this when Ben and I met you?" I asked.

"The agreement collapsed," Clare said. "With Alexander and Ed passing, Steven and Mom's generation didn't want to continue. They seem to have regressed to thinking people from outside the area have nothing to offer and are only out to cheat or harm us."

"Then why are you here?"

"Because people are complex," she said. "I don't believe it's wise to let your fears isolate you to what you know. We are richer as people when we make the effort to understand each other. As I listened to you describe what was happening with Leo, and saw how Steven closed you out, I got angry. I want to change how people are treated when they come to us for help."

"I appreciate it. We wouldn't be able to attempt this without you taking a chance on us."

Clare nodded. "You're welcome."

Ben came into the kitchen, and I handed him a sandwich. "How will you keep Leo and me from messing up the barrier spell this time?"

"I have some ideas," he said.

The idling engine of a car approached from outside. My attention snapped toward the front door.

"Is someone here?" Ben asked.

I nodded and slunk toward the screen door. The engine was cut and a car door slammed shut. Standing beside her cruiser, rifle over her shoulder, was Officer Miller.

25

MY HACKLES ROSE and a growl sounded in my chest.

Ben looked out the window. He appeared as displeased as I was about our uninvited guest. "I can tell her to leave."

I didn't want him facing her alone. "Let's go out together."

Miller heard the squeak of the screen door. She didn't smile, but that aggressive vibe I related to Hunters was also absent. "Hello again, Miss Steward, Mr. Sharpe. Mind if we have a candid chat?"

I eyed the rifle. "We were told you've been following us. Why?"

"I'm trying to locate a lupine that's running rampant," she said, "and he happens to turn up wherever you two are."

"That's our problem. We're taking care of it," I said.

"He severely injured a Commoner at that beach party," she said. "So now your problem is also my problem."

I lifted my chin and narrowed my eyes.

Ben turned his back to Miller and lowered his voice. "Your Grandpa worked with her dad. Maybe she and her father are different from other Hunters."

"Different?" I scoffed, not bothering to hide my reply. "After she kills Leo, because she will, we can't trust she won't kill us next."

"I'm here to restore order by eliminating only Leonard Whelan," Miller said. "We can either help each other or get in each other's way. Which do you prefer?"

My own experience with a Hunter, and what I'd heard about them, struck fear into my heart. They murdered people like me.

But if all Hunters were terrible, why would my grandfather partner with one to help struggling lupine?

I thought of my lost friendship with Anne. She'd agreed to carry a Hunter's key within her body, giving her the abilities to track, fight, and kill supernatural beings. If all Hunters weren't zealots, was there a chance Anne and I could make amends?

"Leave your gun there. We'll grab it once you're in the cabin." I hoped I wouldn't regret opening our door to Miller.

She hesitated. "I'm not sure I'm comfortable with that."

"I don't care," I growled.

Frowning, she took the rifle slowly from over her shoulder. "If this is going to work, there has to be a bit of trust between us." She crouched, laying the rifle on the ground but not taking her gaze from Ben and me.

"If you don't provoke or attack us, there's no reason to hurt you." I opened the screen door. "Would you like a sandwich? We're having lunch."

I SAT AT one end of the couch and Miller at the other. The rifle leaned against the wall between me and the kitchen.

"We think Leo's botched tether caused some type of infection in his body," I said. "It smells terrible, like it's rotting his insides. Even after Ben removed the tether, Leo's brain still seemed scrambled. We want to try to heal him and see if he can be reasoned with before any other drastic measures are taken."

"He nearly killed that man in Silver Lake," Miller said.

"But he didn't." I picked up and opened one of the photo albums. "Did you know your dad used to stay here with my grandfather? For some reason, Grandpa trusted him."

She accepted the album, her features softening as she viewed the photos. "During my apprenticeship, Dad told me about working with a lupine here. I didn't realize it was Alexander."

"Does Dottie know about you and your dad?"

"No, she doesn't." Miller carefully turned the old album's page. "Uncle Theo knew. Dad asked his permission to propose to Mom."

I struggled to believe that wouldn't cause a problem. "But Theo was lupine. He didn't have a problem with his brother-in-law being a Hunter?"

"I asked about that when I first considered following in Dad's footsteps," she said. "Uncle Theo said if his sister was going to fall for a Hunter, he hoped to hell it would be someone like Dad."

"So Ed didn't make a habit of murdering supernatural citizens?" I couldn't help the edge in my tone.

Miller's jawline tensed. "After you left town, I dug out files on Dad's unsolved case of the livestock slaughterings. I ran dates by Mom. The summer that case was marked unsolved was the first summer Dad and Alexander stayed here." She closed the album and tossed it on the couch between us. "No, my dad wasn't murdering supernatural citizens. He was making cases go away so no one discovered the Dogman was real. In fact, Dad almost sank his law enforcement career on that unsolved case to protect a lupine, your grandfather."

My pulse lurched. "No, that's wrong. Grandpa wouldn't mindlessly kill those animals." My hands trembled as I grabbed his box from the end table. I set it with the photo albums and pulled out the news articles, spreading the clippings across the tabletop. "All these dates line up with the list of Dogmen." I pulled out the CCC's handbook and flipped to the back page. "Look."

"What's that?"

"We think it's a list of lupine that acted as the Dogman." I read off the years of the articles, setting each aside as I found a name in the book within the same year. "Ed and Grandpa tracked down and confronted the lupine responsible for the livestock killings mentioned in these articles. Instead of Ed executing them like most Hunters would, he and Grandpa brought those lupine here to find balance again with their wolves. The rehabbed wolves got a second chance by acting as a cryptid, the Dogman, to protect these forests. And by protecting the forests, they protected the lupine and hamadryads living here."

I was left holding a single article, the oldest from the collection. I scanned the list of names twice. Miller opened the photo album she'd looked through to its first page. Beneath the first photo was the date that matched the publication date of the newspaper clipping I held.

I dropped into my seat and blinked back sudden tears. It was true. The part of my grandfather that was wolf had slaughtered a herd of livestock. And then he was saved by a Hunter, a type of person I only knew as an indiscriminate murderer.

I hated crying in front of Miller, but seeing Grandpa as anything but the wonderful man from my childhood shattered my heart.

"My dad and your grandpa were veterans," Miller continued. "Dad knew firsthand what warfare can do to a person's soul. When he investigated Alexander, I assume he saw a person hurting like he'd hurt. He wanted to help."

Grandpa wrote in his letter he received help for his PTSD, or Post Vietnam Syndrome as it was called at that time. I assumed it was therapy at home, not a helping hand extended by a Hunter. "And when the cabin and these woods helped Grandpa rebalance the dark and light of his wolf, that's when Ed and Grandpa guided the other lupine."

Miller nodded. "That's my best guess."

My emotions were spinning all over. It was difficult to reconcile the different versions of my grandfather: the soft-spoken and kind man I remembered, and a lupine who brutally butchered a herd of animals. Was my recent and tentative comfort with the wolf in me premature? Letting my wolf run resulted in a dead deer, but I'd spared the Commoner in his hunting blind. I numbly collected the articles, put them back in the box, and replaced the lid.

"I'm sorry. I need air." I wanted to distance myself from Miller, the albums, and the box.

I found myself outside taking deep and slow breaths of fresh air. Ben stood in the open area in front of the cabin speaking to Clare. Overhead, the sky darkened and the wind picked up.

Ben spotted me and jogged over. "Is everything okay?"

I nodded, my arms wrapped around myself. We had a difficult task ahead of us dealing with Leo. I didn't want a discussion about all my conflicting emotions to distract from that. "How's it going out here? Almost ready?"

"We're finished. Your car is going to get caught inside the barrier. I would have moved it, but . . . " He gestured to the tires lying in the grass.

"It's fine. There isn't a big enough space anywhere else."

He glanced upward. "We may be getting soggy tonight."

A distant roll of thunder rumbled toward us across the sky.

26

CLARE HANDED ME a packet the size of a tea bag. "Make sure it passes down his throat."

It reminded me of my parents teaming up to get our dog, Grommet, to take a pill. I wondered briefly if cheese would help. A strangled laugh escaped me.

I tried to rein in my nerves and looked between everyone. "Are we ready?"

Miller and Clare stood at the front of the cabin, Miller with her shotgun in hand. Both nodded.

Ben stood opposite the open area near a tree inscribed with a sigil. "Are you sure you don't want me inside the barrier?"

"No, wizards are too squishy," I said. "Plus, you need to make sure the barrier doesn't fall."

"Okay." He didn't look pleased but didn't argue. "I'm ready."

"Remember, Miller, you're insurance only if everything goes south," I said.

She calmly acknowledged the statement with another nod. Rain pattered lightly around us, and another roll of thunder announced the storm's swift approach.

I walked into the area of barely-there lawn within the boundaries of Ben's spell. Standing in a t-shirt and underwear, because I preferred not to get naked for anyone but Ben, I wiggled my toes into the soil and pine needles. The raw earth beneath my feet helped me to feel grounded. A gust of wind lifted my hair, and I focused on the sensations it created while traveling over my skin. I took a deep breath.

The part of me that was wolf and the part of me that was woman were more intertwined than they'd ever been. But there was still room for mistakes. Is that what happened to my grandfather?

I slowly exhaled, expelling the doubt from my body. I'd spared the deer hunter. If I was going to wrestle Leo into taking Clare's homemade pill, I would need all my strength.

The wolf in me pressed up through my consciousness and the confines of my warming body. The usual snap and pop of cartilage came from my hands and ears. A burst of adrenaline dulled the pain of the more dramatic change in shape. Breaking bones. Stretching and slipping muscles. Cracking skin and emerging fur. Fabric ripped, unable to contain the larger form I took when fully shifted.

The rain fell on my large fur-covered body. The energy of the arriving storm turned everything electric. The colors of the scents and shapes around me vibrated like the lightning. Thunder cracked and tumbled through the sky. I raised my muzzle and let loose a long howl.

From the woods, a reply was given. A wavering howl ended in an agonized scream. My hackles rose. I spun in place, nostrils quivering. The sounds of snapping twigs and congested growling came from the woodline. In the murky light, two glowing red eyes watched me. The scents of rot and rage reached my nose.

I stood to my full height, pulling my lips back to bare my jagged teeth and snarl.

Leo slunk from the woods on all fours. He'd again chosen to confront me in his full lupine form. The wounds I'd given him from previous fights still hadn't healed. His thick fur was missing from those areas. The lesions from his throat were opening on his muzzle and flank. They pulsed the same furious red from his eyes.

I vocalized another round of snarls. Lightning flashed above, punctuated by a tremendous crack of thunder.

Leo leaped up onto two feet. Even in my full lupine form, he stood a head taller. Eyes wild, he charged. I widened my stance and braced myself.

A prickling sensation rushed along my hide. Ben shouted his incantation. Sigils flared up along the trunks of four towering pines. They weren't carved into the trees, but created within the pattern of the bark. Clare's work. Shimmering walls of blue light flashed into existence around Leo and me before fading.

Leo was on a collision course with me. I pushed at the outside of his arm and stepped around him. His momentum sent him flying past. He struck the barrier. It shuddered. Maybe I could wear him out instead of directly fighting him. I tightly held Clare's packet in my hand.

All my senses trained on Leo. I backed to the center of the enclosed space, hoping to draw him with me.

He smashed a palm against the barrier's wall. It crackled and sparked but remained intact. Leo roared and slashed at the magical barrier with his claws. Blue fracture lines burned bright on its surface.

Ben launched into casting another spell. The cracks in the barrier started to heal.

Leo's panicked reaction was familiar. I'd done the same when the spell trapped me in a confined space at my Committee trial. I let loose a bark. Leo snarled, and his attention was back on me.

I laid my ears back against my head and slunk toward him. I stopped, extending my hand with the packet. Leo's red eyes narrowed. He stretched forward, squinting at the small object in my palm. His nostrils quivered to investigate the scent.

My bunched muscles twitched. I struggled to stay focused on the goal. The wolf in me understood this man wanted me dead. He'd crossed the state and traveled many miles with that goal.

Leo tentatively reached out with his enormous clawed hand.

I lunged, seized his forearm, and drove my heel into his shin. He yelped and toppled. I dropped to a knee beside him and tried to pry his jaws apart. Leo bucked and snarled on his back, kicking up mud. He twisted his head side to side. I couldn't get clear access to his open mouth. His claws sliced at my arms and hands to free his muzzle.

Slick with saliva, my hold on his lower jaw slipped. He snapped his mouth closed. Leo threw a punch to the side of my head. I stumbled to my feet and away from him, shaking my head, my ear ringing.

"Alex, look out!" Ben's voice carried over the thrumming downpour of rain and Leo's growling. I turned back to Leo. A car tire collided with my face. White-hot pain exploded over my cheekbone and brow bone.

I dropped the packet.

He swung the tire again, but I caught it between us. Leo leaned forward over the tire. His jaws snapped at my face. My muscles strained to hold him at arm's length. His brute strength was too much. I leaped back away from him.

Leo stumbled forward. He rushed past me and swung the tire into the barrier. It crackled as the tire bounced off it. I sliced and snapped at Leo's flanks to divert his attention again. He ignored me and smashed at his prison with his fists. Fissures leaking bluish light pulled open on the magical surface.

Ben swore and tried to shore up the barrier again. His spell couldn't mend it fast enough. Leo's claws, increased strength, and repeated attacks were rendering it to ribbons.

"Shit!" Ben stepped back. The spell-rendered barrier collapsed. Discharged energy exploded outward and dissipated, lifting his hair and the hem of his jacket.

Miller lowered her rifle at Leo.

Wait!

My voice came out as a bark. Miller's rifle cracked. Leo grunted, and his hand flew to his chest. His eyes took a moment to refocus on Miller. Released from the barrier, he lumbered toward her.

I snatched the packet from the ground and sprinted after him.

Miller's rifle fired again. Leo screamed. He sprang at Miller, teeth and claws bared. She still had her rifle trained on Leo. I tackled him. The gunshot went over our heads. We rolled into the side of the cabin, taking Miller off her feet.

Leo staggered to his feet and crashed back into the woods. I tightened my hold on the packet and dashed after him. He moved at a type of limping jog. I gained on him, deftly bounding through the forest.

We reached the gully that slanted down toward the river. The rain made the hill slick with mud and wet leaves. Leo tripped, fell forward, and rolled down toward the water. I tried to follow but slipped and slid the rest of the way on my ass.

Leo's hulking form lay at the river's edge. I hurried to his side and turned him onto his back. His shallow breath escaped in short steamy bursts. The smell of rotting flesh was overwhelming.

My ears swiveled. From somewhere up in the woods, my name was being called.

I set Leo's head on my lap and slipped my fingers between his lips. I carefully pried his jaws open. Taking Clare's packet, I shoved it past his tongue to the back of his throat. Leo whined and weakly tried to lift his head. I closed his jaws and put my hand over his nose to block his airways. I gave a low growl.

Swallow... Swallow...

He swallowed.

Whatever Clare had mixed up, it worked fast. Only a few minutes passed before Leo's eyes rolled up into his skull. His breath quieted and became more even. I pushed his head from my lap, crawled into the shallow river, and sat in the water.

With the loss of consciousness, Leo's body released its wolf shape. What was left when his form realigned itself was a ghastly shell of the man he'd been. His eyes and cheeks were sunken, and his complexion sickly.

Steam rose from my body into the autumn air. I turned my face to the sky, closed my eyes, and let the rain fall on my upturned face. Though the river water was cold, it felt good to let the current cleanse the clumps of mud and leaves from my fur. I rolled and stretched, pushing my arms and head underwater. Reemerging, I stood and shook the water from my body in a mist.

The wind carried my name to me again from somewhere up the hill. I lifted Leo from the riverbank and began the climb back up the hill to the cabin.

27

WE SETTLED LEO into one of the cabin's empty bedrooms. While he was unconscious, Clare tended to him. She extracted bullets, washed his wounds, and prepared an herbal salve for the lesions. We took turns keeping watch at his door as he slept.

Miller refused to leave. She insisted on staying until she saw Leo wake and was convinced he wouldn't cause more problems.

"You used regular bullets in your rifle," I said. "I expected silver from a Hunter."

"Those were in my pocket," she said.

After twenty-four hours, the wounds Leo received from Miller, Steven, and me, began to knit closed. The inflammation around the strange lesions receded. Clare became confident they'd disappear if we continued the regimen of redressing the areas with her herbal salve.

Almost forty-eight hours after I hauled Leonard Whelan's ass up that slippery hill in the rain, he opened his eyes.

I was sitting with him. As soon as his breathing changed, I jumped to my feet. With every muscle taught, I stood ready. There was no guarantee he wouldn't fly into an immediate rage and attack me and the others.

He slowly turned his head and saw me at his bedside. His voice was a deep rumble. "You."

"Me."

"It's so quiet. Am I dead?"

"You're not. The tether is gone. Clare's medicine is drawing the infection from your body." I hoped my mantra provided similar comfort for his wolf as it did for mine. "It's okay. You're safe."

Leo's smile was small. "My head isn't full of fire anymore." Then he wept.

It was filled with relief.

Peace.

***

JESSICA STOOD IN front of the busted Camry with her arms crossed. "And he did this?" She jabbed a thumb over her shoulder.

"Yeah." I winced, realizing it was less than a week since the car had been in her shop. "He's lupine, like me."

Leo towered behind her. The bits of his face not covered by beard or eyebrows were scarlet with embarrassment. "I got mad."

Jessica pivoted to face Leo, looked him up and down, and stated. "I found your fur in the door assembly."

Leo's mouth opened, then closed.

"Do you get mad a lot?" Jessica's tone was neutral. She wasn't judging him, simply discussing facts. "If you work at my shop, you can't get mad. It's unprofessional."

He quickly shook his head. "I won't. I can do better now."

"I fix cars at my shop." She pushed a business card at him.

"I like cars . . . and baseball."

"Baseball is okay." Extending a hand, she said, "My name is Jessica. It's on the card if you forget."

"I'm Leo." He accepted her handshake.

She narrowed her eyes, studied him for an awkward moment, then concluded. "You're very large."

His mouth opened and closed again.

"Help me fix Alex's car. Then I'll know if I can give you a job." Jessica walked like a woman with a mission to the bed of her truck. Leo followed.

We'd been at the cabin for two weeks, and for most of that time, Leo hadn't spoken. He said he liked the quiet. The lesions were gone from his body, leaving extensive scarring similar to those from severe burns.

Ben called Jessica while on a grocery run for us. We needed the car repaired, and I'd gotten the idea of her hiring Leo. She loaded her truck with the necessary tools and drove to meet us. The job would give Leo some purpose and be within driving distance of the cabin if he became overwhelmed and needed a break.

I watched Leo pick up one tire and then the other. He carried them to where Jessica placed jacks under the car. Footsteps, as well as a familiar scent, approached from behind me. My body tensed.

"Lunch?" Miller stopped at my side. She offered me a plate with a sandwich.

"Thanks."

"You think this is going to work?" Miller watched the two at the car. "He's a big guy. It could get dangerous fast."

"He should get another chance," I said. "People shouldn't be expected to think straight when they're hurting so much."

Miller took a bite of her sandwich.

"How does he look?" I knew Hunters could identify supernatural beings using special sight they possessed.

She chewed thoughtfully, watching the car repair. "When I saw him that night, his head was full of darkness. That's common in tethered lupine. But it had spread into his chest. The growing dark reached into the rest of his body and oozed from those wounds. There was so little light in him, I didn't think there was anything left to salvage. Now he's a diffused gray. There are still fissures of dark running through him, especially in his head. Those may not disappear completely, but it gives me hope he might make it."

I swallowed and willed myself not to tear up. Knowing we'd helped a fellow lupine begin healing from the effects of a tether meant a lot to me. Reginald said Leo and George were tethered for kidnapping and killing a prominent wizard in Chicago. Having been tethered for a short time, I still didn't wish the punishment on anyone.

"What about me?" I'd wanted to ask Miller since she arrived at the cabin but didn't quite trust her. Or maybe that was an excuse because I was scared to know.

Miller hesitated.

"Please, tell me."

"Your light and dark aren't as mixed as most lupine your age." She paused, leaving space for my explanation.

"My wolf woke late. I was twenty-two." I set the sandwich aside, the roiling acid in my stomach decimating my appetite.

"Much of it has diffused to gray." She hesitated again.

"Tell me." My demand was edged with a growl.

Miller's eyebrows rose and her tone cooled. "There's a dark mass about the size of a fist in your chest. It's not spreading, but it's opaque, like a tight knot."

I'd lived with that seed of rage lodged inside me for eight years. I was relieved to hear: *It's not spreading.*

"Be careful of that." She took another bite of her sandwich.

"I will," I promised.

For the first time since finding my grandfather's box with the tarnished key, I was confident in my ability to keep that promise. If the dark part of my wolf grew deadly, my life didn't have to end. There was a path forward.

I thought of Grandpa's letter. He hadn't shied away from mentioning the fears and danger of living life as a werewolf. But he also stressed not to face those alone.

The wolf makes us strong in many ways, Alexandria, but if you are struggling, please ask for help from your family or someone close to you. There is no weakness in this. A wolf relies on their pack. And you will be a better person for those you care for. I wish I would have done so sooner.

"I'M SORRY I hit you in the face with a tire." Leo sat at the firepit with us, the lawn chair bowing under his mass.

"Apology accepted," I said. "You were ill. We were all a little ... stressed."

"The tether made it so the storm in my head couldn't get out." He grimaced and touched his temple. "Then I could turn into a werewolf again, but my head was full of fire."

Ben spoke from beside me. "Leo, do you remember who altered your tether?"

Leo's face screwed up, and then he grunted. "The fire made my brain fuzzy from that time. The blond guy who hired us had a wizard do it. My pal George would know. He's pretty smart and remembers things better than I do."

"George Moreno?" Miller sat across from me on the other side of Leo.

"Yes. He's a wizard," I said.

"I miss him." Leo wiped at his eyes with a huge hand.

I reached out and gave his shoulder a pat. My encounters with George led me to believe he was a rotten person and didn't treat Leo kindly. I didn't understand their friendship, but I did know how it felt being separated from your closest friends. I missed Emma terribly, and Anne ... Our more difficult parting still pained me.

"After I ran away and couldn't find George, I got the maddest I've ever been," Leo said. "When I saw a poster in Detroit with Ben's name, I thought Alex would be with him. I'd make her tell me where to find George."

"We told you we didn't know where he was," I said.

Leo shook his head. "It was too late. The fire kept getting bigger and sharper inside me. It hurt my guts so bad that I couldn't concentrate. I almost lost my chess game."

"What chess game?" Ben asked.

The image of the scorched chessboard popped into my mind. "Leo, did you beat the antique shop owner at chess?"

Ben gave Miller a nervous glance. "That's not poss—"

"Yes." Leo scratched absently at his belly. "My Nana taught me how to play chess when I was a kid."

I raised my eyebrows and grinned at Ben. He gaped at Leo, struggling with the idea a lupine could outsmart a dragon.

"I won, so she gave me a magic sticker," Leo said. "I put it on your car so I would know where to find you in case my head got worse. I don't remember too much after that."

"Do you still feel that anger?" Miller asked.

He seemed to turn this over several times in his mind. "Not really. My head is clear now, so I know Alex was protecting her friends when she fought with George and me."

"Do you feel rested and ready to start again?" I asked.

"Yes. I like cars, and Jessica said I learn fast. She said I got the job, and we can go tomorrow." Leo gave Miller a shy glance. "Lucy said Traverse City is really pretty, too."

Miller blushed at his use of her first name. Ever since Leo found out Miller was a Hunter but chose not to put a silver bullet in his head, he'd developed an endearing type of respect and fondness for her.

"No one has ever let me try again to get it right," he'd said.

"And then in the spring you and I can meet back here, and I'll introduce you to Steven, another lupine," Miller said. "We'll all talk about what to do next."

"That's when I can be a Dogman," Leo said. "That sounds pretty fun."

"If all goes well, yes." Miller stood. "Welp, I'm going to turn in for the night. Sleep well, everyone."

"I'm tired, too." Leo stood. The lawn chair gave a pitiful squeak.

"Good night," I said.

Ben nodded. "Sleep well."

Leo and Miller walked from the halo of firelight and into the shadows toward the cabin. I watched them leave, hoping our tentative plan for Leo worked.

Ben slipped his arm around me. "It's out of your hands."

I leaned into him. "The whole thing reminds me of what I learned about Grandpa. He did these terrible things, but got help and did the work to better himself for his loved ones. That's why I could have a happy childhood with my grandparents."

"Do you think Leo will make it?" Ben asked.

"I hope so," I said.

"Even though he made our lives hell and tried to kill us on multiple occasions," Ben said. "I do, too."

I sat up and turned to face him. "I've been thinking about us."

Ben raised an eyebrow, searching my features. "You have?"

"I still want to live with you in Hopewell, but in a new space with a bedroom." I took his hands in mine. "Even though you may be traveling."

He shook his head. "I don't have to tr—"

I interrupted by kissing him. He fell silent with a smile.

"You don't want to help rebuild like I do," I said. "That's tough because it's something important to me. I like to share what I love with the people I love. But, I understand your feelings about Hopewell are complicated."

Ben dropped his gaze to our clasped hands. "I'm sorry."

"Please, don't apologize." I lifted his chin and gave him another soft kiss. "I want you to be happy. If that means leaving to entertain your legions of adoring fans, I'll figure out how to be okay with that." I smiled. "But I also want to be the home you come back to. Can we try that and see what happens?"

Ben looked at me in that way that made my stomach flip. The way that warmed my whole being, let me know every part of me was loved, and made me feel I'd be terribly missed if gone.

"Absolutely," he said.

Thank You

Thank you for reading *Track the Wolf*. If you enjoyed the book, please consider leaving a reader review.

For updates on the Alex Steward series, simply scan the QR code or visit the author's website at **stefaniegilmour.com**

Acknowledgements

THANK YOU TO my husband and first reader, Josh. Alex's story began as one novel in my head and now we are at four! Your support during every part of this writing journey, spontaneous road trips across Michigan included, is appreciated.

Thank you to the publishing professionals who guided me: Lenore Appelhans for leaping into the middle of a series and strengthening the story's bones, and Rebecca Cooper for using her eagle eye to ensure readers receive a polished book.

The *Track the Wolf* beta readers made sure all my ducks were in a row and not out at the club. You each gave me feedback that made the story stronger. Thank you to Emily Bevilacqua, Kelly Bungee Rogers, Hailey Fournier, Matthew Gatesy, Jen Hefko, and Robin Iknayan.

I'm grateful for the family and friends who support me and my writing in too many ways to list. Thank you!

Finally, to the readers who've been with me since the beginning of Alex's story: Thank you, thank you, thank you. Your purchase of my novels, notes of encouragement, reader reviews, fun chats at live events, and ongoing support are why I continue to write.

Stefanie Gilmour

STEFANIE IS A graphic designer who enjoys creepy and fantastical stories. Her short fiction has been published in *The Quiet Ones* literary magazine.

Plants, concerts, books, and writing are a few of her favorite things. She's a Midwest native and lives there with her patient husband and their tolerant cat.

stefaniegilmour.com
Facebook.com/AuthorStefanieGilmour
Instagram: @StefGilmour